Coming Together

*Johnson Road
Book 1*

Fearne Hill

Copyright © 2019 Fearne Hill

All rights reserved, including the right to reproduce this book, or portions thereof in any form. No part of this text may be reproduced, transmitted, downloaded, decompiled, reverse engineered, or stored, in any form or introduced into any information storage and retrieval system, in any form or by any means, whether electronic or mechanical without the express written permission of the author.

This is a work of fiction. Names and characters are the product of the author's imagination and any resemblance to actual persons, living or dead, is entirely coincidental.

The views expressed in this work are solely those of the author and do not necessarily reflect the views of the publisher, and the publisher hereby disclaims any responsibility for them.

ISBN: 978-0-244-54037-1

PublishNation
www.publishnation.co.uk

CHAPTER 1

SOPHIE

I have two burning questions as the black cab stalls behind a grubby double decker bus advertising cheap pine furniture. Question number one: who the hell is Brian Clough? And, probably more importantly, how could it be that on the university open day, six months earlier, the city of Nottingham had not looked anything like this? Because if it had, I would not right now be making small talk with a garrulous taxi driver as he negotiates his way around the centre of his hometown. Instead, I'd be sitting in a boho café in Durham, St Andrews or Bath, sipping a latté and thinking I was pretty special as I discussed the finer points of Florentine fifteenth century architecture with my new, cool friends.

The rain outside the window is being thrown down in biblical proportions. The windscreen wipers are working furiously. Grey concrete office blocks loom large on either side of the busy ring road, and drably dressed office workers and miserable shoppers hurry along the wet pavements, heads firmly down. I idly study the low budget shops and fast-food outlets lining the road, familiar from every British high street everywhere. Subway, TK Maxx, Costa, WHSmith, Subway again, fairly depressing actually, although you can find some decent stuff in TK if you can be bothered to trawl through the racks. I think about the quaint cobbled streets of Durham, lined with quirky vintage clothing emporia and *avant-garde* art galleries.

'You're the fourth student I've picked up today, love,' announces the cabbie cheerily, eyeing me through his rear-view mirror. 'Let me have a guess at what you're studying - the effects of an excess of cheap vodka on human biology, is it?'

He sniggers, highly amused at his own joke. I bet he used that line on the three previous students too, although I doubt the repetition makes it any funnier. We stop at a set of traffic lights and he's still looking at me, apparently expecting a proper answer.

'Art History, actually,' I reply, primly. God, I sound stuck up, that's what five years at a posh boarding school can do to you.

He laughs easily. 'That's a new one on me, love. Is that a real degree? Nah, you're having me on.'

I refuse to rise to the bait, so I say nothing and concentrate on looking out of the window. The Nottingham that I fell in love with on open day was a leafy green campus, with a huge boating lake, surrounded by elegant period buildings, home to thousands of eager students. Not this dark, wet cityscape, and definitely not this talkative cab driver either. We halt once more, just beyond the city's main square.

'There's all the art history you need, me duck,' he states triumphantly, and indicates with his thumb to a corner just beyond the busy pedestrianised area in front of the imposing town hall. My eyes follow in the direction that he is pointing and come to rest on a larger than life bronze statue, supported on a raised plinth. It is a statue of man, an ordinary looking, slightly overweight middle-aged man, inexplicably wearing tracksuit bottoms and a sweatshirt. He has the appearance of being caught in the moment of unscrewing a lightbulb just above his head, but on closer inspection, he is actually clasping his hands together in a sort of victory salute. Somebody has draped a red and white football scarf around the statue's neck.

'Brian Clough, that is,' announces the cabbie proudly. 'Best football manager England never had.'

I belatedly notice the cabbie is wearing a football shirt in the same colour scheme as the scarf. 'He managed Forest for eighteen years,' he adds, changing gear. 'Bloody footballing genius.'

He nods at his own wisdom. 'It's a better statue than the shit they let some clowns put up, over there,' he growls angrily, as the taxi finally picks up speed again.

We chug past yet another bronze, this one smaller and depicting a quartet of people, each facing in different directions and seemingly oblivious to each other's presence. Two men and two women also dressed in modern day clothing. They look as if they have been captured going about their daily business – walking purposely to work or on a shopping trip. None of them look particularly happy, a simple and effective summing up of the mood in the city around me, particularly on a dreary day like today. To my as yet untutored eye, however, it looks like quite a good piece; seeing as I'm going to be studying Art History, I should probably return and study it more closely.

Fortunately, the driver has become distracted by the bigoted views of an elderly lady on a phone-in radio show, and so I sit back and consider my impressions of the city from the taxi window with my hazy memories from six months earlier. I wonder what the weather forecast is in Bath today, whether the sun is beaming down on the Roman baths and the elegant Georgian townhouses.....

We have now taken a series of left and right turns through almost identical streets of two and three-storey red bricked Victorian semi-detached houses. A few of these big homes have been converted into flats, but I can see that most have turned into student lets. Front lawns have been paved over to make way for parking spaces and wheelie bins, the brick frontages are much shabbier, I imagine, than when they were spacious homes for affluent middle-class families. This is the suburb of Lenton, I see from a sign, and the houses are shared digs for thousands of university students - nearly every street corner boasts a dingy corner shop, with music festival flyers and adverts for cheap alcohol plastered across the windows.

'Johnson Road wasn't it, love?' he asks, and I confirm with a nod.

He sucks through his teeth. 'You're just about alright living up that end of Lenton, love, although I wouldn't turn left out the top of your road if I was you, not at night anyway. Gets a bit rougher down towards the Hyson Green end of town. A student got stabbed last year down that way. In the wrong place at the wrong time.'

He sees the slight look of alarm on my face. 'All about drugs, isn't it, the stabbings?' He tries to reassure me, 'You'll be alright, me duck.'

I feel a mild panic. Nearly all of the first-year students, particularly the ones straight out of school like me, automatically take a room in the campus halls of residence, the better to settle in more easily and make friends. However, after eight years at boarding schools, surrounded by hormonal girls, smelly dorms, canteen cooking, endless rules and communal lounge areas, I'm keen to go it alone, albeit with unknown housemates. This seemed a good idea when I was filling out the form but is now feeling like a pretty brave plan the closer we get. Have I made a monumentally poor decision? Is it too late to ask him to turn the taxi round, return to the train station and enrol on the Art History course in St Andrews? Or should I embrace this big rainy city, with knife wielding psychopaths lurking around every corner? For all I know, one of them could be masquerading as my new housemate!

The rain has lessened to a more familiar British drizzle as the car slows to a halt outside a red brick semi. It is no different to any of the others, apart from the thin young man in a rain spattered grey suit hovering anxiously outside and furiously tapping on his mobile phone. Number 5, Johnson Road, Lenton. I settle with the cabbie and add a small tip. No way am I taking any more cabs until the return journey at the end of term, it's far too expensive. He rewards me with helping to lift my two suitcases from the boot and placing them on the pavement outside the house.

The young man hurries over. 'Sophie Ashworth? Hi, I'm from SLA, you know, the Student Lodgings Agency? They said you would be the first to arrive. I haven't got a lot of time - I've got to be at another one in twelve minutes. Busiest week of the year for us.'

He looks down at his phone, thumbing another text message. He has the same accent as the taxi driver, that I presume is local to Nottingham. I like it - Brummie mixed with Manchester is the best way I can describe it. No one at my school had a regional accent, apart from the irritating fake estuary voices beloved of overprivileged boys everywhere.

I fish out my confirmatory letter from a side pocket of my bag and he gives it a cursory once over, then carries on. 'Here's the keys. You need to sign for them. Can you let the others in when they arrive? I think one's coming today and the other maybe tomorrow. We've put you in the upstairs room - we always recommend the girls have the upstairs rooms - safer, you know, in case of break ins? We get a few around here, especially at the start and end of term when they know people are coming and going.'

Yet again, I feel doubt creeping in. Have I got a target on my back or something? Two locals in the space of half an hour have

4

warned me about the suburban crime rate. It is a good job my father isn't with me; I'd have definitely been put back on the train. Major-General Robert Ashworth has been scathing enough as it is regarding my 'wishy-washy' course.

The chap from SLA thrusts three sets of keys into my hand and I scribble my signature on his paperwork. 'It's really nicely decorated this one is - you'll think you've hit the jackpot to be honest, love. They're not all like this, you know, not by a long shot! A girl from the Middle East - Saudi or somewhere - had it to herself last year and had it all done up. Lived like royalty apparently, and then just left all the furniture behind afterwards. She must have been loaded, never seen anything like it myself for a student house. It's nicer than any house I've ever been inside, in fact. You know that song, 'I want to live like common people'? I reckon she was like that.'

I politely nod my recognition of the song. For someone in a hurry, he can certainly talk. From my limited experience of the Nottingham natives so far, I conclude that they are chatty and mostly friendly. I smile at him; he seems a nice guy. I know plenty of people like the Middle Eastern girl after boarding in the Dorset countryside. Money grew on trees at that school. It was a rarefied environment, but I'm ready for a change. Maybe I'm subconsciously choosing to live out the story of the song too, by coming to the heart of this midland city.

I reach down for my cases and he turns to go.

'Bye then, hope it's okay. The agency is open until six tonight if there are any problems - the number is on the key ring. Oh, before I forget – another bonus: the bedding and towels are changed weekly, and there's also a weekly cleaner thrown in too! Can you believe it?'

He is looking as incredulous as I am feeling. 'One of your new housemates organised it with the agency before you got here and paid for it all upfront - I reckon he don't sound very normal either.'

With a backward wave, he hurries off to his car and I drag my cases onto the step and through the front door.

The man from the agency certainly hasn't exaggerated about the decor. The long narrow hallway has a polished oak parquet floor, which probably wouldn't look out of place in a stately home. The walls are covered in a brilliantly patterned wallpaper, which appears to have gold leaf woven through it. I put my hand out and stroke it, feeling the velvety texture of the material.

Immediately ahead, a staircase reaches up into a darker landing. I put down my bags and cautiously open the door to my right, revealing a much more plainly decorated square room. It is a decent size, and I think that the previous occupant had probably used this as a lounge or a guest bedroom.

The walls are a thick cream and the floor is richly carpeted in luxurious dark wool. Better than the hallway, I decide. An inviting double bed with a dark blue upholstered headboard and piled high with pillows sits opposite the netted bay window, which opens up on to the quiet street. Two matching dark blue deep easy chairs complete the look and face an enormous widescreen TV fixed to the wall. A tasteful wooden desk and chair make up the remainder of the furniture. It is simply, but evidently expensively furnished.

I would have liked this room for myself, however it is assigned to another housemate; the door has a temporary paper sticker attached to it, with the name 'A.G.W. Van-Zeller'. Very exotic! I think, and place one of the sets of keys on the desk.

Under the stairs is a downstairs loo, more of a mock-Victorian wooden throne really; the hand basin next to it has ridiculously over stylized ornate brass taps. I continue down the hallway to the only other room on the ground floor. This is a long galley kitchen, extended so that it opens out at the far end to accommodate an attractive chunky oak table and four chairs. On three sides I am surrounded by sleek white units and black granite worktops. I laugh out loud in disbelief and start opening cupboards at random to find pristine saucepan sets, matching dinner plates, elegant crystal wine glasses and a set of lethal-looking kitchen knives.

I have never been a student before, but even I know that these are no ordinary digs! It's the most bizarre student accommodation imaginable! I walk through to the end of the kitchen and peer out of the windows into the tiny garden beyond, half expecting to see a jacuzzi and a tiki bar, so I'm almost relieved when it reveals a small enclosed area, simply laid to grass, with a bike rack screwed into the side wall.

My boot heels tap loudly on the parquet as I retrace my steps and begin lugging the cases up the stairs, pausing to feel the smooth sweep of the polished bannister. At the top, leading off a small landing, are three closed doors. The first opens into a compact bathroom, but again, this has been designed far beyond student expectations. Instead of a cheap white suite with cold lino flooring and green mould around the shower tray, the room is dominated by a vast slate-tiled walk in shower with a huge sprinkler head and a complicated array of taps and dials. The coordinating grey tiled floor feels warm through my thin-soled boots and three fluffy white towels neatly hang from a heated towel rail.

The next-door room also has a sticker on the door, bearing the much simpler name, 'J Coutts'. I briefly peer into that room too. It is decorated in the same colour scheme as the one downstairs, but without the TV and with just one comfy chair, so it has a more spartan feel. More normal in fact. Putting down a second set of keys, I head to the room furthest away. Plain old 'S. Ashworth' announces the sticker. I plonk my cases down with relief and then look around in wonder.

This bedroom, although of average size is possibly the most extraordinary bedroom I have ever seen. If I thought that the hallway was the stuff of grand British manor houses, then the inspiration for this comes from Far Eastern palaces, thousands of miles away. Maybe the Saudi girl recreated her bedroom from her own home, but what makes me shake my head with amazement is the sheer opulence of my surroundings.

The walls are a nice dark blue-grey. Nearly every inch of wooden floor is covered in thick Persian rugs in a myriad of colours; I slip off my boots and sink my toes into the luxuriance underfoot. A bed dominates the space, and by dominates, I mean it is absolutely enormous, at least seven feet or more across. A hideous crimson upholstered satin headboard stretches high up the wall and is flanked by delicate fluted crystal wall lights. Slim marble topped tables frame the bed.

I perch cautiously on the edge of the bed, and immediately sink into the deepest realms of the yielding mattress, topped by the softest of duck down duvets. Bloody hell, that headboard is ridiculous! I carefully lie back and study the ceiling, reminded of the princess and the pea, one of my favourite childhood fairy stories, where the young princess sleeps on layer after layer of the finest bedding. But there is no uncomfortable pea here; the bed caresses my travel-weary body as if it were moulded specially to fit.

I lie back for a few minutes, breathing deeply, my eyes closed, enjoying the silence and the complete and utter comfort. I might get stabbed or burgled overnight, but at least I'll be suffering in comfortable surroundings. I stretch out into a star shape, but my fingertips don't come close to reaching the edges.

I reluctantly heave myself upright, to better appreciate the rest of what will be my home for the next year. I take some photos on my phone - no one will believe me otherwise. It probably isn't exactly how I would have designed the room, given the choice and a whole load of cash, but hats off to this unknown girl, she certainly knew how to make herself cosy. Even if I imagine the headboard is more suited to a high-class brothel, although I don't actually have a clue what one of those would look like.

Opposite the bed is an ornate silver leaf ceiling-to-floor length mirror, its heavy frame decorated with plump cherubs and angels. I sit on the bed a while longer, studying my reflection. My blonde hair lies long and straight, naturally darker at the roots and lighter at the ends after the long hot summer. It needs washing. I like my thinness, mum thinks I'm too thin, but my angles are currently covered in charcoal skinny jeans and a navy hoodie, typical student uniform, so if I am underweight, it's difficult to see. I peer a bit closer at my face, bare of makeup. My skin looks clear today. I look better with a tan - I think my skin has a yellowish tinge in winter.

The tan is courtesy of my father's latest posting. He has recently been promoted to the prestigious role of Major General of the British Forces in Cyprus. We are all very proud of him. I have spent my summer enjoying hot sunny days around the pool at the officers' club or riding ponies through the scrubland next door.

It was fun being on the army base, lots of the senior officers have kids of a similar age and short of any other company, we soon got to know each other. Of course, some of the younger officers weren't much older than me, and I'd be lying if I pretended that I hadn't noticed them watching me in my bikini from time to time.

I'd had a brief summer fling with one of the more persistent ones, a fit second lieutenant not long out of Sandhurst. It was fun whilst it lasted, the clandestine assignations, meaningful looks exchanged in plain sight, and quick fumbles after dark. When it was over, when the young man had been assigned back to the UK, I had felt sad for a while, but now I realise I'm quite relieved he won't be there when I go back. He was unquestionably hot, but his unbounded enthusiasm for everything military was boring, and even worse, I'm fairly sure my very conservative father was becoming suspicious.

Swinging my legs off the bed, I begin arranging my stuff in a slim wardrobe. I place a recent, framed photo of my parents and younger twin brothers on the desk. They are all smiling in the sunshine, my folks' arm in arm and two cute little boys beaming out at the camera. I don't miss them yet, of course, but I probably will at some point. I've always been an army brat, so I'm used to long periods away from them. My brothers are adorable, my mum is sweet and my father a little more challenging. I quickly choose a couple of pictures I've snapped of the room and post them on the family WhatsApp group.

It's quiet in the house and very few cars pass through the street, despite it not being far from the town centre. I go back downstairs, once again fingering the embroidered wallpaper and conclude that the texture feels weird. I grab my purse from my bag, pick up my keys and close the front door behind me. There is no-one lurking with intent in the sparse foliage, so I wander down to the corner shop. A bell rings as I enter, and a young girl appears as if from nowhere behind the counter. I smile a hello, am not acknowledged, and begin gathering a few basic foodstuffs off the shelves, aware that I'm being stared at in silence. The shop smells musty, the choice is extremely limited and I'm glad when I pay up and re-emerge into the brighter daylight. Hopefully, there is a proper supermarket nearby.

I spend the next few hours having a shower (the powerful jets are as satisfying as they look), catching up on school friends first days at uni via Instagram, and then check my route to campus for the following day. It is just turning dark outside when the doorbell rings. I'm in the kitchen making a cup of tea, still scoffing at the sleek worktops and how incredibly lucky I am to be allocated this strange house. The sound of the doorbell gives me a brief thrill of excitement - I'm looking forward to finding out who will be sharing my new life. I open the door wide, a welcoming smile ready on my face.

A young man, but maybe three or four years older than me, stands on the step, a piece of paper in one hand and two hold-all bags seemingly effortlessly balanced in the other. My first impression is one of size, his broad shoulders fill the doorframe and I clock the rather lovely muscular definition of his arms through his thin grey long-sleeved T-shirt. He's well over six feet tall and he gazes down at me intently for a moment, his soulful brown eyes framed by thick curly black hair. His expression is neutral, neither friendly nor unfriendly.

'Hi, is this number 5?' he asks.

'Yes,' I reply, still smiling politely.

'I'm Jasper Coutts,' he says, putting out his hand, 'I think we are probably housemates?'

His voice is soft and low, and so quietly spoken that I can barely hear the last few words. But, my goodness, what a voice! The accent is soft southern Irish, and I feel an unexpected flutter in my chest as I step back to let him in.

'Hello, Jasper, hi, I'm Sophie, Sophie Ashworth. Please, come in.'

I wince inwardly at my girlish formal tone; the same one I was aware of in the taxi earlier. He's studying me as I speak, the faintest of smiles plays at his lips. He ducks slightly as he passes through the doorframe, his wide shoulders almost touching the walls on both sides of the narrow hallway. We are unavoidably in close proximity and his broad chest brushes passed the bare skin on my arm as we briefly share the confined space. I catch a cool snatch of freshly laundered clothes, mixed with a muskier, darker scent. He raises his eyes again and indicates to the bags.

'Which is my room? I'll take them up.'

That voice again. I feel my face flushing and stammer over my reply.

'Follow me up the stairs - I'll show you. I must give you your keys too.'

I make my way up the stairs ahead of him, aware of his heavier tread following closely, imagining those dark lashed eyes boring into me from behind. I indicate his room and the bathroom too.

'The tour doesn't take very long,' I laugh apologetically, 'And you'll see that the house is probably not what you were expecting, although obviously I don't know what you were expecting, because I don't know you, but anyway…..' I trail off lamely and am rewarded again by a faint smile, revealing even white teeth.

His jaw is angular with a few days' worth of dark stubble. Whilst he fiddles with the keys and his bags, I quickly study him. His natural handsomeness is difficult to ignore, but he looks dog-tired, purple shadows pool beneath those brown eyes. As if he can read my thoughts, he sweeps a hand through the front of his hair and looks up at me again.

'I'll call it a night then, Sophie. It's been a long journey.'

And with that, he steps into his room and closes the door quietly behind him.

I awake before my alarm next morning and luxuriate for a few minutes in the vast expanse of the bed. The house is still. I have slept ten hours straight, despite my misgivings last night, when I had climbed into bed and realised that a complete stranger was on the other side of the wall, and that my door doesn't have a lock. But I had survived the night unscathed, and from the size of the stranger, a would-be burglar would probably think twice about attempting to rob this particular student let.

I am disappointed that our encounter was so brief. I am starved of conversation and want to find out more about this mysterious man, with his sad eyes and world-weary demeanour. I replay his low sexy accent on a loop in my head and feel something akin to excitement as I recall his intense, serious brown-eyed gaze. And amazing biceps. And strong thighs under the denim of his jeans.

I don't think my new housemate has yet surfaced, as I am unaware of any signs of movement from the room next door. So, when I tiptoe very quietly to the bathroom, careful not to disturb him, I am surprised and not a little disappointed to see that his bedroom door is open, with no sign of the occupant. He has not unpacked his bags and the bed is carefully made. In fact, apart from a folded towel and a pair of battered brown boots neatly lined up next to the desk, there is no sign that he has spent the night there at all. An upturned glass drying next to the sink is all the evidence in the kitchen too. And the downstairs bedroom is still clearly unoccupied. I make myself a quick instant coffee, grab an apple and my shoulder bag, and head out.

The first day of university passes in a blur of essential administrative tasks. The campus is about three miles away and I enjoy the brisk morning walk in the hazy late September sunshine. It is well signposted, and even if it had not been, then the throngs of other young people walking or cycling or being deposited from the frequent buses in the same direction are a giveaway. I am pleased to spot a Sainsbury's sign down one of the nearby side streets and decide to pay it a visit in the next couple of days.

Easily locating the red brick humanities building, remembered clearly now from my visit last spring, I register my details with the Art History administrator. I consider purchasing a takeaway coffee at the tiny café in the foyer, but they are a bit pricey, so I sit on one of the benches outside the entrance without a drink and study the syllabus, appreciating the warmth of the sun on my face. Thankfully, this little corner of Nottingham is exactly as I recall it.

The first year of studies is vaguely entitled Appreciation of Antiquity and will focus largely on sculpture and architecture throughout three eras: Archaic, Classical Greek and Hellenic. According to the syllabus overview, by the end of the first year, students will be able to confidently fully distinguish between the three styles and develop a complete understanding of how the works evolved.

It all feels a bit ponderous. And daunting. My knowledge so far of this period is extremely limited, although I have a reasonable comprehension of how the Italian Renaissance sculptors, such as Donatello and Michelangelo reintroduced these classical styles to a modern world. Before becoming a full-time army wife, my mother had taught art history at A-level, and I had spent many a childhood holiday sweltering in the streets of Florence, instead of building sandcastles in Cornwall, like all my classmates.

I still wasn't sure why I had chosen this course. Apart from to irritate my father, who would have preferred if I'd chosen something else - something more substantial were his exact words. I wasn't even sure why I had decided to go to university at all come to that, except that it was the expected thing to do, and I hadn't been able to come up with a viable alternative. I should probably have had a gap year to figure out my life, but my closest friends hadn't, and I didn't want to travel on my own.

Lectures aren't due to start for another two days, so I find myself wandering through the freshers' fair alone. For the first time I regret not being in halls of residence, as there are lots of groups around the stalls, who all seem to know each other already and are having fun. It is a bit like the first day of school, but on a bigger scale, and with easier access to alcohol.

Second and third-year students are trying to coax newbies to join their drinking society, political society, sports team or church, thrusting flyers or vouchers for free drinks into the hands of anyone who passes by. I'm not really tempted by any of them, although I do toy briefly with joining the miniature schnauzer appreciation society, if only because I feel sorry for the nerdy bloke manning the unpopular stall alone. If I had been with others, if my mate Fi had been here, then I would have signed up for plenty of stuff, but on my own, I just feel shy and awkward.

By late afternoon, I am ready to escape. I am cross that I haven't had the nerve to walk up to people and start chatting, but that's how it is, and so I begin a slow meander home. I stop off at Sainsbury's for some groceries on the way, and as an afterthought, I add a couple of the cheapest bottles of wine on the shelf, one red and one white.

I have resolved to make an effort with Jasper Coutts - try to loosen him up. The alcohol will help. Maybe he had simply been extremely tired yesterday, or perhaps he is just exceedingly shy. I wonder why his hazy image has entered my thoughts quite so frequently throughout the day; after all, I have only spent one or two minutes in his company and exchanged no more than about three sentences. I am fairly sure he hasn't given me a second thought!

By the time I insert my key in the front door, I am ready to drop the awkward bags of shopping. I have also decided, yet again, to be more frugal, starting from tomorrow. There is also an Aldi in Lenton, and I will find that and shop there next time. As I open the door, a blast of what sounds like French reggae burns my ear drums. What the hell? I stop, dead in my tracks. Why oh why, is Heath Ledger's absolute double standing topless in the kitchen, ironing a shirt and nodding his head in time to the music? If this is the all-inclusive cleaning service that the SLA guy mentioned, then the company have found themselves a very workable niche in the market.

The god-like figure looks up as he hears the door close. He instantly reaches to turn down the music, unplugs the iron and leaps towards me, hands outstretched.

'Goodness, let me take those bags, they look far too heavy!'

Snatching them out of my hands, he plonks them unceremoniously on the kitchen table. Turning back, he looks me up and down, beaming from ear to ear.

'Wow! Now I am very much hoping that you are S. Ashworth!'

I nod cautiously. He carries on enthusiastically,

'I guessed - and hoped - that you would be female, as I've already peeked into that amazing bedroom and seen some of your stuff. This house is fucking great!'

I wince inwardly. Had I left yesterday's pink knickers and threadbare grey sports bra out on the bed? And the bumper box of tampons on the desk? Quite probably. He is still talking.

'Bloody hell, S. Ashworth - we could get all three of us in that bed! Hah! Maybe I'll settle for just the two of us. Only kidding. Hi, I'm Alex Van-Zeller by the way, and I have the greatest of suspicions that we are going to become most excellent housemates!'

He somehow manages to say all of this whilst enveloping me in a tight hug, smiling mischievously and continuing to openly appraise my face and body. I am still in shock from the awesome physical specimen standing in front of me and his total lack of shame by admitting that he has already checked out some of my undies. I feel myself blushing furiously.

His hands are now on his hips and he is grinning widely at me, perfect white teeth in a tanned face, crystal clear blue eyes and a shock of blond wavy hair that almost reaches down to his shoulders. Even more glorious than the actual Heath Ledger, if that were possible. He looks like he has spent the last three months surfing somewhere very warm.

His golden torso, at which I am trying not to openly gawp, is a perfect 'v' - an elegant triangle framing a broad hairless chest and defined abs. Fi, my old friend from school would have described the upper half his body as 'a giant arrow, pointing the way towards his cock' and on this occasion, she would have been one hundred per cent correct. His belt-less faded blue jeans hang loosely from his angular hips, his slim feet are bare.

Alex's voice is a mix of public-school drawl, and something European – German maybe? Definitely foreign and very seductive. In fact, everything about him hints at foreign, and at lots of money too, from his sexy confidence, the expensive shirt he is ironing, his Armani jeans, the slim white-gold watch on his wrist (is that a bloody Cartier?), and his seemingly effortless charm. He definitely isn't the new cleaning lady, but I would bet my student loan that it is him paying for the domestic services.

I rapidly try to compose herself - I have spent the last few years at boarding school with many, many versions of Alex, although admittedly, none quite so bloody gorgeous. I'm not going to collapse in a heap of jelly at his feet just yet, even though I can feel a hot flush coming on.

'Hi, yes, I'm Sophie Ashworth, pleased to meet you. You've obviously made yourself at home. I'll just put this shopping away. I was going to cook for the three of us tonight - don't expect it every night! Unless you have plans of course? We could get to know each other, although you may have already met Jasper. I've been out all day, I need a shower first, how long have you been here?'

I realise I'm prattling and distinctly uncool. Alex seems oblivious, however.

'Dinner would be fab, Sophie, I'm famished. We can cook together and chat, or maybe you could cook, and I could just chat? I'm fairly useless in the kitchen. Have you got any booze in those shopping bags? If not, I can probably find a few bottles of fizz somewhere in my trunk, although I haven't unpacked yet. I've met our friend Jack Reacher, he's definitely the strong silent type, isn't he?'

He tilts his head towards the ceiling and rolls his eyes. I relax and smile back at him conspiratorially,

'I'll go and ask him to join us,' I answer. 'Let's see if we can liven him up with a couple of glasses of something.'

An hour later and I am showered and changed into dark leggings and my favourite oversized light grey cashmere sweater. I am determined not to be seen to be making too much of an effort, although I do apply a little eyeliner and some lip-gloss. And then a thin silver chain around my neck. And also, an array of jangly silver bracelets, purchased in the tourist market near my temporary Cypriot home.

I have dried my hair with more care than usual too, and it now hangs in a what I hope is a glossy dark blonde sheet down my back. As I appraise my reflection critically in the gigantic mirror, I hope I have struck the right look - relaxed and casual but definitely not trying too hard to make an impression. These two men are going to be housemates for heaven's sake, and despite the fact that I have spent the whole shower fantasising about Alex's perfect lean body, I am determined to banish any such thoughts from now onwards. I wish Fi is with me as confidence booster though, but I will be fine I tell myself. Posh kids like Alex are familiar, at least one of my housemates will hopefully be relatively easy to read.

Wrapped in one of the fluffy white towels on my way back from the shower, I had spied Jasper sitting hunched over his desk through the half open door. He seemed to be staring at a small photograph in a silver frame, but I was too far away to see the subject matter. Taking a deep breath, I tapped hesitantly.

'Jasper....hi, sorry to disturb you, how are you?'

He looked up at the interruption, those deep brown eyes resting momentarily on my own. He was still pale and seemed just as knackered as last night.

'Hey, Sophie, I'm good, thank you for asking.'

He looked as if he were about to turn away again, so I blurted out, 'Er.... sorry to disturb you, but Alex and I are cooking together tonight. Do you want to eat with us? We thought it might be nice for our first night altogether?'

I felt nervous, more nervous than when I had spoken to Alex and I could feel my face burning - why did that soft voice have such an effect on me? He placed the photograph carefully in his desk drawer.

'Thank you, Sophie, you are very kind. I think I would like that, very much in fact. I'll be down soon.'

CHAPTER 2

ALEX

Fuck me, who the hell is this beautiful creature coming through the door? I quickly switch off the iron. I can see she's struggling with some carrier bags and leap to help. Christ, she's even better close up. I've hit the jackpot here if it's who I think it is. I'm not sure I've ever clapped eyes on such a stunning girl in all of my life, and trust me, I've seen a few.

I take the bags from her, like the perfect gent that I am and dive in to give her a big hug. I can't stop myself; I need to touch her, to check that she's real. Christ, her hair smells good. Vanilla. Fresh air and vanilla. I keep breathing it in. I'm babbling like a twat and have to force myself to pull away. She must think I'm a fucking weirdo holding on to her like that. Those cheekbones, though. Fuck me! Green eyes, wow! And those collar bones! I love an elegant pair of collarbones. Tits are marvellous too, from what I can see under her top. Small, but marvellous.

My cock has turned to solid concrete. I'm flying commando and it is threatening to introduce itself out of the top of my jeans. I don't think she's ready for the Van-Zeller manhood quite just yet. Give it a couple of days though.

I retreat back behind the ironing board, hoping that my trouser situation is concealed. She doesn't seem to have noticed; she's talking about dinner. She bloody cooks as well! I think I've died and gone to heaven.

Right, I've got an hour to get my act together and calm the fuck down. She's gone to have a shower. I grab some sheets of kitchen roll and go back to my room. How am I going to get through a whole evening without trying to jump her? I need to get rid of some of this tension and to do that, I need to sort out my raging hard on. I grab myself and start pulling. Finally, some relief. Shit, I can hear the shower turning on upstairs. Sophie Ashworth is naked, in the shower, not twelve feet from my fucking head. Now there's a vision.

I close my eyes and concentrate on my pleasure, conjuring up images of her showering, blonde head under the hot jets, soapy water coursing over that perfect smooth skin. Job done – over very quickly in fact, and I clean my belly then screw up the soggy tissue and throw it towards the bin. Straight in with a satisfying thunk, now that's a good sign. There are going to be a hell of a lot more bedroom poppadums joining that one if I see her every day.

I'm calmer now, in control again. Suave, sophisticated Alexi is back, thank God. I have put on a clean shirt, my favourite pale blue one. I can't take my eyes off her. We're chopping veg together and it's all I can do not to kiss her on those fucking luscious lips. She gives me the onions to slice, which isn't my first choice to be fair, but I don't make a fuss. She's wearing a soft grey sweater, which I am itching to pull over her head. And that arse when she bends down to get something from the bottom of the fridge has me hard all over again. I keep staring at her, I can't help it. She must think I'm very strange. I'm surprised I haven't chopped my finger off, I'm so distracted.

The huge bloke from upstairs has come to join us. He watched her arse when she bent over too. Miserable bugger, although he contributes to the wine and we all neck a couple of glasses quite quickly. He looks knackered. Good body though, he must work out. I reckon he needs a decent nights' sleep and a proper seeing to. Not by my bird though. He can't have her; she's going to be all mine.

The food isn't bad. I think I can take most of the credit. The onions were perfectly chopped. Not only is she a babe, but she's funny too. I like her. No, scrap that, I'm in love with her.

Chat around the table goes surprising well considering we're all strangers. Jasper doesn't say much, but he listens and nods and smiles at my jokes in all the right places. We get the background information out of each other fairly early on, although Jasper doesn't contribute much, so it's left to me to do most of the chat. This is his third year at medical school - he's retaking the year after dropping out and having some time off. Family bereavement back in Ireland apparently, but he clearly doesn't want to talk about it, and we don't push him. He looks upset actually, even just giving this much information. He stays on the periphery of the conversation after that, although he seems happy enough just being with us in the kitchen. Occasionally, I glance across and observe him staring into space, as if transported to a different world, and by his sad expression, not a very nice one.

I tell them about myself up to a point. I'm not embarrassed about who I am, but I'm not planning on laying it all out. And I can't pretend I'm skint, because they've probably spotted already that I'm not. So, I pretty much tell the truth, I say that papa works in banking back in Zurich and that mama was a former London socialite until I came along. I'm a doted upon, spoilt only child - I didn't need to spell that out, they worked it out for themselves. And to their amusement, mama has already phoned twice to check I am okay, which is less than ideal, but hey, she loves me, and they will have to get used to it.

I reassure them that the accent isn't German, but Swiss, and that we divide our time between our homes in Zurich and Notting Hill. I received most of my schooling at an international school in Geneva, before having two years in the sixth form at Harrow. I know when I say all this that I sound like a posh twat and I can see that conclusion plastered all over Jasper's face, but I've thought about it a lot before coming to uni, and getting it all out first means that they won't ask any more questions about my background as they will assume everything has been covered already.

'So why did you come to Nottingham then, Alex?' asks Jasper, which is almost the longest sentence than he has strung together all evening. I bet the girls really go for that accent, even I'm finding it a turn on. 'Shouldn't you be somewhere, I dunno, a bit fancier?'

I laugh, 'Come on mate, you must know that Nottingham has the highest female to male student ratio than anywhere else in the country? And with a bit of luck, most of them will be studying English with me.' Jasper nods his assent, although I'm getting the impression that he's not made his way through many of them.

'That can't be the only reason, Alex,' protests Sophie, and maybe me saying that has annoyed her a little. It is a bit crass, even by my standards.

'Nah, it's not the only reason,' I agree. 'After Harrow and Geneva and stuff, I just want to try living like a normal student for a bit.' As I say it, it sounds even more crass, and Jasper scoffs.

'From what I've seen and heard of you so far, Alex, I'm not sure that is going to happen. You've organised a bloody cleaner for chrissakes!' And him saying that pisses me off a little, as he is right of course, I won't actually live like a proper, hard up student, even though I'm surrounded by them. But I do want to try to keep a low profile for a while, although I don't need to explain that to him.

'I can arrange for the cleaner not to bother with your room, Jasper, if it is a problem for you?' I say with the sweetest of smiles. I actually like him; I like that he's challenged me already. But I don't want to piss him off, he's bloody enormous.

'So why did you choose to come here, Sophie?' I ask, to switch the conversation. I plan on giving her my full attention, which isn't difficult, as I am mesmerised by her blue-green eyes.

She looks confused for a moment and is struggling to find an answer. It surprises me, she gives the impression that she is cool and sorted, but maybe it's just a good front. The wine most likely makes her reply honestly,

'I don't know, Alex. I think I'm looking forward to starting my course, I hope I become interested in it. But what I want, what I want to achieve…Maybe I'll find out whilst I'm here.' She shrugs and looks away.

Fuck, I've got to go out in ten minutes. I wish I wasn't going now. It will make me look cool though. And there's no rush here. Let's face it, she isn't going anywhere. I'm going to see her every fucking day! How good is that?

A blast from a horn outside that will be for me. I've arranged to hit the town with a couple of guys I know vaguely from Eton, who are starting in Nottingham too - friends of friends. Wine bar, club, maybe the casino later.

I kiss Sophie on the forehead as I get up to leave. I can't help it; I need to touch her again. Her skin is so soft, her hair smells so good, I nearly change my mind and stay behind. Jasper - he's not so bad, either. A bit quiet, but I'll loosen him up with a few beers sometime. I ruffle his hair as I go, he's not sure what to make of it, I can tell. Then I'm out the front door and into the night.

CHAPTER 3

JASPER

And with that, like a whirlwind, he's gone, the front door slamming behind him. The energy in the room drops considerably with his departure. Sophie stands up and wordlessly starts clearing away the remains of the dinner and I do the same. We work in what I think is companionable silence, washing and drying. But I sense I make her nervous, probably because I don't say much. Standing side by side at the sink, I'm aware of her proximity and I'm relieved when it is all done.

'Better call it a night, then,' I say wearily, 'I've got an early start tomorrow.'

I feel her eyes on me as I disappear down the dark hallway. She's pretty, really pretty, and I know I'm not the only one that has noticed. Alex was all over her. He'll have a crack at her sooner or later, I can guarantee it. He's very pretty himself, not that I tend to give blokes the once over, but even I can spot one as good looking as him. Great body too, I guess he works out.

I hear Sophie in the bathroom and then settling down into her room. She seems really nice too, a bit bewildered maybe, but trying not to show it. I'm surprised she's here living with us and not in the halls on campus - it would be much easier for her to get into the swing of things. Alex is alright too, not the sort of bloke I usually spend time with, but alright. I think he knows he can be a dick sometimes but can laugh at himself easily.

I sit in my chair for a bit, looking at the little photo of Christian. I've got others, loads of them, but this is my favourite. I look at my textbooks too - I've got loads of them as well. I know I'm not going to sleep anytime soon, so I open a neuroanatomy one and make a start.

Sometime after midnight, I hear the front door open, some loud whispering and girlish giggles from Alex's room below. I can smell fags, I bloody hate that smell, I might tell him not to smoke in the house if he does it too often, and if I want to appear a total fun sponge. It could be his girl smoking, I suppose. Eventually they go quiet. They must have disturbed Sophie though, because I see her tiptoe across the landing to get a glass of water. Fantastic legs, she's only wearing a T-shirt. She looks surprised to see me still up and gives me an embarrassed wave.

I'd never really thought about insomnia until I had it myself. Everyone has a bad night once in a while when they can't sleep - worried about exams, a big curry dinner or whatever. But this isn't the rich pasta and red wine from earlier keeping me awake, this is me, every fucking night. I reckon I'm averaging three, four hours max, and most of that is in a chair, head on my desk. And it's been this way pretty much since Christian died. Every time I close my eyes, I see him. White, lifeless, cold. And I see me, hugging that little body to my big chest, rubbing him, shouting at him, begging him to wake up. But he never does, and he never will.

I watch the clock tick round until six am. The gym at the boxing club in Hyson Green opens at 6.30, and that's when I can forget trying to sleep and start to get through my day. It's my only unnecessary expense and I can't afford it, but it's the only thing that keeps me sane. I must have had a couple of hours kip at some point, as I see that my face has red lines across it from lying across the papers on my desk when I stare at myself in the bathroom mirror. I look like shit; God knows what Sophie and Alex think of me.

I've got a routine, and so I don't see much of the other two for the rest of the week. After the gym, I cycle to med school, sit on my own in lectures or hide/sleep/cry/study, or do all of those things in one of the library cubicles there. I don't reappear at Johnson Road until dusk, slipping quietly back into my room. I don't really know anyone in my new year at med school, apart from a couple of the lads I played rugby with before I left, but that's okay. I'm going to start rugby again this week, it will be good for me, and give me something to do at the weekends. But I don't feel like making small talk at med school, and so I get left alone. There are more than one hundred and fifty of us, so no-one really notices.

Occasionally, I bump into people I was friends with before I left, good friends, drinking buddies, rugby mates, my old on-off girlfriend Samira, who seems determined to track me down. They make a fuss of me, back slaps, hugs, promises to meet up for drinks soon. But it's awkward, they don't want to mention Christians' death and neither do I. Dead brothers don't make for good corridor small talk. And they can see that I've changed. So, the promised drinks don't happen, and that's fine with me too.

Sometimes, I come across Sophie in the kitchen, preparing a sandwich or a cup of tea, and she tries to exchange a few pleasantries with me about her day and her course, but our conversation peters out, because I rarely offer anything in return. I could tell her that I silently wept in the shower for half an hour at the gym this morning before pulling myself together enough to go to med school. Or I could say that because she is so pretty and gentle and normal, would she mind just holding me in her warm bed all night, because I can't sleep on my own in mine? But of course, I do none of those things, I just listen and nod politely and excuse myself, and she is left alone, probably thinking I'm boring and miserable and relieved that she's got Alex for company.

Although neither of us have Alex for company very much. From what I have seen, on the rare occasion that I have come home early and from what Sophie tells me, he appears to be asleep all day and out partying all night. I hear him stumbling through the front door, alone or with a girl, and not the same girl from their voices, most nights or in the early hours of the following morning. And Sophie says the way he sleeps during the day is unbelievable! Maybe I need to ask him for some tips. Bin lorries, meter readers, the cleaning lady, Sophie's music, the postman; apparently Alex can snooze eight hours straight, morning and afternoon, and wake up looking as fresh as a daisy. I'm envious that's for sure. His English degree clearly isn't proving too onerous.

CHAPTER 4

SOPHIE

I'm glad to actually finally get going with my course. It's tough not being in halls and a big part of me is beginning to regret my decision to be in Lenton. There are lots of parties organised this week for freshers, but I can't exactly turn up by myself - that would be mortifying. Clearly, I can't ask Jasper to go with me, and it seems that Alex has his own social agenda completely sorted already. The thought of asking him if I can join him on a night out makes me cringe.

Everywhere I go on campus, I go alone, but am surrounded by groups of two and three, who seem to have been friends for like, forever. It's not that I'm feeling homesick - I saw my folks recently, and I'm used to being apart from them for terms at a time. No, it's more of a familiarity sickness. It's hard work not knowing your way around, and not having found a new friend to do it with you. I miss having my old school mates that I can flop onto the sofa with, and just chat about crap, or not chat at all, and that's fine too.

And I'm not the friendliest of souls anyway - Fi would agree with me on that point. I have a social awkwardness with people I don't know. I'd like to be friendlier and just breeze into a room and introduce myself like Fi can, but it's not me. I struggle with that. Although he seems really miserable, and is very unforthcoming, I actually enjoy my little chats with Jasper. And it's not just the honey voice and the distracting biceps. If he gives me a chance, I think I could get comfortable with him, and maybe reach that relaxed familiarity that is missing. It wouldn't be difficult to get that familiarity with Alex either, because he's so easy to talk to, if he was just awake more during the day and not out every night.

So, the course starting is good. The teaching is split into regular group tutorials, from which I will receive assignments and explore individual artworks in an in-depth fashion. The high point of the week, however, is the 'grand round' lecture, held in the main auditorium.

These lectures are delivered by the Head of Art History, a man named Professor Mackie, and a world-renowned expert in sculptural antiquity. He is a funny-looking little man, approaching retirement age, but still dressing like a member of the Beach Boys. He has a vast selection of Hawaiian shirts – by the end of the term I will not have seen the same one twice, which he pairs with scruffy jeans and Converse Hi-Tops. His thinning grey hair is pulled back in a ragged ponytail.

At the start of each lecture, he bounds energetically onto the stage, his eyes glinting behind round silver frames. He gesticulates wildly and paces the stage throughout the lecture, his clipped Edinburgh tones rising and falling briskly as he endeavours to share his passion with us all. It is a captivating performance.

The first lecture covers a sculpture I'm pleased to see that I visited in the British Museum over the summer on a shopping trip with my mother. We had popped inside for an hour, to escape the busy crowds and hot streets, and I'd found myself daydreaming in front of it. It is a colossal stone statue taken from the mortuary tomb of Rameses II of Egypt. All that remains is his head and torso, carved from exquisite pinky-grey granite; it is an impressive three metres high; the whole body would have stood at seven metres. His sightless eyes gaze down expressionlessly, his facial features are utterly devoid of emotion. Whatever life or death, feast or famine, love or loss that Rameses has embraced or endured, his impassive stare ensures his secrets remain forever.

I like him a lot, I like how this enormous stone carving has suffered so much, from being shot at by Napoleon's troops at the end of the eighteenth century to surviving a treacherous ocean journey to this final resting place in London.

The undergraduate course is small and friendly; there are only about twenty-five first year students, and so over a couple of lunchtimes, I plaster a smile on my face and try really hard to get to know a few of them. I dread that my awkwardness comes across as aloofness, but it seems to go okay, and I'm hopeful I'm going to get somewhere.

In my tutor group, I sit with two girls who are in halls of residence together and already seem firm friends. They are very welcoming. Katy is a slight, elfin girl from Manchester, with short black hair, black jeans, black sweaters, thick black eyeliner and Doc Marten boots. I warm to her immediately, as she has a direct humour - she calls a spade a shovel, as my father would say, and her cheery, confident outlook belies her dark attire. Her friend Amy is much more reserved and probably more like me on the natural warmth front. Shorter and curvier, with a peaches and cream complexion, she has a slightly breathy laugh, lots of freckles and a mass of unruly red hair.

On the second Friday of term, the tutorial group arranges a bonding night out at the main student bar on campus. This is nothing special for people who have already survived freshers week, but for me it's a big deal, and I'm excited. I meet up with Katy and Amy in Katy's room first, for cheap wine and takeaway pizza, before making our way across campus to join in the throng. It appears that just about every other student on campus has the same idea - the bar is heaving with freshers, still heady and overexcited about being away from home, and making the most of the cheap beer and fishbowl cocktails. It is noisy, rowdy and fun. I relax and enjoy myself.

Katy is cheekily assertive, and has somehow managed to bag a table, and we find ourselves a bit pissed and giggling about nothing and eyeing up the best-looking blokes.

'My God, Sophie, can I just say how brave I think you are, moving into Lenton on your own and not knowing anybody?' says Amy, sucking the dregs of her cocktail noisily through a straw. 'What are your housemates like?'

'They are two blokes,' I reply. 'One is a first year like us, studying English, and the other is a medical student, but he's a bit older and in his third year.'

'Are they fit?' asks Katy, crunching an ice cube.

This is about the easiest question I've been asked since arriving in Nottingham. 'Bloody gorgeous, and I'm deadly serious, but I hardly get to see them! Jasper, the med student, is working all the time and Alex is either asleep or out with his mates!'

'I'm coming over!' says Amy, giggling. 'To wake him up! Do you think they are up for anything? They're not gay, are they?'

'Alex definitely isn't,' I reply, 'He's got a different girl every night as far as I can tell. I don't think Jasper is either, he doesn't seem to have a social life, but I think he did mention he had a girlfriend a while ago.'

'Great,' says Katy, 'I'm coming over too!'

Both of her new friends are decidedly single, but judging by the looks our table is receiving, it is unlikely to last for long. Amy is an outrageous flirt when she has had a drink, and whilst not as pretty as Katy, she certainly knows how to attract a boys' attention and then hold it. Her impressive cleavage probably helps considerably, and she uses it to great effect. I wish I had half the same level of confidence. I'm loving being with these girls.

Katy looks around at the various groups of boys with disdain, 'I'm not sure there's anyone here tonight who floats my boat.'

The art history boys shamble over, lining up rows of Jägerbombs. I decline, to a chorus of boos. I know I'm not endearing myself to anyone, but the last time I had one of those had been speech day on my last day of school and I had woken the next morning in my own bed fortunately, but with no idea how I had got there. Plans are being made to go clubbing. Sounds good, I think I may have just found my gang.

It is after two when I thank the Uber driver outside 5, Johnson Road - so much for no more taxis! -and quietly unlock the front door. I've sobered up quite a lot - the booze in the club was so expensive that most of us just danced and drank water. Alex's light is turned off and his room empty - no surprises there, he will still be out hitting it hard somewhere. I turn out the hall lights and head up the stairs, quickly brushing my teeth and changing into an old baggy T-shirt.

Maybe it is the lingering effects of the early glasses of wine followed by a barrel of sugary cocktails, but when I walk past Jasper's room and see his door is ajar and the light still on, I stop and peep inside.

As usual, he is in his chair at the desk with the lights down low, but this time there are four empty beer cans next to him. He looks to be sleeping, with his head on his arms folded across the desk. The little framed photograph is face down next to him, as though it has fallen from his hands as he nodded off. As usual, the double bed is neatly made. I am convinced more than ever that he has never slept in it. The rest of the room is also neat and tidy; no attempts have been made to add any personal touches.

It's way too late to be working, he has obviously nodded off in his chair. It can't be very comfortable, so I tap on the door gently and say his name. He wakes with a start, looking around blearily, then smiles awkwardly at me, clearly embarrassed at having been caught unawares. He rubs his face once then rearranges his facial expression immediately back into the usual one of bland politeness, which I find irritating. He reminds me of Rameses from my earlier lecture - a complete emotional void, determinedly keeping all of his secrets deeply hidden.

'Hey, Sophie, is everything ok?' he asks, stifling a yawn. His amazing voice is raspy from sleep and underuse.

'Hi Jasper, fine thanks.' I reply, awkwardly. 'I've just got back, and then I walked past your room and saw you weren't in bed. You might sleep better there.'

I pause and then add, with a little laugh, 'Actually, do you ever go bed?'

He leans back and folds his arms defensively, so I hastily clarify, 'I don't mean to pry, nothing like that. Sorry, forget I asked, it's really none of my business.'

My face goes red, I can feel it and I'm unsure whether to plough on or just back out of the room.ABwishing fervently that I hadn't bothered now, I steel myself.

'I suppose I was just wondering if you are okay, you seem tired all the time and well, I noticed you don't seem to sleep much……?' I trail off, avoiding his eye, sinking deeper into a hole filled with awkwardness.

Jasper sighs and gives me a half smile. 'Come and sit down, Sophie. Have a beer with me if you like.'

I step inside and perch uncomfortably on the end of the bed, aware for the first time how short my T-shirt is - it barely skims my thighs. He glances down quickly at my thighs too, before looking away, and I feel exposed and vulnerable - alone in the house with this virtual stranger, and we are both extremely conscious of the fact that I am half undressed.

He reaches down to the floor under his desk, producing a can of Sainsbury's own brand lager, and opens it before passing it to me. He takes one for himself and drinks thirstily.

'I think I owe you an explanation, and Alex too.' His words come out in a rush, as if he will change his mind halfway through if they don't, and he'll clam up again.

'You probably think I'm really weird. I don't know if you'll believe this but being here in this house with you two is as good as it's been for me for quite some time. You have no idea how beneficial you are for me, actually - you're both so ....' he searched for the right word and took a swig, 'So normal....and well.... happy.'

I nod and take a swig of lager myself, not sure where the conversation is leading. The word 'normal' and the divine being known as Alex Van-Zeller don't really fit into the same sentence, but I think I know what he is getting at.

'I've not spoken about this to anyone here in Nottingham yet, because, well, it's too hard to say the words out loud, but I had to leave university last year and go back home. I'm from just south of Cork, by the sea, from a small town called Kinsale. Have you heard of it?'

I shake my head. He carries on,

'It's beautiful, really beautiful, you should go there some time, it's surrounded by hills, there's lots of walking and fishing. The tourists love it, it's very pretty.'

Another swig and a deep breath. 'I've lived there all my life, apart from uni, with my mam and my little brother, but last year.... he.... he died very suddenly.'

I stare at him. He had mentioned a bereavement, but beyond that, Alex and I know nothing. He rubs his chin with his hand and turns his head slightly so he's looking away from me at the far wall. He exhales deeply.

'Bloody hell, I think that's the first time I've actually said that out loud. Anyway, he died.... and now I'm back here and it's really hard. I'm struggling to get up every day and carry on, to be honest.'

He looks at me helplessly. I'm stunned. I have no idea how to respond. I had absolutely not expected this conversational direction at all and realise how ill equipped I am to provide any sort of appropriate grown up response. I reckon that even Alex would be better.

Here I am, worried about making friends, worried I can't find my way around in this protected environment of university, with my capable parents just a phone call away. And this man, who I hardly know, this poor man sitting across from me, who I had thought was probably just a bit shy, who has been politely smiling at me and Alex, and cooking with us, and listening to the two of us rabbiting on about nothing, has all the time been carrying around this awful burden.

'I'm so sorry for you Jasper,' I say eventually. It is a useless response. 'I don't know what to say. Gosh, I'm a bit rubbish, I'm afraid.'

He smiles at me sadly, those big brown eyes resting on my face.

'There isn't anything to say, Sophie. He's dead and I've just got to carry on and get through. Can I tell you about him?' he asks, looking at me shyly.

I nod to him to continue.

CHAPTER 5

JASPER

I can't believe I'm doing this. It's nearly three am and I'm choosing now to open up to someone. And I'm choosing Sophie, this beautiful young girl that I only met a couple of weeks ago and who now definitely thinks I'm weird. But she is still here, and still listening, and I need to get it off my chest. I have a feeling she is a good listener. Some girls talk a lot, to fill a space, but I don't think she is one of those.

'It's quite a long story. I'm not sure where to begin. He was younger than me, eight years younger, and he was beautiful, everyone loved him, he was so cute. He had hair like mine, but even curlier and he had a wicked laugh. Look, I've got a picture of him here, when he was a toddler.'

I hold the photo of Christian out to her in its silver frame and she looks at it properly, not just pretending.

'He was a cute baby, Jasper,' she says with a small smile. 'I can tell he's related to you - his eyes are just like yours.'

She hands the photo back to me and I carry on.

'He was a normal, happy, bouncing baby. When he was two and a half, just after this photo was taken, he choked on a grape whilst having his lunch one day. He was just sitting in his highchair as usual, but he choked and nearly died. I was at school, my mam was there, but she couldn't do anything to stop it.

'It was awful, as you can imagine, although I actually don't remember much, because I got sent to live with my aunt for a bit after it happened. When I got back, he had changed. Everything changed. He was still beautiful, he never stopped being that, but...but...They said he'd never get better and they were right, cos he never did.'

I stop speaking for a while and stare at the far wall, trying to keep my shit together. I take a gulp of lager.

'As he got older, he was in a wheelchair, as he couldn't walk, and he couldn't do anything else at all really - he couldn't talk or feed himself or anything. After a few months, because he'd suffered this brain injury, he started to have lots of fits, lots of them and they were awful to watch, sometimes they went on all day, on and off. My dad left after a year, he couldn't hack it anymore, so it was just me, my mam and Christian - that was his name - Christian. He loved us, we'd sit with him and he knew it was us, I know he did, and me and mam, we worshipped him.'

This is by far the most I have actually said about anything to anyone since returning to Nottingham. But now I've started, I can't stop, I don't care what she thinks, I've just got to get it all out. I swallow some more of my cheap shitty lager, clear my throat and carry on. My voice is shaking with the effort to hold back my tears, but I'm beyond caring.

'As he got bigger, it got harder and harder for mam to look after him - he got heavy and she's only little - so I helped a lot when I wasn't at school. I'd carry him up to bed, and after a while, I put him in bed with me every night so that if he had a fit someone was with him. I handled the fits better than mam, I think. I didn't want him to be ever alone and frightened. Then, last Christmas, when I went home to see him, he........'

Tears are running freely down my face now and I make no attempt to brush them away. I don't care that she sees them. I'm gulping the lager down and continue, my voice cracking, but I'm going to get through, I'm going to get to the end.

'In the middle of the night, he had yet another fit and then another one. The fits had been getting worse all week and they wouldn't stop; they went on and on and we had tried everything. Eventually that night he went to sleep, with me cuddling him.

'Later on, in the early morning, with him still in bed next to me, I woke up and he was cold. He was dead, Sophie. The ambulance people tried everything, but they couldn't bring him back and he.... he was just fucking dead. I was there, cuddling him and I couldn't get him to wake up and now he's dead and mam and I haven't got him anymore. We haven't got anything anymore - or anyone. And my mam – she's there in Kinsale, all alone in the house, and I'm here and I should be with her.'

I get to the end and put my head in my hands and weep, great ugly sobs. It's a horrible sound. I see Sophie's long, tanned bare legs walking over to me before she cradles my head against her, and I can feel my wet tears soaking through the thin cotton. I smell fresh laundry and her skin. I don't know how long we stay like that, but her touching me, it feels so nice.

'You have got someone Jasper, you've got me,' she whispers, 'And Alex too. We're probably pretty crap, but we're here for you. Tell me what I need to do, and I'll do it - anything.'

I don't want to move, having her arms around me feels so comforting, but I lift my head and wipe my tears away with the back of my hand.

'I'm so sorry Sophie, I didn't want to do this to you. I never cry, I promised I'd never cry again, but you're being so nice. I can't keep it in anymore. And I'm so bloody tired! I can't sleep; I can't even face getting into bed. I sleep in this chair because every time I get into bed and go to sleep, I wake up and Christian's not there next to me and it's like a fucking constant reminder every bloody night.'

I can see how it is making sense to her now - the bed always made up, the side light on throughout the night, and of course, my exhausted face.

'If you can't sleep,' she says, 'You can always come and sleep with me.' She blurts this out, then looks like she'd like to retract it. 'I mean...., I don't mean like that obviously.'

Her face is reddening. 'What I mean is, I've got that ridiculous, enormous bed that's big enough for three people, with room to spare. I wouldn't even know you were there, and then maybe you wouldn't feel quite so...quite so .... alone.'

She finishes lamely and busies herself with the dregs of her lager. I put down my empty can and blow out my cheeks loudly. I study her face.

'You're a very sweet girl Sophie. Thank you, and thank you for listening to all this. Just promise me that you and Alex will carry on being normal around me. I need it, I really do.'

She stands up to go. I would like her to stay. 'Okay Jasper, I'm going to bed now, but honestly, I'm next door if you need anything, any time, I'll do whatever I can.'

I smile at her gratefully and she slips out of the room, closing the door quietly behind her.

CHAPTER 6

SOPHIE

I wake late next morning, having slept soundly, more due to the excessive alcohol than the late-night revelations from Jasper, which if I had been sober, would have undoubtedly kept me tossing and turning for hours. I lie there, revelling in the warmth and space, thinking about him and everything that he has told me. It strikes me that he is about as far from soulless Rameses as it is possible to get - so much for my emotional intelligence.

I think about my own home life and happy childhood. I'm blessed, and I resolve to try to be more grateful for my own lively, irritating, noisy little brothers back home.

Needless to say, Jasper did not come to my room - what a crazy suggestion! and I hadn't expected it, although I wonder whether a small part of me is just a little bit disappointed. There is definitely something extremely attractive about him and not just his pecs, brown eyes or his honey coated voice. He has something I can't quite put my finger on – a stillness and self-assurance, despite his grief – he seems much older than his twenty something years. Living through tragedy means you grow up pretty quickly, I suppose.

I will tell Alex all about Christian as soon as I can, and we will make sure that we include Jasper in everything we do together. Which up to now, to be fair, isn't much. Thinking of Alex, I am surprised that I can hear him moving about below, clashing the pans in the kitchen, and the tempting smell of bacon wafts up the stairs. He rarely seems to surface before lunchtime, so I climb out of bed, put a brush through my hair and go down to find him.

He is standing with his back to me in the kitchen, preparing a fry up for breakfast. He is clad in a pair of black Calvin Klein boxer shorts and absolutely nothing else. Couldn't he put some clothes on more often, I think? Honestly, pictures of his body jostle for space in my head enough as it is, without adding yet another unbelievable image to my mental photo album.

He hasn't heard me come downstairs and so I lean against the kitchen door frame for a few moments, ogling him. Blimey, this man's physique is perfect! He'd give any Greek God a run for their money. His long lean thighs are deeply tanned, the hard muscles covered in fine blond hairs. He is still completely oblivious to my presence, so I continue enjoying the rounded shape of his buttocks and the well-defined contours of his back and shoulders for a little while longer.

'Morning, Alex!' I say eventually.

He doesn't turn around but carries on separating rashers of bacon and placing them in the pan, totally absorbed in the task.

'Hey, Alex, morning!' I say, a little louder this time.

Still no response. I am extremely puzzled. I walk towards him and tap him lightly on the shoulder,

'I said good morning, Alex!'

He is completely startled and drops the scissors he is holding with a loud clatter.

'Gosh, Sophie, hi! Sorry, you made me jump. Hang on a second.'

He reaches across the counter for a small black leather case. Taking out what look like a couple of circular brown plastic discs, he quickly clips one behind each ear and they disappear into his thick blond waves of hair.

'That's better,' he says, grinning at me, 'I can hear you now.'

I am astonished. 'Are you....er ...deaf?' I ask him, incredulously.

'Well, since I've put my hearing aids on, no, I can hear you perfectly,' he replies innocently.

He grins at me mischievously and strikes a silly pose.

'You, Sophie Ashworth, have the great honour to be living with the one and only Alexander Gottfried Wilhelm Van-Zeller: international playboy and sexy, genius poster child for cochlear implant surgery!'

He pulls back his hair. 'See? I have two electrodes inserted under my skin, and then these microprocessor things just clip onto the outside. They are held on by a magnet. I'm surprised it took you this long to realise!'

I laugh. 'Gottfried? Where the hell did that name come from?'

He pretends to look wounded. 'I like Gottfried, it's my grandfathers' name. I'm from a long line of Gottfried's!'

I laugh again. 'No, but seriously, Alex, I had no idea, why didn't you tell me?'

He carries on putting rashers of bacon into the sizzling pan. 'There's nothing to tell, Sophie. I was born completely deaf - still am without my implants, obviously. When I was a kid, I had an operation to have them fitted in America, luckily my folks had the money to pay for these special tiny ones, that don't have the wires or anything, and I have been seducing girls ever since. They love it of course, poor damaged Alex blah blah blah. I wouldn't have it any other way. I'm proud to be me and proud to be deaf!'

I smile back at him. It is beginning to fit together actually, the way he manages to sleep all day without being disturbed, the way he sometimes stares at me so intently when I speak.

'Do you lip read?' I ask him, curiously.

'Yes, I have to sometimes,' he admits. 'Particularly if I'm in a noisy room. I'm not as good as some people though, because I had my implants quite young. I find that I can either concentrate on hearing or lip reading, but I am not very good at doing them both at the same time. And although I can hear really well with my aids, I don't always catch everything everyone says, especially if it's boring and I zone out a bit.'

He expertly cracks two eggs with one hand on the side of the pan. For someone who apparently can't cook, he has certainly mastered the art of a decent fry up - my mouth is watering. He carries on explaining to me.

'I like putting subtitles on the telly too, I find it much easier. And sometimes, like today, I don't always feel like hearing anything at all. When I'm back at home in Zurich, I can go the whole day without putting my aids on - it drives mama mad. Although, trust me, if you had to spend whole days with my crazy mama and papa, you would wish that you could do the same thing too. And also, when I'm studying, which isn't very often, as you've probably noticed, I can concentrate better if I block out everyone else's noisy world.'

He gives my body an appraising look, then winks at me lasciviously. 'To be honest, Sophie, I perform a lot better in most areas when I don't put my aids on. The complete silence lets me concentrate solely on the one thing I'm doing.'

His voice drops lower and he steps closer so that he can take my fingers in his, his gaze moves from my eyes to my lips and the tip of his tongue runs over his full lower lip. His smooth golden chest is inches from my face, I want to lean forwards and kiss it. He smells of coconut shampoo.

'If I also then close my eyes, Sophie, the entire world is completely shut out. So, if I were to find myself lucky enough to be kissing a girl like you, for example, it's as though my other senses go into overdrive - I would be able to focus only on the feel of her.........the taste of her........the...'

I cut him off - I am blushing furiously and hope he hasn't noticed. 'Alex, stop it! You really are the most ridiculous person. It's fairly amazing, though.... wow! I'd never have guessed.'

He brings my fingertips briefly to his lips before reluctantly letting go of my hand and resuming his frying, a smile playing at the corners of his mouth. He knows the effect he has on me; he knows the effect he has on most women and he is just playing games. He beckons me to sit.

'Come and share this breakfast with me. Jasper and I have decided that we need to get a bit of fat on that skinny arse of yours.'

CHAPTER 7

ALEX

Jasper and I develop an intimate relationship rather more quickly than either of us intended. I'm having a weekend off from hitting the town with Hugo and Seb. My throat is dry from too many fags and I'm knackered. It's Saturday afternoon, and I'm in my room, sprawled in my favourite chair, sweatpants pushed down to my thighs and wanking contentedly. He walks in to check the football results on Sky. I haven't bothered with my hearing aids and so I don't know he's there until he's virtually standing in front of me. He is mortified - I couldn't give a shit really - but I apologise anyway. I decide to take him out for a drink.

We walk to the Wheatsheaves - his suggestion. It's a proper blokey drinking pub, more his thing than mine, with a big selection of independent cask ales. I offer to buy him a drink and see him hesitate.

'Don't get the cheapest, get the one that you want - my shout.' I say.

I quite fancy a gin and tonic, but I have a feeling he'll think less of me, so I have the same as him. Fuck, I'll be growing a hipster beard and becoming a vegan if I have too many of these. We play pool and he thrashes me repeatedly. I always fancied myself as quite a decent player, but clearly not.

'Not much to do in the winter in Kinsale,' he says apologetically, giving me his satisfied smile. 'I'm surprised you haven't got one of these tables in one of your houses, Al, to be honest.'

I have one in two of our houses but keep quiet. I reckon he's the sort of bloke that's naturally good at everything. He runs his hand through his thick curly black hair frequently between shots. It's not an anxious thing - he is very comfortable in his own skin, that's for sure. The barmaid would like to get in his skin too, I think, the way she keeps looking at him, which pisses me off a little. But he is utterly oblivious to the attention he gets, which is sort of sweet.

We have another pint and then another. I can feel a beard actually sprouting. I refuse to let him pay, I know he watches every penny, I've seen his shitty lager in the fridge.

'What do you think of Sophie, then?' I ask, aiming for a neutral tone.

I don't want him to know how keen I am, although I'm not sure why. She had breakfast with me a few mornings ago and I nearly asked her for sex afterwards. She looked so fucking cute in her pyjama shorty things. I flirted with her outrageously, she loved every second of it. It's only a matter of time, and I'm in no rush.

'Bloody gorgeous, mate,' he replies. 'She comes and sits on my bed sometimes and we have a chat about all sorts of things. Well, she talks, and I imagine her in my bed instead of on it.'

Fuck, I think. Why didn't I get the upstairs room? I laugh appropriately. 'She's definitely out the top drawer,' I agree.

We have good laugh after that. He loves his rugby and there is a game on the telly in the pub, so we make a whole afternoon of it. I like watching it, but I'm shit at playing it. I had a go at Harrow, but I had to take my hearing aids off, and the refs didn't like it when I was apparently ignoring them. I played a bit of fives instead and start to explain the rules to Jasper. I'm clearly talking a foreign language and he takes the piss out of me for being so posh.

'I'm sorry about your brother,' I say on the walk home. I'm a dick, because we had had a great afternoon together and I realise I want to spend more time with him. But now he's clammed up again.

'But I'm cool if you don't want me to mention it. I just want you to know that I'm sorry, and if there is anything I can do to help, then I will.'

His hands are deep in his jeans pockets and he takes a big breath in. 'Cheers, Al. I'll be able to talk about it soon, just not yet, I don't think. We should do this again, though, sometime, it's been great.'

CHAPTER 8

SOPHIE

I'm alone in my room, stressing about an assignment. I had spent an evening over at the hall of residence with Katy and Amy, instead of getting it done, and now I'm regretting it. We have been looking at examples of works from a period when sculptural styles were moving away from the emotionless, static Archaic pieces, like Rameses, but had not yet attained the realistic expressions, clothing and lifelike poses of later Classical stuff.

To emphasise the point, Prof Mackie transports us on a wonderful mental journey through thick olive groves, high on the steep hillsides of the small Greek island of Aegina. 'Close your eyes, my children,' he urges in his clear Scottish tones, 'And imagine yourselves travelling up a winding rutted road, feel the heat from the scorching sun on your pale skin, taste the salty sea breeze sweeping in from the Aegean. In front of you lies the ruined Temple of Aphaia, part hidden amongst the trees.'

It is warm in the stuffy lecture theatre and I have no trouble imagining the heat, the olives, the sea breeze and nor does Katy - she is sound asleep. He interrupts our reveries by showing an illustration of the honey-coloured stone temple. Although much damaged over the years and the roof long gone, the east and west facing pediments have been preserved, along with the numerous intact relief sculptures adorning them.

The Prof highlights one example in particular, which catches my eye. Almost hidden in a corner of the eastern pediment, it is a small, simple relief sculpture of a soldier, known as the Dying Warrior. He is lying on his side, propped up on one elbow, and with his other hand he is captured forever in the act of vainly attempting to remove a spear from his bleeding torso.

The smooth curvature of the stone body, defined musculature and the elegant draping of his garments hints at living flesh and blood underneath, the clear poignancy of the scene easily conveyed to us amateur art historians. But his facial features remain stoically unanimated, the eyes unseeing, his lips fixed in a blank, Archaic smile. He is plainly beautiful, and I almost want to reach out and comfort him; such is the depth of pathos.

Alex is out somewhere, and Jasper is in his room as usual. I've just walked past his door earlier and all seems okay. He's studying at his desk but has Radio 4 on quietly in the background and he's waved at me companionably.

Since his extraordinary, sad revelation, I've sat on his bed a couple of times, just chatting about nothing much, and I think he's welcomed the diversion. He's been out with Alex for a few beers too, and I hear them sometimes in the kitchen, fooling around and the occasional burst of laughter. They have even discussed teaming up on a lad's night out in town, although Jasper makes an unlikely wingman for Alex. And clearly, at some point, they have discussed the shape of my bottom, as I discovered when Alex and I shared breakfast. He has no filter that boy.

Despite being apparent polar opposites, they seem to get on really well and have discovered a shared love of rugby, so much so that they have begun to spend quite a lot of time together in front of Sky Sports on Alex's massive telly.

I filled Alex in on the details of Jasper's brother and his horrific death. Neither of us can even begin to imagine the horror of waking and finding your brother dead beside you. His insomnia is more than understandable. Alex has surprised me with his evident concern for Jasper's wellbeing. Despite coming out of his shell a little, he still sleeps in a chair as far as I can tell, and his face remains pale and haunted.

I give up on my essay and settle down into bed for an early night, turning out the light. The heavy brocade drapes across the window prevent any light or noise from outside entering the room, and so I usually fall asleep quickly. Tonight is no different, but my dreams are unsettled, filled with jumbled images; Jasper's face, with vacant unseeing eyes, superimposed on a hard, stone body, Jasper with a bleeding hole in his chest, blood pumping across his abdomen, valiantly trying to save himself from a mortal wound.

I wake with a start and sit up, feeling sweaty and disoriented, and the alarming realisation that it isn't only the vividness of my dream that has woken me. A tiny scraping noise is coming from the direction of the bedroom door, the handle turning ever so quietly. I lie back down on my side, facing towards the door and stay stock-still, suddenly completely alert in the dark, blood drumming in my ears and I fight to bring my rapid breathing under control.

The door is slowly opening, and I am acutely aware of footsteps padding very softly towards the far side of my bed. The duvet lifts and the mattress dips slightly as someone climbs in so very, very carefully next to me. I don't move, not even when an achingly beautiful Irish voice whispers,

'It's only me – it's Jasper - don't wake up.'

I don't respond and carry on feigning sleep, all the while my heart pounding and pounding in my chest. I am convinced that he must be able to hear it and stay paralysed in the same position for what seems like forever.

Eventually, my heart slows a little, and I can hear his breathing become heavier and more regular. Inch by inch, when I am sure he has fallen asleep, I turn myself over, so I am facing him. He doesn't stir. I prop myself on one elbow and study him as he sleeps, my eyes gradually getting used to the dark.

He is lying on his back, with one arm flung above his head and the other resting on top of the covers. His broad shoulders are bare, and I realise I have no idea if he is wearing anything on the bottom half of his body. I'm certainly not brave enough to look, and this thought excites me.

He looks at peace, his curly black hair spread out behind him on the pillow, his pale face relaxed. His lips are slightly parted and his long dark eyelashes, like a small boys', rest on his cheeks. I wonder what those soft lips would feel like if I were to lean over and kiss them, but I resist the urge.

His firm jaw is covered in a dark bristle; he could probably grow a full beard in under a week. He is really beautiful, I realise, but not with the boyish, stunningly handsome, film star beauty of Alex, but the beauty of a full-grown man. I watch him for a long time, my eyes feasting on him, but my mind thinking back to the tortured Dying Warrior, until eventually I fall asleep, turned away again from him.

Next morning, I wake early, snuggling down in the warmth of the duvet, before taking a sharp intake of breath as I recall the events of the night. I sit bolt upright and look around, but I am alone, the room is empty apart from me, the covers lying neatly on the far side of the bed. I shake the sleep out of my brain. Had I dreamt it? No, definitely not, he had been there, and when I lift the duvet, I can see an indentation of where his body has lain. Placing my hand on the white cotton sheet, I can feel it is still warm.

Leaning across, I press my nose to the pillow next to me, breathing in an aroma of fresh laundry and what I have started to think of as '*eau de* Jasper'. The smell of him and the recollection of him in my bed turns me on, I can feel warmth between my thighs. My heart starts beating faster again, I bury my face in his pillow enjoying my body's awakening, and my hand strays to touch myself under the covers.

CHAPTER 9

JASPER

Am I really doing this? Yes, I am, and that first night I got six hours straight sleep. I felt like a new man next morning, stronger. I am confident that my tears are unlikely to ambush me at inopportune moments. So, I have done it again the next night and the night after that.

I join her when it is very late, and most evenings she is already asleep, and probably only dimly aware of my body next to her. And I am gone before she stirs in the morning. I want to tell someone, to sense check my behaviour, to find someone to tell me that her invitation was true, and she wasn't just trying to stop me from crying. I think of telling Alex, as I have no-one else, but I know he would be pissed off with me - I've seen how he looks at her.

The person I should really discuss it with is Sophie, but neither of us mention it when our paths cross, either on the stairs or in the kitchen. We are both too shy to bring it up. My unspoken gratitude comes out in my solicitude towards her - offering tea or coffee, even cooking pasta for us both one night when Alex is out. Our conversation stays on safe subjects; our studies, rugby, Alex's roster of female consorts.

Over dinner one night, she started to tell me about Alex's deafness, but I cut her off with a smirk. I recounted the story.

'You were out with Katy and I wandered downstairs to make a sandwich one afternoon. I saw that Alex's door was open and so I had a quick look in, to see if he'd got the football match on the telly.'

Sophie had nodded encouragingly. I went on to relate, laughing softly as I spoke, how I was greeted by Alex, hand jammed down inside his sweatpants, energetically giving himself what I euphemistically refer to as a 'hand shandy', whilst watching a Transformers film with subtitles and the sound muted.

'I was absolutely mortified!' I recall, shaking my head at the memory. 'I tried to pretend I hadn't seen anything and backed out through the door. But typical Alex, he wasn't bothered at all – he didn't even take his hand away!'

I laugh incredulously. To have that level of brazenness. 'He just casually winked at me, and said something like, aah, alright Jaz mate, awfully sorry I didn't hear you come in - not wearing my hearing aids mate. I'll try to remember to close the door next time. You can come and watch Transformers with me if you like - I've just reached the good bit!'

I do a rubbish impersonation of Alex's posh Swiss-English drawl and Sophie thinks it hilarious.

'I'm assuming that it's Megan Fox in a tight T-shirt that turns him on and not cars that change into robots!' I joke, drily 'Although he also has a fondness for old Top Gear re-runs, so maybe he has some weird fetish we don't know about!'

'Nothing would surprise me with Alex!' replies Sophie, rolling her eyes.

I relate this story in a deadpan fashion and realise how much I enjoy the few conversations we share together. It is as if the invisible wire that draws me inexorably to her at night loses all of its tension by morning and we revert back to simply being agreeable housemates. Although I'm not sure that is enough for me. I feel better after a few good night's sleep - my pale face is less drawn and the purple circles under my eyes have almost disappeared. Even Alex has noticed. 'I'm guessing you're getting your end away at last!' he speculates. I blush and rapidly change the subject.

It is evening again, and Sophie has said her goodnights early and gone up to her room. Alex has had Hugo and Seb round all afternoon and we've shared a few beers. She hasn't felt like joining us tonight, I can tell. We are settled with more beers and a bumper bag of Bombay mix to watch Champions League football, an armchair each. She doesn't mind the football, but she absolutely loathes Bombay mix. She's been irritable and moody for the last couple of days and her period cramps have started. I know this because she was in the kitchen earlier, as soon as Alex's mates had gone, in her oldest, baggiest T-shirt, swallowing a couple of paracetamols, and filling a hot water bottle.

I'm trying to concentrate on the football - not easy as Alex prefers to watch it muted with subtitles, but I really want to see if she's okay. I'm sure there are times when she wished she lived with girls - tonight is probably one of them. As soon as the match is over, I go up.

She is lying on her side in the darkness as I slip into the vast space behind her. It is earlier than usual, much earlier, and she pretends to be asleep. I am paralysed with indecision. I sense her misery. The bed smells of her, I can smell her vanilla shampoo and my need to touch her grows. My dick is hard, when was it ever this hard? I make a decision that I hope I don't regret tomorrow. I shift my weight in the bed so that I am lying on my side and I boldly snake my arm over her hip. I am scarcely breathing; my fingertips burn where they brush over her smooth skin.

Wordlessly, I gently and deliberately lift the cooling hot water bottle away from her tummy. Casting it aside, I place the palm of my own warm, dry hand tenderly in its place on her lower belly. She takes an involuntary sharp intake of breath; I hear it and freeze. It feels unbelievably good, and it is all I can do not to gasp at the feel of her. My dick is twitching for attention and I wrap my other hand around it. If she is going to sit up and ask me what the hell I'm doing, then that moment is now, but she is silent.

I draw her body back towards me across the expanse of bed, so that I am spooning her from behind. She fits beautifully. My face is almost in her hair, I breath in her thrilling scent. She continues to lie perfectly still, I'm scarcely daring to breathe, focusing on the gentle pressure of my comforting hand on her abdomen, easing away the cramping pains. Neither of us speak for a few minutes - I am too terrified.

'Does that feel better, Sophie?' I ask, and my voice is hoarse.

She nods in the dark, and I am overcome with the sensation of my naked body pressed softly into her back. I cannot trust myself to speak. I am more turned on than I have ever thought possible without actually, well, doing anything with someone, and it takes every fibre of my being not to press into her more.

'Go to sleep sweetheart.' I whisper eventually.

CHAPTER 10

SOPHIE

I awake next morning, alone as usual, and definitely confused. I need to work out what is going on. The straightforward sleeping thing is fine, a true friendship is emerging between us, albeit a slightly unconventional one. But last night was on another level entirely. Was that his version of making a play for me? If so, then I can't deny that I am very attracted to him, physically anyway. Indeed, my body seemed to be crying out for his touch; just thinking about him spooning me makes me feel aroused again.

I need to track him down and we need to talk. He's troubled, hurting and still in the depths of his grief, which is no basis on which to begin a relationship. He is nowhere near ready for that and I don't think I am either. But it's not as if we're having a relationship anyway - we haven't even kissed or held hands or been on a date!

Yet I cannot ignore the fact that we share a bed night after night, and last night was possibly the most erotic encounter I have ever had - and we hadn't done anything! I can still feel the weight of his hand lying against my belly and the light pressure of the length of his muscular warm body against mine. At least now I know whether he sleeps naked.

I go downstairs to be greeted by a note scribbled on an old envelope propped up against the kettle. It is addressed to me and is very short.

'Dear Sophie, gone on rugby tour to Manchester for a few days, back on Monday. Hope you are feeling better. Look after pretty boy for me.' It is signed 'Jx'.

No mention of last night, no kiss, no emoji, no hint at all as to his emotions. Typical man, I think, disappointed. The handwriting is scruffy and barely legible. He'll make a good doctor, I reflect. Our chat will have to wait.

Alex wanders into the kitchen (predictably only wearing those black Calvin's) to make a cup of tea. He indicates to his ears that he is in what he refers to as his 'powered down' mode, which means either his batteries in his hearing aids are being recharged or more likely, that he isn't ready to join the hearing world yet. Probably the latter, as he seems to have collections of little circular batteries everywhere, and several sets of hearing aids.

This morning I don't blame him for not wanting to talk - I feel much the same. Without Jasper, and knowing he isn't just down the road at the medical school but is actually out of town, the house seems empty, even though he is the quietest of the three of us. I hold the note up to Alex so he can read it.

'Never mind Sophie, you've still got me. Alone together at last - mmmmm! There are girls queuing up to take your place!'

He beams at me to show he is joking, although studying his devastating body, I know that he is probably right. His voice takes on a slightly nasal quality when he can't hear, which I find unbelievably cute. I think about waiting until he puts on his hearing aids and telling him about Jasper and his night-time visits, but decide to keep it to myself, my secret, for the time being. Maybe I should just start telling him now to get it off my chest, knowing he can't hear, but he has already taken his cup of tea back to bed.

'Dainty pricks!' intones the unmistakable booming voice of Prof Mackie at the start of his weekly lecture. 'You lot need to see beyond the dainty pricks!'

He repeats the bizarre phrase, rolling the 'r' of the word 'prick' in a dramatic fashion as he strides purposefully across the stage. Behind him, displayed on the huge whiteboard, is an image of a giant marble statue known as the Farnese Hercules, the mythological hero depicted as a rugged man mountain, now weary from completing his famed twelve labours and resting his bulk on his sturdy club.

Our studies have completely moved forwards from the Archaic period, of which I have become extremely fond, to the study of Classical Greek statues, of which the Farnese Hercules is an excellent example. This period in time was a celebration of fabulous Greek heroes and young gladiators - athletes in their prime, forever immortalised, never to grow old. These statues paid homage to the vibrancy of the youthful male, unashamedly displaying their nakedness and taut rippling muscles, to be admired by all who came to marvel at their sporting prowess.

Under Prof Mackie's expert tutelage, we become fluent in the language used to describe these idealised forms; musical Italian words, such as contrapposto, (my personal favourite) which describes the incredible ability of these early sculptors to craft believable human poses from huge slabs of rock, and merely by a subtle shift of body weight onto one leg, to effortlessly represent the influence of gravity on the leg muscles and limbs.

We learn an appreciation of rhythmos - harmony and balance captured in a moment in time, such as seen in Discobolus, a beautiful sculpted youth forever frozen at the point of hurling his discus high into the admiring crowds.

What it seemed the Italians have failed to supply a romantic term for, and which the Prof is now helpfully supplying, was the tiny penises that seemed completely out of proportion on these hulking giants. He was definitely warming to his theme.

'Big pricks were distasteful to ancient Greeks, belonging only to fools and barbarians, those poor characters lacking in any self-control. By contrast, it was considered a virtue of a real hero to have modesty in all areas including the control of his most base desires. From henceforth, you shall be seeing many, many dainty pricks. Let that be a message to all you rampant students out there with your hormones running freely out of control. You must learn control your base desires, you young barbarians!'

It is the end of October. Amy and Katy have plans to get a gang together for a big night out at Cripps Hall, one of the male halls of residence. A couple of live bands are playing, and it is probably going to be the last outdoor student gig of the year, as the nights are drawing in and the clocks will soon go back. The weather is set to be dry and the booze will be cheap. I'm looking forward to it. Jasper is still away until tomorrow and so we are yet to talk.

I spend the day shopping in town, treating myself to a new pair of skinny grey jeans from Zara to wear with my old black biker boots. I check in with my family, phone Fi to catch up on her news, and take a long shower, washing and drying my hair carefully.

On my way out, planning on catching the bus at the bottom of Johnson Road, I meet Alex on the stairs (just a little white towel hanging off his hips, naturally) and he looks me up and down, as only Alex can get away with.

'Not bad Sophie Ashworth, not bad at all! Who's the lucky man?'

I explain that I am meeting the girls on campus and he studies my lips intently as I speak. It is clear he is on the way to the shower.

'Fab! Give me two seconds and we'll go together. I'm going up to Cripps too and I've got an Uber coming in ......' He glances at his watch and frowns, 'Shit, three minutes.'

In no time at all he is with me in the back of the car, looking amazing, smelling amazing and clearly in party mode. He produces a well-worn, brown leather hip flask from the inside pocket of his jacket, takes a long swig and passes it to me. I take a cautious sip. Delicious, sweet syrupy sloe gin.

He carelessly drapes his arm across the back of the car seat and around my shoulders and, in the confined space of the cab, I am enveloped in the rich scent of Chanel, expensive coconut shampoo and the warmth of his arm. I inhale deeply and snuggle closer. Alex is completely oblivious to the effect he is having on me and is bantering with the driver over Nottingham Forest's home defeat this afternoon. I study him in profile, his flawless skin, high cheekbones and angular jaw. He laughs out loud at something the driver says and turns to smile down at me.

'No mate, she's not my girlfriend, unfortunately. Too good for me! Nah, we're just housemates. One day perhaps, when she realises what she's missing!'

I giggle and prod him in the ribs. He gives my shoulder a friendly squeeze then leans his head down to my ear, whispering,

'Maybe a goodnight kiss later though, hey baby?'

I freeze, acutely aware of the proximity of his sensuous lips to my face and his warm breath on my cheek. I look up at him - he studies my face seriously for a moment with those wicked blue eyes, then sits back again, smiling to himself and looking out of the window.

When I alight from the taxi, I see Amy and Katy looking around anxiously for me.

'There you are!' cries Katy, with relief. The girls hurry over. Alex climbs out of the other side of the car. He saunters round to my side, waves a hand at the girls in greeting and gives me one of his customary quick forehead kisses before sloping off towards the bar.

'Did I just see who I thought I just saw? How the hell do you know him?' Katy demands at once, giving me a welcome hug.

'Oh.... that's just Alex,' I reply with a grin, trying to be cool and failing miserably. My friends stare at me incredulously.

'What do you mean, that's 'just' Alex?' says Amy in wonder. 'That is Alex Van-Zeller, possibly the hottest bloke to ever go to Nottingham University like...ever! Oh my God, he's absolutely gorgeous! Imagine getting naked with him!'

Katy and Amy dreamily watch his retreat into the packed bar where he is instantly surrounded by a throng of mates, both girls and boys. I laugh.

'I live with him, silly, he's my housemate! And actually, I get to see him almost naked all the time, as he never seems that keen on putting on many clothes. In fact, tonight is about the most dressed I think I've ever seen him!'

I laugh again with glee as I take Katy's arm and steer her into the bar. 'And ladies, let me tell you, you would not be disappointed. He is as gorgeous underneath as you are imagining!' The girls are very impressed.

'Bloody hell, Sophie, when you said you lived with a bloke called Alex, we didn't realise it was that Alex! We're coming around to visit asap! Where did you say you lived again?'

I'm having a really great evening. I'm wanting to tell them both about my extraordinary night with Jasper, but it's too noisy and busy and not the right moment. I down a couple of cheap cocktails early on, which after the sloe gin in the taxi, goes straight to my head. Amy and Katy seem to know everyone, and we all dance crazily, right in the middle of the mosh pit to both of the bands.

A bloke called Ben, one of Katy's brothers' mates from home catches my eye. He's drinking with the art history boys. Every time I look up, he seems to be watching me from across the crowded bar, looking away awkwardly when we actually make eye contact. I'm rubbish at this sort of thing, Amy is brilliant, so mostly I just enjoy the music, the dancing, the company of my lively new friends and the drinks, which are definitely much cheaper than in the bars in town.

I spot Alex a few times, his height and blond hair standing out in the crowds of people, always surrounded by girls, sometimes bending lower to catch what they are saying, with his hand resting on their shoulders, or throwing his head back and laughing with his mates. It is probably well after midnight when the live music stops, the drum and bass start thumping, and the bar staff are ringing for last orders.

We have lost Amy a few minutes ago to a rather intense Scottish engineering student, who she has been stalking all night. Personally, me and Katy are struggling to see the attraction of him. He is big and muscly, but in that gorilla-ish sort of way, with chicken drumstick thighs and overgrown deltoids. He has mean piggy eyes and has scowled all night at anybody who has accidentally glanced in his direction.

Katy has just excused herself to go to the loo, and I wonder whether this is a tactical toilet trip, as Ben approaches and thrusts a plastic beaker of warm white wine into my hand. He is pleasantly pissed.

'Don't see you out much, Sophie?' he states, nervously taking a gulp of his own drink.

Not the most exciting of chat up lines, but I am having such a great time, I don't care. And anyway, he seems nice, and quite good looking in a typical, brown haired and boy next-door sort of way. He is standing quite close to me, one arm resting on the bar, his body facing towards me. He is slightly invading my personal space in the way that we all do when we are drunk, and I detect a whiff of stale sweat.

'Maybe I could see you again sometime?' he tries again. 'You should come out more! Are you going to Amy's birthday thing on Wednesday? Or better still, can I walk you home now?'

I concentrate on taking a sip of my wine to buy myself some time, unsure how to answer. But I will never know how I choose to respond, because before I open my mouth, I am rescued by a pair of strong arms circling my waist from behind. Gasping with shock, I turn to see Alex giving Ben a hard stare across the top of my head. He forces a tight smile, then leans down and speaks into my ear from behind.

'Sophie, gorgeous, can we go home now? My left battery ran out ten minutes ago and the other one has just beeped a twenty-minute warning. I haven't brought any spares and so I'm going to turn into a pumpkin very soon.'

As he speaks, his lips ever so slightly brush the hairs on the back of my neck, and I shiver involuntarily. His hands stay at my waist, his thumbs caressing my hipbones through the thin material of my top. Ben immediately ceases to exist, backing off into the crowd, his face and body blurring into the background with everyone else.

We start walking off the university campus towards Lenton. There isn't a taxi in sight. I left my phone at home and Alex's phone is out of charge. But it is a clear, cloudless night with just a slight autumn chill, so it is refreshing to be out in the fresh air after the fug of people crammed into the bar. We link arms loosely as we begin the half hour walk home. Alex doesn't ask me who Ben is and I don't really expect him to, so mostly we walk and talk about nothing much at all. Almost fifteen minutes in and Alex puts a hand up to his right ear and fiddles with the plastic disc.

'That's it, no more talking Sophie, the right one's gone too.'

We have just crossed the busy hospital roundabout so still have a fair distance to go. Leaving the bustle of the main road, we pass through a quiet, more residential area. Without warning, Alex stops abruptly and leans against a low red-bricked wall. Reaching for my hand he pulls me to him, the other arm now around my waist.

'Seeing as how we can't talk anymore, Sophie, I think it's time for that goodnight kiss that I mentioned earlier.'

He leans down so his mouth touches mine, his soft lips cool from the night air and gently probing. He is gauging my response and as I don't pull away, he kisses again, more firmly, pulling my body even closer to him. I close my eyes and surrender to the kiss; I hear myself softly moan and I return the pressure. The world around us vanishes, as my body responds in a way that I know I have never responded to a kiss before. It probably only lasts a minute, but I could let it go on forever. He pulls away, breathing heavily, his face flushed. Cupping my face in his warm hands, he gives me a serious look.

'I told you that I do my best work when I can't hear anything.' He breaks into giggles, and I love that the cool, sophisticated Alex Van-Zeller giggles.

I don't want it to stop and reach to kiss him again, pushing the length of my body against him, my arms around his neck. This time it is Alex who groans involuntarily, and the kiss becomes more heated, I can feel his erect penis bulging hard through our layers of clothing – no dainty prick there! His hands move to my rear, exploring the shape of my denim clad buttocks and drawing me in nearer still. We stay like that for several minutes more, he is pushing his penis up against my belly. Finally, reluctantly, I pull away.

'Home?' I mouth, and he nods his assent.

We set off, arm in arm this time, closer, the electricity between our bodies almost palpable. Once through the front door, we kiss again and again, each time Alex's hands move lower, his long fingers begin caressing the skin around the low waistband of my jeans and he starts undoing the top button. I put my hand over his to stop him going any further. He looks surprised.

'We can't do this.' I say to him, enunciating carefully and making sure he is looking at my face.

'Why not?' he pants, leaning in again, his busy hand still working determinedly at my jeans.

It is a fair question, and every inch of me wants to continue, but I think of us, sharing this house together. How will it feel in the morning, and for the rest of the year? I'm not ready for that. I force myself to step away from him and do up the button on my jeans once more.

'Because........because you do this to lots of girls,' I gesticulate with my arm as if to an invisible audience of eager girls. 'And I don't want to be just another one of them. And....well...I live with you! It could be awkward! We need to think about this! Do you understand what I'm saying?'

Alex pulls me back to him and buries his face in my neck.

'I do understand,' he says in a resigned, muffled voice, 'But I don't like it. I want you Sophie!' he beseeches.

I love the way he says my name, his Swiss accent making it sound sexy and alluring instead of plain and dull and English. I nearly succumb there and then. He kisses me again, but the urgency of the moment has passed, his touch is soft and gentle as he traces his fingers across my lips.

'I want you too, Alex.' I murmur, into his mouth, but obviously he has no idea as he can't see my lips. I break off again and wait until he looks straight at me.

'Still friends?' I ask.

He grins, back to his normal, playful self. 'More than friends now Sophie! I'm going to expect this more often!'

I am too agitated and wide-awake to sleep, despite the late hour and the alcohol. My groin and lips are still on fire, and I replay the passionate kissing over and over in my mind, sorely tempted to rejoin him downstairs after all, as my stomach flips over with each memory. But surely I have been wise by stepping away, no matter how difficult it has been to say no. I know Alex - Jasper and I hear him at night - he changes girls like he changes his socks, and I have too much self-respect to join the growing list of girls of whom he's grown tired.

And what about Jasper? I feel guilty that he hasn't crossed my mind all evening. But why should he? We aren't having a relationship; I am helping him overcome his bereavement insomnia and he gave me a late-night cuddle when I was feeling sorry for myself! Maybe there is nothing more to it than that? Just because I had found our spooning session intensely erotic didn't automatically mean that he had too - for all I know, he could be in bed with a girl up in Manchester right at this moment! I realise how little I know of him. I have no idea what he is thinking.

I toss and turn a little while longer, too many conflicting thoughts crowding my brain. My nerve endings still burn from my encounter with Alex, my body reminding me how frustrated I feel. I am so close to joining him downstairs. He is completely irresistible, everything about him is utterly arousing, and sex with him will undoubtedly be everything that those amazing kisses promise. I feel the wetness - even now- between my legs, and my nipples tingle with the memory of his expert touch. I reach down under the covers and relieve my frustration as best I can.

I'm up early on Sunday morning and start the day with a brisk run in the fresh air. It clears my muzzy head. I should do this more often - it's too easy at university to do bugger all between lectures and home and the pub, without teachers or parents encouraging more worthy activities.

Back at Johnson Road, Alex is still sleeping - I don't expect him to surface for several hours more and am relieved that I can put off facing him a little while longer. Jasper is yet to return, so I spend the next few hours catching up on some assignments and checking in with family and friends. I plan on steering clear of questions about boys, but my old friend Fi knows I'm hiding something. She pretends otherwise and is keen to share the details of her latest crush with me. After nearly an hour of chat, I feel that I know this Fraser bloke about as well as Fi herself does.

'So, Soph,' she says finally. 'Spill the beans then.'

So, I do, but I don't mention Jasper and I don't know why.

'Well, I snogged my housemate, Fi, but I don't want to take it any further. Actually, let me rephrase that. I do want to take it further, because he's absolutely the best-looking man on the planet and he's really sweet and funny and Swiss and deaf....'

'Deaf?' She is surprised at this.

'Yes, totally deaf, unless he's wearing his hearing aids - he's been deaf from birth. He's unbelievably cute actually. He says it makes him a better lover as he can concentrate better than any other bloke, because he can't hear. He's a bit of a comedian.'

I realise I'm almost drooling when I talk about him - until I say these things out loud, I don't appreciate how much I like him.

'I'm struggling to see the problem, Soph,' says Fi sensibly.

'Er.... well, I live with him, Fi? Which could be a problem if it doesn't work out, as we've got another two and a half terms to go. Oh, and he is an absolute man whore, to put it bluntly. You wouldn't trust him as far as you can throw him.'

'Aaah,' says Fi, and she goes silent for a moment. I could add at this point that in addition to Alex, I am becoming ridiculously fond of a beautiful sad man that soothes away period pains with the palm of his hand, but I don't, and funnily enough, she doesn't ask.

'Well, Soph, if you want the sex of your life, then go for it, but be prepared to have your heart broken and the house dynamics a little.... strained.'

Fi and I are in tune, because it is exactly the conclusion that I've drawn too, out on my run this morning.

I go downstairs in search of company. Alex is leaning back in a chair at the kitchen table, engrossed in a rare moment of study, predictably shirtless and in a belt-less pair of old jeans, that hang beautifully off his narrow hips. The fine trail of blond hair leading south from his navel is beyond gorgeous. Not that I am staring, naturally. His face lights up, and I feel a familiar thrill.

'Hey beautiful!' he smiles at me, blows a kiss, then returns to his book. I start preparing a rather complicated Thai recipe I picked up in Sainsbury's, and we work happily alongside each other. Alex is absentmindedly eating his way through a dish of plump black olives as he studies, and it amuses me to see him place each stone carefully into a heart shaped pattern on the table after he's sucked on it. Neither of us allude to last night.

Just as I am putting the finishing touches to the meal, the front door rattles and Jasper comes shuffling through, dropping his sports bag onto the floor and collapsing into the nearest chair. He looks flushed and knackered, but in a good, healthy way. He has a small cut at the corner of his mouth and the faint outline of a fresh bruise below one eye. I feel a rush of pleasure at the sight of him.

'Bloody hell, that smells great!' he sighs, contentedly.

'Good time?' queries Alex, pushing his books aside to clear a space for an extra dinner plate.

'Brilliant thanks mate, really great, but I'm absolutely beat. We played five games and narrowly lost in the final and that's only because their ref was biased.'

He grins happily at us both and it is the first genuinely relaxed smile I have ever seen on his face. Alex evidently notices it too, because he gives me a slight nod of satisfaction. We dish out the food together; Alex helps himself to a bottle of beer and offers one to us. I accept, but Jasper declines.

'Bloody hell, it must have been a good tour!' suggests Alex. 'You've not missed much here mate. Actually, yeah, a load of us went to that party up at Cripps last night. The bands were pretty good; it was a decent night out. Of course, at one point I had to rescue young Sophie here from some absolute tosser who was trying to make a move on her...'

I roll my eyes at them both. Jasper smirks.

'I'm sure she was thrilled that you were around to save her, Alex,' he says sarcastically.

'I'm sure she was!' retorts Alex, 'He looked a right twat!'

I harrumph at him and try to sound indignant.

'He is called Ben, and I don't know him very well, but he was only asking me out for a drink! I don't know if he's a twat or not, but I guess I'm never going to find out now, thanks to your alpha male display!'

'Good!' replies Alex in a satisfied voice.

It takes only half a beat for me and Alex to realise that Jasper has said good at exactly the same time. Alex casts him a curious look, a half smile playing on his lips, but Jasper has quickly turned away and stands up, wincing in pain as he does so, and puts his plate in the sink.

'Thanks Sophie, that was delicious - my turn tomorrow. I'm off for a shower and a couple of ibuprofens.'

Alex stays in his seat, helping himself to the remnants of the curry. Neither of us speak.

'It would appear that you have maybe two admirers in this house, Sophie,' he ventures at last, his eyes watching my reaction carefully.

I say nothing but feel myself reddening. I could tell Alex now about Jasper, but I don't. Alex chooses to stay quiet and we carry on eating. The conversation moves onto other things and we clear up together. He likes art - I don't know why he didn't choose an art history degree, as his knowledge is already halfway there. I talk about the temple of Aphaia at Aegina - he knows it.

'How come you know so much?' I ask him.

He shrugs. 'Mama is obsessed, and we travel a lot, we go to a lot of galleries. I'm an only child, remember! I've spent a lot of time with my parents doing adult stuff.'

'We'll have to go down to London together sometime,' I say, and he nods.

'I'd like that a lot, Soph.'

He finishes his beer. Putting the empty bottle down next to the bin, he stands in front of me, blocking the doorway.

'I think I just need to check if last nights' kiss was as good as I remember it being. I've been preoccupied by it all day.'

He leans in and kisses me softly on the lips, his hand trailing its way slowly down the side of my body, coming to rest on my hipbone. The other is lightly playing with my hair. I close my eyes and sink into the kiss, instantly feeling my own response. Goodness, he's bloody good, so good. When we pull apart, Alex whispers, 'Not bad, darling Sophie, not bad at all. I think I could get used to this.'

He starts gathering up his laptop and books, humming to himself cheerfully. He doesn't try to kiss me again, and I'm almost grateful, I feel emotionally drained, what with last night still fresh in my mind and now Jasper's interesting response to the story of poor Ben's attempt to ask me out. So much to think about! I retire to bed early, flick through a couple of news stories on my phone and turn out the light.

It is probably an hour later when I stir to the sound of my door being pushed slowly open. I am lying curled on my right side as usual and feel the familiar bulk of Jasper slip in behind me, on the far side of the bed. I giggle in the dark as I hear him wince in pain.

'It's not bloody funny, Soph!' he scolds in a whisper, but I can tell he's smiling too. I wait for him to settle onto his back in his usual pose. But tonight, he gingerly rolls onto his side and his hand gently finds its way over my hip, before taking up position across my lower belly, just like it had done once before. It feels as wonderful as it had the last time. I automatically snuggle back into the warm curve of his body and close my eyes again.

'We need to talk, Jasper,' I say in the darkness.

'We do, Sophie,' he agrees. A pause.

'I missed you, Sophie. Did you miss me?' his lilting voice whispers, and I smile happily to myself in the dark, feeling my heart melt.

'Yes, Jasper, yes, I did.'

CHAPTER 11

ALEX

'So, here's the thing, Hugo,' I say to my good pal as we lean back against the bar. 'Why is it that the bird you really want to fuck, more than any other, is the one that won't fuck you?'

Hugo grins and pinches one of my olives. This isn't a student bar obviously, we're at one of the big hotels in town. Seb will be here later, and we can drink our gin and tonics in peace, without mockery.

We don't mind the student places every now and again, but we recognised early on that we're kindred spirits, the three of us. We don't like cheap booze and grimy pubs and can afford to avoid them. If people think that makes us atypical students, then we're not apologising. But, more importantly, we're here tonight because Hugo has a thing for the older lady, he is already making eyes with a fit blond across the bar. By older, I mean about twenty-five.

'Must be a new experience for you, Al,' he says laughing.

'It's not bloody funny, Hugsy! I have to see her every day!'

I share a kiss with Sophie most nights, unless I'm out late, like tonight. Occasionally, I surprise her when we are washing the dishes or sitting with our notes spread out at the kitchen table. It only happens when Jasper isn't around - I have a feeling that she wouldn't like him to know.

I'm losing my touch. I can be minding my own business and then I find myself gazing at her, and it's followed by an uncontrollable urge to grab her by the wrist and kiss her. My hands generally stray to the line of her knickers, just to remind her what I'm really about. My cock is always rock hard, obviously.

The passion of these moments catches her by surprise too. I press her against the kitchen cupboards, the fridge, the kitchen door. These heated encounters are brief, only lasting a few minutes and only ever longer if they take place in my room, behind a closed door. She wanders in sometimes and finds me sprawled in my chair, sometimes sleeping, sometimes working. These are the best times; the ones that test her resolve the most. I can see her wavering. Often, I have removed my hearing aids and kiss with an urgency that leaves her panting and wanting more. I pull her hand down to my cock, its warm length straining against the material of my jeans.

'Come on Sophie, babe,' I murmur breathlessly, 'You're bloody killing me here.'

I don't say all this to Hugo and Seb, of course. 'I just wish she'd bloody try it once - she won't look back. Once she's had the Van-Zeller manhood, she won't want to try anything else. Ever.'

They smile at me pityingly. They've heard it all before, every time we go out in fact.

'What's so special about her anyway?' asks Hugo. 'I mean, I know she's fit, but there are plenty of fit girls out there.' He's talking to me, but still looking over at his woman. He'll go over soon, I sense he's building up to it.

'Apart from the challenge of getting her into my bed?'

'Yes,' says Seb, 'Apart from that.'

'Let me think.' I pause, not sure where to begin. 'Well, for starters, she laughs at my jokes - she has a really dirty laugh, like she smokes twenty fags a day, and it's a big surprise the first time you hear it and you want to make her laugh so you can hear it again. And she doesn't pander to me, she doesn't try too hard. She's so kind to Jasper - she worries about him as much as I do. She loves art, like I do, she hasn't a clue what she wants in life, she gets anxious over silly little things, she's a bit shy in groups, she loves sloe gin, she doesn't mind Sky Sports, she kisses me like it's the first time every time, er....what else?' They are staring at me, clearly wondering if I'm losing the plot. I think I probably am.

'You'll get over her, Al,' says Seb kindly. He's a kind man, I'm very fond of him. Of both of them, actually.

'Yeah, probably,' I agree, but I'm not convinced.

I'm not hanging around pleading with her though, that's for sure. I've stopped bringing birds back to Johnson Road, but it doesn't mean I can't go to theirs.

CHAPTER 12

JASPER

The first term is already more than halfway through. The nights are becoming cooler and the leaves have fallen from the trees. I feel like Kinsale is another world, but it is always there, at the back of my mind. I can concentrate better now though, and I'm officially not exhausted. I can't imagine that there has once been a time in my life when I haven't known Sophie and Alex.

We still need to talk. I know that, but I'm scared what she will say and where the conversation will take us. I join her religiously every single night. I wrap my solid presence around her. Our relative positions in the enormous bed remain unchanged, my hand flat and warm against her belly, her bottom tucked in against my naked flesh. She sleeps with my cool breath caressing the back of her neck. Sometimes, when she is asleep, I press my hardness against her, and my heartbeat catches in my throat. And on other occasions, I inch my hand ever so slightly lower, my fingers more splayed down towards the juncture of her thighs. I need to talk to her, soon.

I am always gone by morning, carrying the delicious warm scent of her body with me. Does she dream that my fingertips reach lower? During the day, I am friendly, relaxed and definitely more cheerful, but we stay slightly distant, as if our night-time closeness has never happened. I am content to listen to her and Alex dissect the day. I like an opportunity to take the piss out of Alex about pretty much everything, but I still need the peace of being alone in my room, with the radio humming in the background, reading or having a couple of quiet beers by myself.

It is the middle of the afternoon and I'm at med school. Actually, I'm standing outside the med school, on the front steps, talking to

Samira. It's chilly, although the sun is shining, and I wish I had my coat with me. Samira often finds me during the day. She would like us to get together again, but I'm not that keen. I've changed and she hasn't - the same things about her that made me call it off before Christian died are still there. She's cross with me, I can tell, her tone is becoming tetchy.

I spy Sophie alighting from the bus, lugging her bag of books across the parking bays in front of the huge building, heading towards the flyover bridge. I think she has spotted us too but is pretending not to. It will be Samira not me, that caught her eye. Samira is stunning, Sophie will have admired her tall, willowy frame, and natural elegance, before she realised the man with her was me. Samira is dark skinned, with sleek black hair, which hangs in a thick glossy ponytail down her back. She has her hand on my arm and is leaning into me, talking urgently, trying to persuade me to come on a night out with her and the old crew. Her voice is raised, but Sophie is too far away to hear what she is saying. She begins walking more quickly towards the bridge with her head down, hoping that I haven't spotted her. I disentangle myself from Samira, just before she reaches the safety of the bridge.

'Sophie, hey Sophie, wait!' I call out.

She turns reluctantly and pretends to be surprised to see me.

'Oh, hi Jasper, how are you?'

I jog towards her, panting slightly from the exertion. She has never seen me out of the Johnson Road bubble before. As if for the first time, she is appraising me, my well-worn loose black jeans, tatty brown boots and my round-necked grey knitted sweater, with a couple of small holes in one of the sleeves. Thoughtlessly thrown on, but I think I look good in this sweater, despite the holes. She looks so pretty - I have no idea what she is wearing, I just see her, her blue-green eyes and the sweep of her dark blond hair. I want to touch it. I push my own hair back from my face, the bruising and cuts have healed.

She smiles at me as I reach her, and I wonder why I have never before specifically noticed the fullness of her lips or the flawless delicacy of her skin. I rub each of my shoulders with the opposite hand.

'Bloody hell, Sophie, it's freezing out here! Have you got time to come in for a coffee?' I colour slightly, 'I mean, only if you're not too busy, it's okay if you have to go somewhere.'

I glance at her nervously. She makes a show of looking at the time on her phone. We need to talk.

We go through the wide entrance of the medical school, which opens out into an enormous atrium and a medical student hangout. The vast medical library is to one side and a bookshop and cafeteria to the other, with several squishy, tired looking sofas and low coffee tables in between, set in lots of separate groups. This central area is a hive of activity as usual, and most of the chairs are occupied by groups of three or four students, slurping coffee, calling out to each other or engrossed in their phones. I find an empty sofa and motion to Sophie to sit.

'I'll just grab us a drink.'

I sense her looking round as I retreat towards the busy cafeteria - I say hi to a couple of people as I walk past. Samira is at one of the tables and I know that she is talking about Sophie to her friend, and not in a nice way. Sophie knows it too and pretends to be busy on her phone until I come back. I flop down next to her, resting my arm across the back of the sofa, and immediately, I am acutely aware of our knees touching.

'Who was that gorgeous girl I saw you with earlier?' she asks, 'She didn't seem very happy with you.'

I sigh and take a sip of coffee.

'That, Sophie, is the lovely Samira. We had a thing for a while, before, you know, before I left and went back to Ireland. I think she'd probably like to take up again where we left off, but I'm not sure I can. I'm not ready. And I've changed. I can't be what I was before. She's generally a nice girl, well, most of the time, although she's behaving like a complete bitch at the moment. She's fit as anything, but you know......she's cross with me, she thinks I'm playing hard to get. But I'm not, I've just been friendly to her and she wants more. Actually, truth be told, she won't leave me alone! And she's going to be even more cross now she's seen me with you!'

My phone pings for attention in my pocket. I ignore it.

'That'll be her, I guarantee it, wanting to know who the hell I'm with. She'll give me all sorts of hell later.'

This is quite a speech for me, and Sophie is silent for a moment, digesting this interesting new information.

'So why don't you tell her that I'm just your housemate and bumped into you accidentally on my way to lectures?'

I turn to study her, my eyes searching hers,

'But, Sophie, I'm not sure you are just my housemate, are you?' I say this so softly. 'I think we are much more to each other than that.'

Sophie is blushing and she looks away, embarrassed. I carry on talking.

'In fact, at the moment, you....and even that ridiculous peacock Alex....you mean more to me than anything. I feel like I'm finally getting back on my feet and it's down to the both of you. But especially you, Sophie, you are getting me through everything. I feel like I owe you so much.'

I feel the prick of tears behind my eyes - they've been absent for a while now. She looks up at me again, as if absorbing every bit of my face.

'You mean quite a lot to me too, Jasper Coutts,' she replies smiling shyly.

'I mean every word, Sophie,' I continue, 'I just.... sometimes I want to take it further with you. I want to make love to you Sophie, I want it so much that it hurts.' I look round at the other students, my face hot, looking anywhere but at her. I shake my head.

'Bloody hell, I didn't think I'd be having a heavy conversation like this in the med school foyer in the middle of the day!'

She is shocked, I think, and waiting for me to speak again. The making love thing, I just blurted it out, because it is all I think about. I need to explain more.

'I'm an emotional mess, I'm not ready for a relationship. I'd be a useless boyfriend at the moment, for you, Samira or anyone. And if I do anything with you, it has to be right. I know that I don't want to spend time with her, but I do need to be with you.'

She takes one of my large hands in hers and we sit like that for a moment. I doubt this conversation was what she was expecting when she'd left the house an hour ago. But I'm becoming attached to this gentle girl. It is more than simple lust; I hope she understands that, I need her to understand.

'I don't want a boyfriend either, Jasper,' she says carefully. 'I like us being just as we are. We'll take it slow, as slow as you like. Let's just see what happens. We don't need to talk about it, well not unless you want to, we can just carry on.' She looks as if she is going to add something else, as if she is going to tell me something important but can't find the right words.

She pauses instead, 'See you tonight?'

I nod and we stand up together. I bend my lips to hers, for only a second, aware that we have an audience, and watch her walk away. She holds her head high as she walks past Samira and her friends, no doubt feeling the daggers in her back. I can still taste the kiss as I turn, collect my bag and head for the library.

CHAPTER 13

SOPHIE

I didn't bloody tell him! Why the hell didn't I tell him? I know the answer of course, but it makes me question what sort of person I am, and I'm not sure I will like the answer to that question either.

He has basically said he wants to have sex with me, but, assuming I want sex with him, is holding back because he wants more than that, and isn't ready for a full-on relationship. Which, with all he's got going on, I fully understand. So, am I going to let him carry on joining me every night? Yes, yes, yes, because I love it. And sex with him? I'm already there in my head, every night when he is pressed against me.

Bloody Alex Van-Zeller. It would be so easy if he didn't exist. I think of those confident, knowing hands, sliding up towards my breasts, his easy smile reaching carelessly down to my mouth, so sure of himself, so bloody good at it. I've got to stop it with him somehow or tell him about Jasper so that he stops it, before I'm in too deep. Those girls' halls of residence are looking so attractive right now.

Katy and Amy are nagging me almost daily to invite them round to the house, mostly I suspect, to ogle Alex. I don't mind at all; it saves me trekking over to campus all the time. I want to get to a point where I can tell them about Alex and Jasper, offload it all.

An evening is arranged, after consulting with Alex regarding his full social diary. The girls arrive promptly, predictably heavily made up and in their best going out clothes. Alex answers the door with me, dressed in my favourite outfit of his, the faded low-slung jeans and bare feet. He has made a small concession to having guests by covering his top half with a brushed cotton, sky blue Ralph Lauren shirt, but then left it completely unbuttoned, to reveal his hairless, golden six pack.

He greets them both like long lost friends, the girls clearly prolonging the physical contact with him for as long as politely possible. I can't blame them - he's pure kryptonite. Even the entrancing vision of Alex, however, doesn't stop Katy and Amy cooing over the incredible opulence of the decor, and they demand an immediate tour of the house. They bounce about like excited school kids on my enormous bed.

'Blimey Soph, imagine what you could get up to in here! It's unbelievable!'

Jasper's room is empty - he is at rugby practice.

'Remind me who is in this room, then?' queries Amy, taking in the lack of personal touches. 'They haven't got much stuff, have they?'

I start ushering them back downstairs.

'Oh, that room belongs to Jasper, he's the medical student I mentioned before. He's a few years older than us. He's really nice. He'll probably be back later, and you can meet him.' I say airily.

'It doesn't look like anyone has ever slept in there,' observes Katy as she follows me back down the stairs.

I smile inwardly to myself. They don't know how close to the truth they are! When we reach the kitchen, we find that Alex has unearthed a few bottles of chilled champagne (as only Alex can), and he augments the first round of drinks with some of his favourite sloe gin. The girls are more than impressed. He cranks up some decent tunes, and a couple of his drinking buddies drop by, to make it more of a party. Hugo and Seb, Identikit posh boys, all floppy blonde hair, good skin and broad shoulders.

I have met them both several times before and they are very sweet. Hugo is loud, irreverent and confident - I can easily envisage him and Alex being extremely naughty together on a night out. The women of Nottingham don't stand a chance. Seb is calmer and less sure of himself, but no less engaging. Introductions made and it isn't long before all six of us are dancing around and singing along.

The arrival of Jasper, freshly showered from rugby and having already had a couple of post training beers himself, is greeted with great delight by Alex, who gives him a big hug and treats him to a trademark forehead kiss. I hang back as Alex proudly introduces him to all of our friends. We are quite pissed now and move the party from the kitchen into Alex's room, where the dance floor is bigger. Alex is in his element of course; he loves dancing and is completely lacking in inhibition. He is a perfect host too, kind and generous. My friends have been made to feel so welcome, from the moment they arrived.

Jasper seems content to watch from the side lines, but I definitely think he is having a nice evening too. We all drink far too much champagne - even Jasper is knocking it back. Amy certainly seems to be pleased to make his acquaintance; at one point she tipsily trips and falls against him. He catches her easily and she seems in no hurry to be put down again, trying in vain to drag him onto the dance floor. She'll not like me very much if she knows what's going on.

Towards midnight, I think I'm feeling a bit too pissed and decide that we would all benefit from some food. As I mooch through the freezer for pizzas, Katy comes into the kitchen and pours herself a glass of cold water.

'Fucking hell, Sophie, you've got yourself an amazing set up here! Why has it taken us this long to find out? And why haven't you shagged either of them yet - or both? I'm not sure I could choose!'

I laugh. It's a really good question. I flunk it. 'We're all just friends; they're a nightmare to live with, honestly.'

I frown to myself at this blatant lie – they are both incredibly easy to live with.

'Well, I'm fairly sure I'd cope!' sniggers Katy. 'I think Amy's in love already, Jasper is an absolute honey! He's a hundred times better than that ugly Andrew she seems to be so obsessed with. Is he single?'

I pause, struggling to come up with a suitable response. I should tell her now about my situation, she might have some useful advice. I don't like the idea of Jasper with anyone else. Which is rich, coming from me.

'Um, I don't know, I'm not sure. I think so, but I'm er.... not sure if he is looking for something serious just now. You know med students, they are so busy, they don't have much time for anything else.'

This is a pretty lame answer, but I hope it will do. Katy is fairly pissed too, so she probably hasn't noticed my dissembling. She carries on,

'Seb's really cute too, and Hugo is hot with a capital H! I shall call him Hot Hugo from now on. But far too posh for me. And Alex is definitely in love with you, by the way, you lucky cow! He can't keep his eyes off you! I heard about what happened with Ben at that Cripps party. He thought Alex was going to hit him!'

I laugh again and pretend to busy myself with some plates.

'That's such an exaggeration, Katy! And now I do know that you're drunk!' I reply, turning away so that Katy can't see my face. 'And anyway,' I continue firmly, 'I'm fairly sure that Alex Van-Zeller is in love with one person and one person only, and his name starts with an A and ends with an X!'

Almost as if he senses we are talking about him, Alex comes into the kitchen. Katy raises her eyebrows at me in an 'I told you so sort of way' and makes herself scarce.

'I've been wanting to do this all night,' he murmurs, circling his arms around my waist and kissing me softly. 'I'm leaving in the morning for Zurich. Don't forget about me over the Christmas holidays, Sophie, otherwise I will be very cross.'

As if I could ever forget about him! Especially after kissing me like this. I feel him hard against me. Preventing my relationship with him from progressing any further is taking every ounce of willpower I possess. I hear someone opening the kitchen door and pull away quickly. Alex adjusts himself discreetly before turning around to see who it is.

'Hi guys, oh shit, sorry to interrupt.' It is Jasper. He halts, looking uneasily at us both. 'I'll just get those beers from behind you, on the table. Sorry.'

I see the hurt in his eyes, even though he tries to cover it up with a smile. Alex comes to the rescue.

'You've interrupted nothing, Jaz, mate,' he states casually. 'I was just giving our gorgeous housemate here a quick goodbye kiss before I leave tomorrow, and I got a bit carried away. Can't blame me really, she's scrumptious! Come and join us for a house hug before we all disappear for Christmas.'

71

He opens his arms wide and beckons Jasper over, who duly receives the same warm embrace that I was enjoying moments before, presumably minus the raging hard-on.

At about two am, I finally call a cab for Katy and Amy. Seb and Hugo have left to go clubbing in town. Jasper has sloped off to bed a few minutes earlier, and despite Amy's best efforts, he hasn't suggested she join him. Alex is crashed out on top of his own bed, most likely his hearing aids have run out, as he is steadfastly refusing to wake up. As the door closes behind them, I start idly picking up some of the detritus of the evening. I wander into Alex's room and watch him sleeping. Even in repose, drunk and dishevelled, he is irresistible. It is a cold night, and I lean over to cover him up, kissing him lightly on his slightly parted lips. He opens his eyes briefly, before closing them again.

'Night, Sophie gorgeous, love you.'

'I'm beginning to love you too, Alex,' I whisper, stroking his hair and knowing he can't hear. 'And Katy is absolutely right, I'm not sure I can choose between you both either.'

I carry some glasses and empty bottles into the kitchen. Jasper has come back downstairs and is stacking the dishwasher.

'Tonight was good, Sophie,' he says, gathering the cutlery from the table. 'Your friends are really nice girls.'

'It was fun wasn't it?' I agree, 'You have definitely found yourself an admirer. Amy was all over you!'

He smiles briefly. 'She's wasting her time on me. You of all people know that.' He is looking at me shyly, assessing my reaction.

'I just want you to know, the thing with Alex. We've just kissed, that's all. A few times, actually. I'm sorry, I should have told you.'

He looks at me, his face inscrutable. 'Are you joining the roster, Soph? I didn't have you pegged as one of those.'

His voice is harsh, he's hurt.

'Of course I'm not, Jasper! I've just kissed him a few times, that's all! It won't go further. And it's not like you and me are an item, is it?'

He sighs. 'No,' he concedes, 'But he's a bugger with girls. Even if he thinks he likes you, he'll drop you from a great height at some point down the line.'

'It won't happen, but thank you for caring, Jasper,' I say quietly.

He laughs and the tension is broken. 'This isn't me caring, Soph, this is me trying to scare you away from the competition!'

I laugh too. Bloody hell, these two boys are something else. How the hell will I ever choose? I change the subject.

'My feet are absolutely killing me now after all that dancing.' I start putting the empty cans in the recycling bin and add as an afterthought.

'Are you not a dancer, Jasper?'

He stops what he is doing for a moment and leans against the sink, sighing.

'I used to dance; I used to quite like it actually, especially when I'd had a drink or two. But, you know, since Christian died, well, I haven't really felt like it. It seems wrong somehow, to do something so... so silly and fun. So frivolous, I suppose is what I mean. I'd feel guilty, it would feel like I've forgotten him, and I never want to forget him.'

I don't reply for a few minutes, but an idea is forming in my mind. I reach for my phone.

'Why don't you dance with me, now?' I whisper, pulling him close. 'Here, in the kitchen, with no one else to see us. We can dance together, and you can think about Christian at the same time.'

I scroll through the menu on Spotify with my thumb, knowing the perfect play list is on there. Here it is: 'Fi's songs for the broken hearted'. I smile inwardly, fondly remembering my old friend for a moment. Hooking up the phone to the little kitchen speaker, I gently take Jasper's hands in my own. The soft tones of Camila Cabello fill the silence as we begin swaying together in the dim light. I reach up and wrap my arms around his neck, pulling him even nearer to me. His head rests gently on top of mine, his arms circling my waist. We stay that way, slowly moving from side to side, wrapped in the warmth of our embrace, lost entirely in the moment. I feel his tears trickling into my hair and pull him tighter.

'I think I'm falling in love with you, Sophie,' he whispers, when he eventually speaks.

CHAPTER 14

JASPER

Fucking Alex fucking Van-Zeller! He can get any girl he fancies and he bloody fancies mine. I knew it of course; I've seen him watching her. I didn't need to see him practically fucking her through her clothes in the kitchen to know that. It's a bloody mess.

If I didn't like him so much, I'd have it out with him, tell him to back off, but I do unfortunately, so I won't. I'm a big strong lad, I've been brought up tough and I'm prepared to use my muscle against pretty boy if I have to. Sophie isn't stupid though; she must surely realise that she's just another fit bird for him to add to his list. The man's a machine, a kind, generous, caring one, but when it comes to girls, just a bloody machine. And he is the only person who uses the phrase 'I've got a bottle of fizz somewhere,' without irony, that I don't want to punch.

In Nottingham, the last couple of days of term are especially quiet. Alex leaves the day after the party, catching his flight home to Zurich. He has overslept and disappears in a hurry – a quick forehead kiss to both of us and he is gone. And he's the only bloke who kisses me too. It's grown on me, to be honest.

Naturally, he is going to be spending most of the holidays at the family ski chalet in St Moritz. He has casually invited us to fly over and join him for a few days, but we both decline. Sophie because her parents are flying over from Cyprus to have all the family together, and me because obviously I can't afford it. I'm going home to get a job for four weeks and earn some cash. I've got a coach to Birmingham and then a short flight to Cork. I'm hitch-hiking my way to Kinsale after that.

I get that the contrast between mine and Alex's family circumstances make us unlikely mates. Since Christian's death, money has been especially tight in the Coutts household. When he had been alive, my mam worked part-time as an orthopaedic nurse at the big hospital in Cork, and Christian spent a couple of days a week at a local school for children with disabilities. Neither me or mam ever saw my da, nor did we want to, but he did bung us a few quid every now and again. Guilt money, no doubt, for leaving, but it had come in useful.

After Christian died, mam wasn't in a fit state to return to work - she still isn't. Her sick pay has run out and da has stopped giving us anything, figuring I'm old enough and ugly enough to fend for myself. We thought about going through the courts, but neither of us has the fight in us these days.

We're scraping by on state benefits and struggling to keep up the mortgage payments on our little cottage. My aunt helps if she can and I'm in debt to my eyeballs.

Sophie sits on my bed whilst I pack my books into my sports bag. After our slow dance, we talked until it was light. But not about us, and not about Alex. I was on the verge of tears again, I told her I was dreading going home. Mam is desperate to have me home once more, and I want to see her, but all the grief will come flooding back the instant I set foot in the house - that's the bit I'm dreading.

I'm going to find it hard to sleep without Christian or Sophie next to me, I'm mentally preparing for a few weeks of insomnia. She makes me promise to call or text, day or night, if I need to. And now, I finish packing my books and we exchange our first proper kiss, standing in my room, my sports bag on the floor between us.

Sophie makes the first move; I think she feels sorry for me more than anything else. I know I look miserable and scared as I half-heartedly gather up my stuff. She reaches across and takes me in her arms, kissing me tenderly. I kiss her softly back, I don't press against her or run my hands all over her like I imagine Alex does, but it's emotional for me and I just want the kiss. I'm so fucking useless, my tears betray me again, they run freely down my face. I need to stop bloody crying! I can't imagine anything makes Alex cry. We stay that way for a long time, just kissing. Eventually I pull away,

'I'm going to miss the coach if I don't go now.'

CHAPTER 15

SOPHIE

Christmas holidays arrive. I'm excited to be reunited with my family again as I haven't seen them since the beginning of September. We're spending the whole of the winter break at my grandparents' Victorian townhouse in Hammersmith, as my dad has some leave from the Army and both my parents want to escape the hectic life on the base for a couple of weeks. My grandparents hardly ever use the house anymore, as they retired to the south coast several years ago, and so it almost seems like our own home, whenever we are back in England.

I love London, I love the noise and bustle of the capital city. The first few days are a whirlwind of activity, the obligatory catching up with aunties, uncles, grandparents and family friends. Fi lives a very short Tube ride away, in a leafy part of Kensington, and I'm dying to meet up with her. I need to tell someone about the two men in my life.

I'm disappointed that I receive no form of communication from either of them. Alex I'm not worried about at all, and truthfully, I don't expect to hear from him anyway. If random pictures posted on his Instagram account are anything to go by, he is having far too much fun to remember to keep in touch with me. He is either photographed in a night club wrapped around various glamorous companions, male and female, or out on the ski slopes, with his arms draped around an extremely sophisticated and beautiful looking older female version of himself, who I presume is his beloved mama. All the captions under the pictures are in Swiss-German, and I steadfastly refuse to be tempted to translate them, particularly the nightclub scenes, knowing I shouldn't care, but secretly dreading what I might uncover if I do.

Jasper's silence, however, is more of a concern to me. He doesn't have any social media accounts, but he does possess a mobile phone, and whilst not an avid user, he has been known to compose an occasional text message if prompted. I message him a few times; just simple, bland sentences saying hi, but never receive a single reassuring reply.

So, I am somewhat delighted when one morning, two days before Christmas, I pick up the post from the doormat. Hidden between the stiff white envelopes containing mostly pointless Christmas cards, is a small postcard, addressed in familiar scruffy handwriting, to Miss Sophie Ashworth. I pocket it before anyone else notices and disappear to my room to pore over it in peace. It is a colour print of Kinsale, taken in the summer months, and Jasper is right when he says it is pretty.

In the foreground, a small harbour is filled with a jumble of colourful fishing boats, rocking on clear blue water, whilst behind, nestled into the side of unspoilt, rolling hills is part of the town itself, made up of row upon row of quaint whitewashed cottages and brown stone terraced houses. I turn the card over. Apart from my name and address, he has written just one sentence, 'Surviving, but missing you. Jx'

There is a single kiss and nothing more. I read it again and again, I even hold it up to my nose to see if any of his fresh, cool, Jasper scent remain. It doesn't, of course, and eventually, I place it carefully under my pillow.

Because of so many family commitments, I don't have a chance to meet up with Fi until after Christmas, when we have a fun day together trawling the Christmas sales. Fi is a dear friend, she talks too much and probably eats too much as well, but she has a heart of gold. Her only aspirations in life are to get married, move to the Hampshire countryside and have lots of horses, dogs and babies. She is still head over heels in love with Fraser, a business studies student in the year above at Bristol. He is coming to her New Year party and she is desperate to show him off to everyone. I am pleased for her; Fi's taste in boyfriends at school had been suspect to say the least, hence the lengthy Spotify play lists full of sad songs. She had her heart broken several times in the sixth form and from the photos, this lad looks like he could be exactly the solid, dependable type that Fi has been searching for.

Over lunch, in a sandwich shop on the King's Road, it is my turn to fill in the details of my first term in Nottingham. Fi is persistent.

'Come on Sophie don't be coy. I want all the Alex details, sex and everything. From that picture you sent me, I'm surprised you're still walking straight - he looks bloody amazing.'

'There are no sex details,' I laugh, shaking my head. I reach for a sandwich. 'God no, it's much more complicated than that.'

So, I tell all, and I'm glad to offload. I don't miss out any detail, not even that I think Jasper's fingers explore a little when he thinks I'm asleep.

'He sounds a bit weird, Soph,' she begins, but I cut her off.

'It does sound weird, which is probably why I'm not exactly shouting about him from the roof tops, but I really like him, Fi - I could see myself with him long term. And when he's in bed with me, it doesn't feel strange at all, it feels right somehow. He's quiet, and sad a lot of the time, but when we talk, which we do a lot, it's like I've known him forever. I could tell him anything, anything at all and he wouldn't judge me or think I was silly or immature or anything.'

'So, you could even tell him about Alex?' she says sceptically.

I nod, 'Yes, I've even told him about Alex. He's not thrilled obviously. But I need to get over Alex anyway - he's bad news, as sweet as he is. I need to keep him in the friend zone, if I can.'

Fi takes a second scone and slathers it in butter. 'Is Alex really that shallow, Soph?' she asks, taking a bite. 'I mean, a gorgeous bloke like him must get girls throwing themselves at him all the time, and he's obviously a bit of a party animal. But what if that's just how he passes the time? Or how everyone expects him to behave? What if actually, given the choice, he'd rather settle down and have a serious girlfriend?'

This hasn't occurred to me, and I ponder it for a moment, considering Alex the party animal and the sweet, amusing, interesting Alex I see nearly every day around the house. 'Maybe, but I don't know if I'm willing to take the risk. He'll break my heart, Fi, if I fall for him, which I will if I let him get to me. And I'll lose Jasper.'

The rest of lunch is taken up with me showing pictures and describing in great detail the amazing house I have been so lucky to rent. Jasper and I metaphorically pinch ourselves regularly to check it's really true.

On New Year's Eve, I do indeed get to meet the much-discussed Fraser and am pleased to see that my first impressions from his photo are correct. He is obviously as in love with Fi as she is with him and he follows her round like a puppy all night. The party is fab - several old friends from school have made the journey and so the evening is spent catching up on everybody's news. As the night wears on and the booze flows, the talking stops and the music cranks up.

Midnight at last, and Fi switches her meticulously prepared play list to Radio 1, to hear the bongs of Big Ben on time. As the bells ring out, everyone joins together in a circle, holding onto each other, jumping up and down and whooping. I am about to join the throng when I feel a vibration in my back pocket and realise my phone is ringing. Alex's number comes up, preceded by the Swiss country code. Blimey, he is the last person I expect to phone - I envision him at a fabulous party halfway up a mountain somewhere, swigging Krug and dancing on tables, rubbing shoulders with the rich and famous.

I quickly pushed my way through the sweaty mass of celebrations and slip into the narrow hallway. It is still noisy; the thump of the music has started again.

'Hi Alex, hi, let me.... just give me a second.... I can't hear you.'

Knowing that Alex will find it impossible to hear me with all the background noise (he struggles with the phone at the best of times), I open the front door and sit down on the freezing stone steps outside. The stillness and cool air of the suburban street is a relief after the heat of the party.

'Hi Alex, I can hear you perfectly now. Is everything alright?'

'Sophie, my gorgeous Sophie,' he sings down the telephone line.

His Swiss accent has definitely become stronger after four weeks back in the motherland. Very sexy, I think, and I'm grinning inanely, forgetting instantly how uncomfortable the damp stone feels through my jeans.

'I am at a mad big party, Sophie, and I am very, very drunk, but I have made two New Year resolutions, Sophie, and I have come outside into the snow - my feet are very wet now - to tell you what they are.'

I laugh, 'Go on then.'

'Firstly, my beautiful Sophie, what are you wearing?' he demands, 'tell me exactly, so that I can picture you? And, where are you?'

I laugh again; he really is ridiculous and definitely very drunk.

'Okay, Alex. I'm sitting on the top step outside Fi's house in London. I'm bloody freezing actually and I'm hoping I haven't accidentally shut myself out.' I glance up at the solid oak door behind me, praying it is still on the latch.

I carry on, 'The reason I'm so cold is that I'm only wearing my skinny grey jeans, you know exactly which ones, because you always tell me that you and Jasper think my arse looks nice in them! I'm also wearing a little sleeveless navy-blue satiny top that I bought yesterday in the sales, and which I'm now wishing was a big baggy jumper instead. And a pair of black kitten heels that I don't think you have seen me wear before.'

I shiver involuntarily.

'And what are you wearing underneath?' he queries, in a determined tone.

I roll my eyes down the invisible telephone wires at him. 'If you really must know, and if I remember correctly, I'm wearing a white lace bra and matching white lace knickers.'

'That all sounds rather lovely, Sophie darling. I think lace probably suits you. I hope nobody at the party is going to see those white lace knickers though, otherwise I will be very, very disappointed.' He says this in a mock teacherly scold.

He pauses, and I hear him walking over crunchy snow at the other end of the line.

'Well, my Sophie, now that I can picture you perfectly, I've just added an extra New Year resolution. It is to have phone sex all the way from St Moritz with you right now.'

He is slurring slightly, and I giggle, he really is the most unpredictable person I have ever met.

'Close your eyes,' he commands, and then a second later, 'Are they closed?'

Feeling slightly foolish, and glad no-one is watching, I shut my eyes.

'Now, my beautiful Sophie, do you remember the first time we kissed, on the way back from that party? I really do hope so, because I remember it extremely often. Concentrate on that.'

I am pleased that he remembers, I myself can't help thinking about it nearly every day, it creeps up on me at unexpected moments and gives me a sudden thrill.

'Now, my Sophie, we are kissing on that dark street, there is no-one about. I am leaning against the brick wall, remember? And you are standing in front of me.'

His silky voice sounds very close in my ear, the thudding music from the party abruptly evaporating behind me.

'I have my hands at your waist, and I am undoing your jeans slowly, all the time we are still kissing. It is making me so hard, you are making me so hard, and I cannot control it. Your jeans are undone, Sophie, and now my hand is inside, and I am putting it lower, between your legs. And your hand is on me, Sophie, and your fist is so good squeezed around my cock. You are wearing thin white lace knickers, and I can feel you with my fingers, and you are wet for me Sophie, my God, and it is the best feeling. I pull aside the white lace and I slip my fingers inside you, Sophie - you are so hot, and I have found the nicest spot, Sophie. I am moving my cock in your fist, I am fucking your fist, Sophie, and you love it, I know you do. But you hardly notice, because my fingers are stroking you inside Sophie, and it's the best feeling Sophie, it really is, and it's getting faster and faster, we are still kissing......and.....my fingers are inside you Sophie, faster and faster....Can you feel it Sophie?'

His voice is getting more urgent and breathier, it is as though he is with me now, and with my eyes closed I can see those beautiful long fingers, and really can imagine them deep inside me, and feel his mouth hard against mine, his penis solid in my hand. A thrill of excitement courses through me and I become aware of my own breathing suddenly loud in the quiet of the night. He has stopped speaking and there is a pause, just his breathing, heavy down the line. He lets out a short laugh, 'Hah! um.... there suddenly seems to be a large patch of something white and sticky on the snow out here,

Sophie, down at my feet. It is very strange, I have no idea what it is, but I think it is all your fault. Fuck, that was good, Sophie!'

I gasp with laughter, 'Oh my God, Alex, I hope you are alone, for goodness sake!'

He laughs again, 'Me too, I forgot to check. Oh well, if not, then someone has had a very lucky night seeing Alex Van-Zellers' phenomenal manhood! Now, tell me that's not the best phone sex you have ever had, although maybe I became rather carried away before we got to the actual sex part!'

I giggle. It is the only phone sex I have ever had, so technically it is the best, but I'm not about to tell him that.

'Not bad, Alex, not bad at all,' I lie. 'Perhaps we should get in some more practice? So, you still haven't actually told me your main two New Year resolutions.'

'Oh, number one is very easy,' he replies, and I can tell that he is smiling down the phone line.

'And I've completed it already. It was to make sure the first person I speak to in this New Year is you. And do you want to hear the second one?'

He suddenly sounds stone cold sober. The tone of his voice lowers and he pauses before continuing.

'My second New Year resolution, Sophie, is to make you love me as much as I love you.'

I sit back against the cold stone, shaking my head slightly. He is so sweet. And so astonishing. Is he really that into me? It is impossible to tell; with anyone else I'd be able to gauge their feelings straight away, but with Alex, he is such a tart, I never know if he is serious or not. Maybe his next phone call to the next girl will be exactly the same. Or perhaps even now, he is going back into the nightclub to find whoever is waiting for him there.

After we end the call, I return to the party. Now that the big midnight moment has passed, the noise levels have settled down, and people are milling about, hoovering up the remains of the buffet, some are putting on coats, and calling for taxis into town.

Fi comes up to me, 'Where have you been? They played our favourite - Mr Brightside, and I wanted to dance with you! I had to make do with Fraser and he's pissed as a fart!'

CHAPTER 16

ALEX

The new term starts with slush on the ground and a frosty chill in the air. Jaz and I are kicking our heels, waiting for Sophie to come back. We haven't actually said that to each other, but it's clear that it is what we are both doing.

My holiday was a hell of a lot better than his by the sound of it. We both got back to Nottingham last night and had a few beers together in front of the telly. I realised I'd missed him.

'How was it, then?' I'd asked, and he'd sighed and run his hand through his thick curly hair before replying. He is thinner than I had remembered, and the familiar hollow circles have returned under his eyes. I was expecting a short answer, but he wanted to talk, and I was happy to listen.

'Okay, I guess. My mam was pleased to see me, but she isn't really getting any better. She hasn't been back to work, and as far as I can tell she spends most days just sitting in front of the telly. I think she only leaves the house to get some food. And the house was a pigsty – I spent the first day cleaning and tidying up. There was about three days' worth of washing up in the sink.'

He had sniffed loudly before continuing, his voice wavering slightly. 'She made an effort when I was there, and I took her out a couple of times, but it's really hard. On Christmas Day, we went around to my aunts, so it wasn't just the two of us, looking at each other and thinking about him all the time. We haven't got anything to say to each other - there isn't really anything to say. And the house is weird without him and without all his stuff, you know; the wheelchair, his cuddly toys and everything. It's like there's a big void and she hasn't got a clue how to fill it. And I'm not sure she wants to.'

I didn't have much to say, I'm not sure anything I could have said would have been adequate. I could have changed the subject, talked about the night in St Moritz when me and my mates took snowmobiles up to one of the mountain top bars and stayed there all night, drinking Kilian vodka and dancing on the tables until dawn. Or about mama's New Year party, when I told Sophie I loved her and wanked in the snow at the thought of my fingers in her pussy.

'I'm here for you, Jaz,' is what I did say, 'I want you to know that, mate.'

I jump up as I hear the front door close and envelope her in a bear hug.

'Sophie, gorgeous, you're here at last, we've waited all day!' I say.

I have my back to Jasper, shielding her from his view, and I kiss her softly on the lips, smelling vanilla, tasting her.

'Good enough to eat, Sophie,' I whisper in her ear, and her warm breath on mine sends a shiver down my spine.

Jasper stands up more slowly, hanging back shyly in the kitchen doorway.

'Hi Sophie, good to see you.'

He smiles as he speaks, and she looks up at him over my shoulder. They exchange a silent message I can't interpret. I wonder if there is something that I'm missing between them.

'We're going out!' I announce, finally releasing her from the delicious embrace.

'We've been back since yesterday and I'm bored. Jaz here has revised all day and he deserves a night off. I have been the perfect house husband and done a huge supermarket trip and cooked a chilli. Let's eat, and then go to the cinema. Come on Jaz, you're always supposed to relax the night before exams, isn't that right?'

They probably think that I relax every single night leading up to exams, and during them as well, and they would be absolutely correct. She takes her bags upstairs and Jaz follows up after her. I hear them talking, but with my hearing, from that distance, I have no chance of knowing what they are saying.

The film selection at the multiplex is fairly dire. There is a romantic period drama – Jasper raises his eyebrows instantly in disdain at that one, and a gothic horror. I am embarrassed to confess that I have nightmares for days after watching any sort of horror movies, so we settle on the latest offering from the Avengers franchise.

We have the auditorium almost to ourselves and select three padded seats slap bang in the centre, Sophie is ensconced in between us. I rest my arm casually across the back of her chair and reach even further and twirl the hair on Jasper's neck occasionally with my fingers, which Jasper manfully tries to ignore. It raises a smile though. I produce my hip flask and feed them both my delicious sloe gin from time to time. I feel relaxed and content to be with my two favourite people. I'm refreshed, tanned and full of energy after my month-long mountain break. I reckon Sophie thinks I'm looking good too, I catch her giving me the once over.

I steal occasional glances at Jasper throughout the film. He seems miles away, his eyes focussed on the big screen, but I have the impression he isn't following any the noisy action in front of him. I'm worried for him; his life is so difficult, especially compared to mine. Sophie has noticed too, and she takes one of his hands, which are resting loosely in his lap and holds it tightly in her own. He seems to visibly relax in his chair. I, however, feel myself tensing. Fuck, I really do not want this to happen, but I have to tread carefully. I lean over to her, my voice full of concern.

'Is he okay? He seemed a bit shit when he got back yesterday, a bit tearful. I've tried to cheer him up, which is why I suggested this trip. I've become ridiculously fond of him, I've realised.'

'Thanks for caring so much,' she whispers back to me. 'It means a lot to him, it really does.'

Maybe I'm reading it wrong, maybe she is just being her usual thoughtful, gentle self. I get that he's attractive, I can see that myself - his physique is incredible and those eyes and that voice, yeah, I see it. But for fucks sake, I'm Alex Van-Zeller! I'm not the vainest bloke that I know - that would be Hugo - but I know I'm bloody gorgeous, because everyone tells me so, all the bloody time! What the fuck is she playing at?

CHAPTER 17

JASPER

I follow her upstairs when she gets home. Alex is on her first, so I hang back, waiting my turn. I can tell he's kissing her, and I want to scream at her not to be so stupid and tell him to fuck off out of her life.

But I understand why she kisses him back, I really do, because look at him, for Christ sakes! He's wearing a thin black cashmere sweater that probably cost more than our monthly mortgage payments, a concession to the worsening weather, and his lean, muscular body is as perfect as it ever was. His smell permeates our lives, and it is intoxicating - coconut and Chanel, all over the house.

And I'll never tell him to fuck off, because he's a really good guy. I'd love to hate him, but I can't, because he texted me every day of the holidays to see if I was okay, and although he hides it from his posh drinking cronies, there is a very considerate, soft side to Alex Van-Zeller that I can't ignore.

He listens intently when I talk about Christian and my home life. He can't pretend to have any comprehension of how it is, just as I can't pretend to have any comprehension of his monied, crazy world, but it doesn't matter, because he listens and cares.

She is in her room, putting away her stuff. She sets down the clothes she is folding and walks over to me, putting her arms around my waist and resting her head on my chest, holding me tight.

'You are thinner,' she decides, and I nod in agreement. 'How are you, how's your mum?'

I fill her in on the details, pleased that I don't get upset.

'At least I'm doing better than my mam, because I've got you and Alex to come back to, and med school and everything. And I worked quite a few shifts at the hotel, so that got me out of the house. The money will come in handy this term.'

I rub my chin; I need a shave before we go out.

'I felt really bad leaving her and coming back to be honest, but it would have killed me to stay any longer. My aunty keeps an eye out for her. Sometimes I think I'm as bad as my dad leaving her.'

Sophie stops me right there. 'You definitely aren't, Jasper, don't say that.'

Her niceness kills me. My bloody tears land on her cheek as I rest my head lightly on top of hers.

'You really need to stop beating yourself up, Jasper, you are not like him at all. You stayed when it was hard and Christian and your mother both needed you. You were the best big brother he could have wished for; you know that.'

I stand back from her and wipe my eyes with the back of my hand.

'I know, but... it's just... it's crap. And I'd promised myself I wouldn't fucking cry this term and here I am, one day in! I'm sick of it! Anyway,' I stand up straighter and manage a half smile. 'I got loads of studying done as there was nothing else to do, so I should be alright for the exams this week. And it's good to see you Sophie, I really missed you... and Alex I suppose. Tonight will be nice, it will be nice to go out just the three of us, it will do me good.'

I appear in Sophie's doorway that night almost as soon as she's climbed into bed herself. It is early, and she is tired after the journey back to Nottingham. Even Alex is having an early night; she'd received one of his intimate forehead kisses before heading upstairs, and I had been fortunate enough to receive one too - I knocked him away, pretending irritation. The house is dark and quiet.

'Can I join you, Sophie?' I ask hesitantly.

If she says no, I'll go and it will be fine, I'll be fine. She sits up slightly.

'Sure, you don't have to ask, Jasper, any time, no matter what.'

I strip off in the dark and slip under the covers next to her, around the far side as usual. I put my arm around her waist, and she snuggles back into me. Alex who? I think to myself and surprise her by kissing the back of her neck lightly. If I think he's serious about her, then I need to tell him about this, it's only fair.

'Thank you so much.... for everything, Sophie,' I say. 'You have no idea how much I've missed this.'

'I've missed it too, Jasper,' she whispers, and I know how true it is.

CHAPTER 18

SOPHIE

The first week passes by in a blur. Jasper has exams every day, and when he isn't working, he is studying in the med school library. He comes home late, and so I hardly see him. He joins me in bed each night though, climbing in when I am asleep and leaving early in the morning. A warm sheet and the fresh smell of his hair on the pillow are the only clues that he has been there at all.

Alex returns to his semi nocturnal state, his hectic social life picking up exactly where it had left off. I am aware that he doesn't always come home after a night out - I'm not going to ask, and he apparently isn't going to tell. I put his amorous drunken New Year phone call firmly to the back of my mind. I am right, I am just one of the many, and I resolve not to fall in love with him any more than I already have done.

I don't have too much time to think about him anyway, my course is picking up speed and it is my turn to present a formal analysis of a classical Greek statue of my choosing to the rest of the tutorial group. The choices are many and varied, but eventually, I settle on the Victorious Youth, a Greek bronze from around 100 BC.

This particular piece was discovered fifty years earlier, caught in the nets of an Italian fishing boat, trawling off the Adriatic coast. It has provided a wealth of new information regarding the ancient skill of bronze casting, which must become the focus of my presentation, and it is stressing me out, trying to grasp the intricacies of the various bygone techniques. Creating the presentation is both laborious and tedious. Even so, I admire the Victorious Youth himself, caught in the moment of victory over all of his competitors. Proudly crowning himself with an olive wreath, there is an arrogant solemnity about him, a pleasing quiet confidence of a young man besting the competition.

Plodding through the techniques of bronze casting, I am easily tempted away from my studies by Katy and Amy, who discover me in the café, hunched over my laptop, becoming increasingly frustrated with the idiosyncrasies of PowerPoint. They are happy to be back at uni - they are both on good form and still single, despite Amy's attempts to snare either the Scottish engineering student or Jasper.

'Too much work makes Sophie a dull girl,' says Amy, rounding on me. 'Come out with us on Friday, everyone will be there.'

'Ben's coming,' adds Katy, and I groan. 'I've told you, Katy, I'm not interested in him, I thought he was seeing someone now, anyway?'

She shrugs, 'He was, but she dumped him. Her loss.'

'And you must come, Soph, because Andrew will be there too, and he'll be bringing his mates and I want to look popular and cool.'

'Ha! I don't make you look cool, Amy! You do that all on your own. I just look grumpy and don't talk to anyone.'

'Exactly,' she says as if I've proven her point, 'Very cool.'

'And chill about the presentation, Sophie,' adds Katy, 'No-one will be listening anyway, it's such a bloody boring choice.'

The girls come around to Johnson Road for a couple of bottles of wine before we head into town and are both clearly disappointed that Alex and Jasper are nowhere to be seen. I explain,

'Jasper has had his last exam today so he's probably getting heavily into the beer in a med student bar somewhere, and Alex - well, he could be getting up to no good anywhere really. I have absolutely no idea.'

I say this about Alex in a careless fashion. I am determined to try and dissociate myself from lustful thoughts I have about him. Apart from the peck on the lips when I arrived at the start of term, he has made no further overtures towards me. I'm not sure why, but I'm sort of glad, because it makes life easier for me and Jasper. Yet at the same time, it is very difficult, of course, not to dwell on his devastatingly handsome face and that perfect golden physique. Especially when he continually wanders around the house half dressed.

We spend the evening in the *Hand and Heart*, my favourite pub, up near the town centre. It is always full of students and most of Katy's crowd are there, including Ben. He has become bolder, and after having checked that Alex isn't about to appear over my shoulder, he approaches me.

'Hi Soph, I haven't seen you in a while, how's it going?'

He is quite sweet in his own way, not bad looking at all, and definitely not a twat. He is a maths student, and whilst his chat up lines aren't his strongest suit, I enjoy talking to him. He is neither deep and complicated like Jasper, nor head-turningly beautiful like Alex, and to his credit, he is prepared to give it another go, Katy must have told him I'm still single. He is exactly the sort of boy I had imagined I would be hooking up with at university.

We discover that we have much in common; his father is in the military and he too, has lived abroad for parts of his life. He has a low opinion of Andrew, Amy's new man, and we bitch about him together and he's funny and observant.

He isn't brave enough to ask me out again, but when I leave the pub for the short walk home, I know I've had a fun night.

I haven't been in bed for very long at all, and am idly flicking though my Instagram feed, when the front door shuts loudly below and heavy feet slowly climb the stairs. I recognise Jasper's tread. He heads straight into the bathroom and I hear him urinating noisily - it seems to go on forever! Two minutes later and he appears at the door, clumsily taking off his boots and struggling with his jacket. I can smell the stale beer on him before he even begins slurring his words; he is clearly very, very drunk. I surmise that the post exam celebrations must have started quite early in the day.

'I'm here, Sophie. I've been drinking all afternoon and I'm fucking slaughtered. Sorry.'

'I'd never have guessed, sweetie.' I reply sarcastically.

He clambers into the bed next to me and rolls onto his back with a big contented sigh.

'Love you, Soph,' he murmurs, and within seconds, he is asleep, snoring loudly. Very loudly. I'm beginning to wish I'd steered him next door, but there is no way on earth I can rouse him now.

I'm not sure how much later it is, when I am woken again by the front door closing beneath my room. Alex this time, and I roll over again away from Jasper, who is still blissfully snoring. I wait for him to use the bathroom and then head off downstairs again, so I am slightly panicked when I hear his much softer, more sober footsteps coming towards my room. This is highly unusual; he generally stays downstairs - I can't remember the last time he was in here and certainly never at night. My heart skips a beat in anticipation.

Because of the heavy drapes and the wintry time of year, the room is pitch black and I am aware of a dim light emanating from his phone screen as he navigates his way to my bed.

'Sophie, it's me!' he whispers loudly. 'Are you awake?'

I sit upright, bringing the duvet higher to cover my chest. I sleep in just my knickers, as despite the cool temperature outside, thanks to the Saudi princess, this bedroom, like the rest of the house, tends towards a sauna climate. He sits on the near side of the bed next to me and extinguishes his phone screen, placing it down on the bedside table. I realise immediately that he isn't wearing his hearing aids, as he appears utterly oblivious to the rumbling snores not two feet away from him.

'I've come for my goodnight kiss, Sophie, I've missed it this week,' he announces, his hand beginning to gently caress my thigh through the bedclothes.

My senses are on high alert as flushed with desire, all thoughts of forgetting about him are instantly abandoned. I have a brief moment of panic and am microseconds away from drawing his attention to the fact that Jasper is asleep across from me, when he leans down, his breath cool on my face. I stretch up to meet his lips with mine and suddenly it doesn't matter that Jasper is within touching distance. His soft lips are on mine and I am subsumed with my need for him.

There is a familiarity now, and the kiss deepens quickly, his tongue exploring my mouth, the urgency intensifying. I put my hands on his narrow hips, revelling in the smoothness of his taut skin as my thumbs massage into his groin beneath. He is only wearing boxer shorts and already barefoot, he slips under the sheets next to me, the length of his body deliciously warm, his hands cool from the night air.

I moan with anticipation, and on realising with delight that I am almost naked, his hands start exploring. His tender kisses cover my face and my neck and I almost whimper as I feel his cool touch on my breasts, cupping them firmly, circling my hard nipples whilst all the time relentlessly punishing my mouth.

'God, you're gorgeous Sophie,' he murmurs, breathing harshly, 'I need you, my beautiful Sophie, I need you right now.'

It is the time to tell him, to say that Jasper is there - he needs to stop, I need him to wear his hearing aids so I can explain.

But his kisses move down towards my breasts, sucking gently first on one erect nipple and then the other, teasing bites and I feel wetness below at his exquisite touch and I arch my back up to him. He is hard against me; his hips start to grind into my thigh as his arousal increases. His breathing becomes even heavier now, and he groans with unadulterated pleasure when I slip my hand inside his boxer shorts and hold the length of his silky penis in a firm grip.

'That's good, Sophie, really fucking good,' he pants as I begin moving my hand up and down its length. I don't want to stop now; I want to give this to him, and he thrusts against me at the same tempo.

His own hand reaches down between my legs, tantalisingly close to the edges of my labia. I gasp out loud as his fingers, those beautiful long fingers about which I have fantasised in my most private moments, finally enter me and immediately find the core of my being. We are both panting hard and fast now, frantically coming to a climax. Alex gets there first - his hot wet semen pumping across my thighs, but I am only dimly aware of the sensation, as I am reaching a climax of my own.

'Jesus, Sophie' he whispers, as he collapses next to me on his back, completely spent, his heavy breathing slowly receding back to normal.

We lie that way, side by side for a few minutes, before he leans toward me again, kissing me very softly on the mouth.

'Well, that escalated quickly!' he giggles - I love his giggles - and I can sense him smiling in the dark as he kisses me again, a hand now returning to my breast for another exploratory visit.

'I made you come,' he observes, clearly pleased with his success. 'I told you that I do my best work when I can't hear anything.'

He smiles happily and kisses me again. I return the kiss, staggered at the speed of my arousal for him and we stay that way for a while, content to lie quietly in each other's arms.

Eventually, Alex props himself up on one elbow. 'That was thirsty work, Soph, let me get some water.'

He swings his legs reluctantly out of bed and fumbles for his phone in the dark. I hear a thud as he accidentally knocks it off the table onto the rug underneath.

'Bugger,' he grumbles cheerfully, and he reaches for the switch to turn on the bedside light.

All of a sudden, I realise what he is about to do. A slow car crash is unfolding before my eyes and I am powerless to prevent it.

'Alex, no, don't turn the light on!' I order in an urgent whisper, trying to grab his arm.

But it is too late, and of course, he can't hear me. The light comes on, and retrieving his phone from off the floor, he turns back to me, leaning in for another kiss.

'I won't be a min.....'

He does a double take.

'What the fuck?' he shouts, angrily. 'What the fuck is he doing here?'

He leaps up from the bed, turning to confront me.

'Sophie? What the fuck is going on?'

I kneel up in bed, all thoughts of covering my modesty with the duvet abandoned.

'Ssshhhh, Alex, stop shouting!' I put my finger to my lips to indicate him to be quiet, but he is most definitely having none of it.

'I said, what the fuck Sophie? Are you telling me that whilst you were giving me the best wank ever, he was bloody in bed with us the whole time?'

Jasper grunts in his sleep, briefly opens his eyes and then closes them again. He turns over onto his side away from the two of us and the heavy snoring resumes. Thank God he's come in so pissed, I think, I'm not sure I can deal with both of them at three in the morning whilst clad only in a skimpy pair of knickers. Alex is understandably still glaring at me.

'Sshhhh, Alex, calm down, for goodness sake,' I plead.

Alex is pacing the carpet now, mussing his hair with his hands and shaking his head angrily.

'No, I'm not going to fucking calm down! This is unbelievable Sophie, what the hell is going on?'

I get off the bed and hold his hand, trying to stop him, trying to calm him down. 'If you were to just stand still for a second, I'll be able to explain.'

Alex stops walking and shakes off my arm. He is still shouting.

'I can't tell what you're saying, Sophie. It's pitch black and I can't fucking hear anything, can I? If I could, I wouldn't bloody be here with him over there, would I? Leave me alone, I'm going to bed.' He pulls away from me and stomps off down the stairs.

My immediate response is to go after him. I get to the top of the stairs and then halt. He is angry and upset - and I am too. And if he refuses to put on his hearing aids, which is extremely likely, then I'll get nowhere with him. Deciding it will be better to wait until the morning, when hopefully he'll have calmed down a bit, I return to bed. I lie there awake, the delicious smell of Alex still on me, the smoke from his cigarette drifting upwards from his room below. I listen to Jasper's oblivious snores, until eventually, I sleep.

Early the following morning. Jasper is still next to me, sound asleep, although thankfully the snoring has finally stopped. I creep out of bed, and pulling on my running gear, sneak downstairs without him stirring. Alex's bedroom door is firmly shut. I stand in the narrow hallway for a second, deliberating, wondering what to do. Eventually I take out a pen and scribble a note to Jasper, which I take back upstairs and prop up on his desk, so he will find it when he eventually surfaces.

'Dear Jasper,

Hope you had a good time last night. Might be sensible to keep away from Alex today - he's in a foul mood. My fault. Will explain all later xx.'

I tiptoe quietly back downstairs and slip out of the front door, closing it gently behind me.

I start jogging through the empty suburban streets, hardly caring which direction I take. My mind churns the events of last night - I have never before experienced such heights of arousal, I ache all over again with the memory of Alex's consummate touch. And then afterwards, his shock and displeasure at discovering a comatose Jasper next to me. I expect him to be angry, maybe to feel a bit humiliated, but the level of pain and hurt, clearly written all over his face, I had not expected. Bloody hell, why hadn't I told him what was happening with me and Jasper before it got to this? He'd have thought it strange, but he might have understood, and at least last nights' farcical disaster would have been averted.

I carry on running hard, past the rows and rows of Victorian houses, through streets lined nose to tail with parked cars. Most of the windows have curtains firmly closed against the daylight, the student occupants sleeping away the excesses of the night before. My phone buzzes in my pocket and I come to a halt as I reach for it, breathing hard. There is a short text from Alex.

'My mother is at the London house this week, so I'm going down to see her for a couple of nights.'

No kiss, no emoji. I quickly text him back.

'Meet me before you go? Please? We need to talk. Sophie X.'

No reply. I let out a sigh and regretfully turn and start jogging back in the direction I'd come. Then it buzzes again.

'Okay, Lenton Park, twenty mins.'

Whoever gave Lenton Park its name had delusions of grandeur. It is actually just a large rectangle of unkempt grass, with a couple of rusty swings and a plastic slide at one end. I imagine most of the kids that I knew at school had bigger gardens. The park is empty when I get there, apart from an early morning dog walker in the far corner, patiently waiting for his black lab to complete his morning business. I make my way past the overflowing litter bins spilling last night's chip papers and beer bottles onto the path and sit on one of the benches next to the empty swings. The morning air is cool, and I shiver slightly in my thin running top.

After a few minutes, I see Alex walking towards me. In the shabby surroundings of the park, he is like an exotic creature from another world, with his shock of blond hair and glowing skin - he exudes life and vitality. His hands are thrust deep in his jeans pockets and he is wearing a thick grey Stone Island parka to keep out the chill. A stylish but worn brown leather rucksack is swung over his shoulders. He has the air of a male model navigating an unusual urban catwalk. He sits down next to me on the bench and fiddles with the straps of his bag, avoiding eye contact. Eventually, he launches into it, evidently still angry.

'So, are you going to tell me what's going on?' He glares at me in an accusatory fashion.

'There's nothing to tell really Alex, you don't need to be so worked up.' I speak calmly, although my heart is beating fast, but he is clearly still full of righteous indignation.

'Hah! Yeah, right! Is he going to join in next time, is that it? To be honest, Soph, I'm happy to try new stuff, but I don't think a threesome is currently my thing. I can't believe I did that last night with you, in front of another bloke! And you let me bloody carry on! You didn't try to stop me!'

His voice is loud in the quiet morning. The dog walker stares at us curiously. I try to reason with him again, my voice firm.

'Please, just listen to me for one second, Alex. It's not what you think. I'm really sorry for last night. I should have told you, but honestly, nothing's going on. It all just happened so quickly, and it was dark, and you wouldn't have been able to hear me anyway.'

He looks at me disbelievingly. 'Yeah, right, blame me for it why don't you?'

'Just simmer down Alex and listen!'

He stares stonily in front him, refusing to meet my eye, but waiting for me to speak. So, I tell him again about Jasper, about the time I went to his room and found out the whole story about Christian. I explain how I'd come to understand over those first few weeks just how much he was suffering and the true depths of his despair. I told him how I invited him in to sleep with me, without thinking it through, but not expecting for a moment that he would actually do it, and then how night after night, when it is very late, he creeps in.

'That's all there is to it, honestly. Come on, Alex, he's so much better now, you have seen it yourself - he's sleeping like a log and... well, he's becoming normal again.'

Alex is sceptical. 'He's playing you good and proper, that's what he's doing, isn't he?' he suggests cynically.

'Alex, it's not like that at all and if you weren't so cross, you'd know that, I think. You know quite well that he's not that sort of person. Nothing really happens when he's there; it's an enormous bed. He just sleeps - we both just sleep. He doesn't even speak to me very often!'

'What, he lies all the way over the other side of that bed and doesn't have a crack at you?'

He's got me, he's watching me intently. Suspicious.

'Okay, don't be cross, but it's a little more than that.' I think it best not to mention the fact that he rarely wears any clothes and that I curve myself into his warm nakedness most nights. Or that I am convinced his hand is moving imperceptibly lower over my belly.

'Sometimes, well, nearly every night, he cuddles me. We go to sleep cuddling.' It's there, I've said it, there's no going back. 'But it's not like you are saving yourself for me, is it Alex?'

He ignores that comment.

'Have you copped off with him?' he interrupts, fixing his cool gaze on me.

'No, no I haven't.'

I decide to come clean. 'Well, we kissed once, very briefly, on the last day before Christmas. And not in bed. It just happened. He was in his room, packing up his stuff and was getting upset. He was dreading going back home, without Christian being there. I gave him a hug, he was crying, and then...yeah, he kissed me, not like we kiss, just a small kiss and just once, but not since, and for your information, I'm not planning on it either.'

'Why not?' he asks reasonably. 'Because he doesn't want to? I doubt that very much, or is it because you don't want to?'

'He says he doesn't want a girlfriend at the moment - he's too messed up, and to be honest, I just don't know what I want, Alex.'

He leans back and studies me, then blows out a sigh.

'Whatever. Although you are going to have to decide what you want sooner or later. But you could have told me before. And you should have stopped me last night - what if he was watching or listening?'

I give a short laugh. 'Alex, he was pissed as a fart! He could scarcely walk up the stairs, let alone watch us and remember it in the morning. And anyway....' My voice drops slightly, and my face reddens, 'I'm not sure I could have stopped you - I didn't want to, it was too good.'

He smiles down at me at last, relaxing somewhat.

'Yeah, it was, wasn't it? We should do it again sometime, but maybe in my room next time? With the door closed?'

I reach for his hand. 'I'm not going to stop him coming into my bed at night though, Alex, he needs it.'

Alex thinks about this for a second. 'Well, maybe I need it too, Soph. Maybe I need you as my girlfriend, how would that work then? It would be a bit odd; don't you think?'

I continue to hold his warm, dry hand in mine, examining those beautiful slim fingers, thinking of what pleasure they had given me less than twelve hours ago.

'We're great together, Alex, we really are. We get on really well and I love being in the house with you. But I'm not going to be your girlfriend, so don't ask me, and it's got nothing to do with Jasper. I've been thinking about this a lot. It would be easy for me just to say yes, I'll be your girlfriend. But at some point, maybe soon, maybe in a year or whatever, I'll stop being your girlfriend, because you'll get bored or someone else you fancy will come by and you won't be able to stop yourself. Girls throw themselves at you all the time, I'm not surprised you can't or don't always say no. And then, when that happens, and I know it will happen, then I'll be sad, and we probably won't be friends anymore. And we could still be living in the same house, which would be horrible. And so no, I won't be your girlfriend, because then there will be a timer on us, and I'll be anxious that you will be about to move on to someone else all the time.'

Alex laughs. 'Blimey Sophie, you don't have a very high opinion of me, do you?'

I pause, considering the question. 'I do, actually,' I reply. 'I think you are pretty amazing.'

I blush and squeeze his hand. 'But I'm not going to fall for you, because then I'll lose you.'

I am embarrassed now and stare at the ground at my feet. Alex leans over and kisses me softly on the mouth, releasing all sorts of fireworks inside me.

'I think you're pretty amazing too, Sophie, but somehow I have a feeling that you don't quite believe me.'

He stands up and hitches his bag onto his shoulder.

'I've got to go, otherwise I'll miss the train. I'm still going to go down to London, I need a couple of days to get my head round it. I'll see you when I get back?'

He turns and I watch him walk away, before getting up stiffly from the bench and jogging slowly back to Johnson Road.

CHAPTER 19

JASPER

Over the next two days, I conclude that Johnson Road without Alex is very quiet, and not in a good way. He brings so much energy to the place, whether noisily taking the stairs two at a time, or shouting up at me through the ceiling, or playing crap German pop music at full blast. We miss his messy cooking in the kitchen and the wet towel on the bathroom floor. The smell of him lingers in his room, permeating from the various items of clothing he's left scattered on the floor.

On the Saturday that Alex leaves, I don't see Sophie at all. I sleep off my hangover and then go to play rugby. Sophie texts to say she is in the library, putting the finishing touches to her Victorious Youth presentation, so I go to med school, to put in a few hours of my own.

I need an early night, and Sophie has obviously decided she needs one too, I join her soon after I arrive home. She still has the sidelight on when I open the door and I smile at her sheepishly, hovering in the doorway.

'Sophie, I'm so sorry about last night. I was absolutely hammered. I should have slept in my own bed. Force of habit, I guess. Hope I didn't ruin your night for you. Is it okay if I join you? I know it's early; maybe you're still doing stuff, in which case I can go next door, or maybe come back later?'

I'm gabbling and I start backing out of the room again.

'Jasper no, don't go, don't be silly, of course you can stay. I was just turning the light out anyway. And also, I need to talk to you about Alex.'

That piques my interest and I come back into the room and start undoing the buttons on my shirt. I hang it carefully on the back of a chair, and as I stand in front of her wearing only my blue jeans, I see her openly admiring my broad pale chest and well-toned six pack. I know I have a good body - all that crying in the gym has to have an upside, and I want her to see it. I reach to undo the top button of my fly and I unselfconsciously begin easing my jeans down over my hips. My dick is growing hard and she leans over to turn out the light, flushing with embarrassment. She usually pretends to be asleep at this point in the proceedings, but now she has a mental image of me that will hopefully replace some of the sad, weepy ones. I climb into bed and lie on my side facing her.

'So, what's up with him? I got your note.'

She turns to face me and props herself up on one elbow. The bedroom door is ajar and casts just enough light for us to see each other properly.

'Alex has gone to London for a couple of days. He's cross with me - and with you actually.'

I'm puzzled. 'Me? What have I done?'

Sophie relates the tale of the night before, and how angry and upset Alex had been when he discovered me sleeping next to her. She doesn't elaborate on all the finer points of her sexual encounter with Alex, and I don't need to hear every detail; my imagination is already in overdrive. She makes it clear they didn't have sex though, which is small comfort, I suppose.

Inside I'm boiling over. He's going to fucking do it, he's going to pinch her from right under my nose. I don't know how to react and she's waiting for me to say something. I swallow my anger and keep my voice light. I'll punch the wall later.

'Jesus, I bet he was well pissed off! I'm not sure Mr Van-Zeller is used to being usurped! It won't do him any harm though, the cocky bastard. He'll get over it.'

I say this in a kindly tone, my friendship with Alex runs deep. I struggle to say anything bad about him, although I have a feeling our friendship will soon be tested.

'You don't seem very surprised, you know, about me and Alex kissing?' says Sophie questioningly.

'I'm not!' I respond, and I hear my fake casualness. I'm trying to stay chilled, although inside I'm starting to panic. 'I guessed when I saw you just before Christmas that it probably wasn't the first time. He's absolutely besotted with you, it's so bloody obvious. Everyone knows it - me, Katy, Seb, Amy, everyone in the English department, probably the miserable bloke in the corner shop if you asked him! The only person who hasn't realised is you!'

I need to up my game, I need to remind her what we have. But I'm too fucking soft, and my confidence is fragile since Christians death. I'm not ready to make my move. And I like Alex.

'Poor bugger, though, I don't think it occurred to him for a second that I might have got here first. Not in that way,' I hastily add, blushing. 'I meant in your bed at night.'

How the fuck can I compete with Alex Van-Zeller? Can anyone? I stay calm.

'He's sort of asked me to be his girlfriend,' she confesses, 'But I said no.'

This is excellent news. I capitalise. 'For what it's worth, and I'm obviously completely biased, I think you've done the right thing. He might be ridiculously obsessed with you, but he's got the attention span of a gnat.'

I sigh feeling more content as she turned him down. If I can't compete, I can take small pleasure from the fact that I've made him jealous. With a bit of luck, he may actually have something to really be jealous about, as God knows for how long I can keep this friend zone thing going with her. It's fucking killing me.

'What do you want, Jasper?' she asks softly. 'Do you want me to tell Alex to stop, and you and I will become an item? Tell me what to do, I'm struggling here.'

She's stroking my chest hair, twisting it gently in her fingers. It takes all of my will power not to take this further, I'm naked under the covers and it would be so easy to....God, she feels so warm and safe and I'm completely relaxed in bed with her. This feels so right. Alex doesn't get to do this, ever.

'This is great, Soph, you, me, doing this - well, doing nothing much at all really, apart from sleeping every night. Which I love, by the way. I want more, but I want it to be right, I want my head in the right place. It's not going to be flash in the pan, a quick fling. It's going to be real and for good. So, I'm not going to tell you what to do, Sophie, that's your choice and you are going to have to choose one day. You know that, don't you?'

CHAPTER 20

ALEX

So, she thinks I'm bloody amazing, but obviously not that amazing, otherwise she'd be with me in my bed right now and we'd be fucking each other's brains out until the middle of next week. Instead, I'm on the fucking train to London and in a few hours' time, she'll be cosied up in bed with Jaz.
But I need time to think.
Mama is great when I get home. I took my hearing aids off the minute I walked away from Sophie, and I have no intention of putting them back on until I've got my head straight. Mama doesn't push me, she knows by now that I can happily stay in deaf mode for weeks at a time, so she leaves me to stew in my room until I'm ready to face everyone.
Anyone but Jaz and I'd be scoffing, supremely confident of my ability to kick his attempt to bag my girl into the long grass. But I know Jaz, I love Jaz, and now it seems that Sophie does too. I fucking knew there was something going on. He may not be shagging her, but he's getting under her skin, slowly and steadily. Not my preferred approach, to be fair, but it's working for him, evidently.
Anyone but Sophie and I wouldn't give a shit.
I come downstairs. I am wearing my aids and I'm hungry. Mama is waiting for me and kisses me and pulls me close. Gloria our housekeeper gives me the evil eye over mama's shoulder - I give her the evil eye back. We dislike each other intensely, so it pleases me to see that mama has asked her to prepare my favourite breakfast. Deborah, mama's stylist/hairdresser/confidante/ friend is there too, and she pulls me into her matronly bosom. I have had my head

between her enormous tits for as long as I can remember, since before I had my cochlear implants, when I lived in a confusing deaf world, and it is one of my favourite places on earth. Sometimes it feels like I have three mothers, and in their own way they are all making me feel better today.

'Do you want to tell me about it?' says mama when we are alone.

'Yes,' I say, surprising her. I reach for a piece of chopped melon. 'The short version is that I'm in love with a girl, and so is my best friend - the same girl unfortunately.'

Mama likes to talk; she never stops sometimes. It is good that papa isn't here, as between them, they fill a room with noise. Jaz and Sophie wouldn't believe that I'm the quiet one in this household. But now, she is listening.

'There are other girls, Alexi, you are very young.'

'I know,' I acknowledge. 'But I like this one, she's special. Jasper thinks she's special too.'

'Have you and Jasper talked about it?'

'No,' I sigh, 'But we will. I don't want to fall out with him - he's special too.'

I fill her in on Jasper's background, it takes a while.

'Sounds like something has to give, Alexi. One of you will have to bend and give way, unless neither of you have her. Which of you does she like best?'

I shrug, I want to think it is me, but I realise I haven't a clue, we are so different, we offer such different things.

'And who is more important - Jasper or your girl?'

And that is the other question that I struggle to answer.

We talk some more, she shows me a small Hockney she has acquired, I tell her about Sophie's course. And then we do what we do best together; she calls to Herman our driver to bring the car round, and we go shopping.

I return to Johnson Road late one afternoon a few days later, signalled by my whirlwind of activity at the front door. Herman has dropped me off.

'I'm back!' I shout superfluously, and come down the hall, laden with expensive shopping bags, to find the two of them quietly working at the kitchen table.

I think I'm completely over it, but seeing their heads contentedly together, his dark and hers blonde, I realise that I am nowhere near over it. I really want to be, but I'm not.

I plaster a smile over my face and beam at the both of them, my animosity pushed aside. Whatever happens, I truly am glad to be back with them both. As always, Sophie looks fresh and mouth-wateringly beautiful. She stands to greet me, and I hug her fiercely, firmly kissing her forehead.

'We've missed you loads!' she cries, and I inhale her divine smell.

Jasper receives a slightly cooler welcome - just the bear hug and a fond hair ruffle.

'It's good to be back,' I declare, 'And I come bearing gifts for my two favourite housemates. And to say I'm sorry that I went off in an immature huff. I'm just going to say this once and then we should try to forget about it. Whatever you two get up to, up there…' I indicate to the ceiling, 'It sounds pretty weird, but I'm cool with it. Whatever floats your boat? And it's not really my business anyhow.'

I thrust a Paul Smith bag at Jasper. 'This is for you. I'm fed up with that grey thing with all the holes in it. It's extra-large, so I'm sure it will fit over that fat beer belly perfectly.'

I flash him a smile and a wink.

Jasper takes a tissue paper covered parcel out of the bag, and proceeds to unwrap it, revealing a simple, but beautiful navy crew neck cashmere sweater. He slips it on over his T-shirt. It fits him like a glove, as I knew it would, accentuating his well-defined gym physique, which definitely has no hint of a beer belly. I let out a low whistle.

'Not bad, big boy, not bad at all, although God knows why I'm trying to make you look more attractive to the opposite sex.' I give Sophie a meaningful look.

Jasper looks down at his new sweater, taken aback by my thoughtfulness.

'Thanks, mate. I'm shocked, it's amazing, no one… no one has ever bought me anything as nice as this.'

His voice cracks as he speaks, he is clearly overcome by my unexpected act of kindness. He lifts his arms and gives me a manly hug.

'And I'm really sorry about Saturday night, I should have told you before about me sleeping there.'

'I'm cool.' I say, 'I've told you, let's forget about it. It's nothing, you sleep where you like, whatever gets you through. And anyway, what's the point of having papa's credit card if I never use it?'

I turn to Sophie, who has observed this exchange, and is probably relieved with how well we are behaving.

'I feel like I've just stepped into a scene from *Brokeback Mountain*,' she smirks.

I had been about to pass a bag over to her, but I snatch it back out of her hand, teasing her.

'I did have something for you too, Sophie, darling, but I might change my mind after that sarcastic comment.'

I pretend to walk off, then turn back, unable to resist any longer.

'All right, only kidding. Here's your present, gorgeous girl. I hope you like it; I've been anxious about it all the way up in the car.'

I thrust a large bag at her. 'Look at it later, when I'm not around, in case you don't like it, or it doesn't fit. I can change it for something else if it's not right.'

Sophie is too impatient for that. 'I'm not waiting until later! I want to know what it is now! I'll go upstairs and try it on, then come down and find you. If I don't come back in five minutes, it will be because it's really horrible and I'm trying to think of how to break it you gently.'

She trips off upstairs. Jasper and I are alone in the kitchen. He knows that I have something to say.

'So, Jaz, tell me. How much do you want her?' I smile as I speak - I really don't want to fall out with him. It's not just that I love him - he's fucking enormous and could do a hell of a lot of damage to my pretty face with those fists.

'As much as you do,' he replies, amused. 'But there is no rush - she's not going anywhere. I'm in it for the long game, Alex.'

This is good, I think, by the time he's got his act together, it will be too late for him.

'Then you won't mind if I......' I begin, but he stops me, a warning hand curls around my wrist. Fuck, his hands are big. My arm is not going anywhere.

'Don't think that I'll just roll over for you, Al.'

I don't doubt it, he's made of strong stuff, much stronger than me. I think this is the most adversity I've ever faced in my young life. He hasn't finished,

'And, Alex,' he continues pleasantly, still holding my wrist, 'Stay out of her fucking room.'

He lets go and I resist the urge to rub my skin where he has left a mark. I stand up and pat him on the back. 'Game on then, big boy.'

CHAPTER 21

SOPHIE

Unsurprisingly, of course, Alex has exquisite taste. And evidently a whole lot of money too. After unwrapping several thin layers of delicate tissue paper, I hold up the most perfect jacket I have ever seen. It is Dolce & Gabbana, a classic American flying jacket. It is crafted of the softest, finest chocolate suede, and with the cosiest sheepskin lining imaginable. It fits me perfectly, as if designed exclusively for me alone. The colour is exactly the right shade for my skin tones.

On the back of the jacket is an intricate and delicate embroidered mosaic pattern of an eagle, in red, yellow and orange, its wings spread across the shoulder blades. I have never owned such a luxurious item and I stand admiring my reflection for a few moments, marvelling at Alex's generosity.

Until Alex came up to my room, I was convinced that I knew what to do. Focus on Jasper, enjoy what we have together, let it develop into more when we are both ready. But Alex has drawn me back to him, with his words and his fingers and his mouth, and I want more. I'm not ready to choose.

I study myself in the mirror thoughtfully for a moment, then slip out of the jacket, and also remove my long-sleeved top and bra. Then, putting just the jacket back on, I fasten the zip all the way up to my neck and go downstairs to find him. He is in his room, putting away the rest of his baggage.

'Wow look at you!' he cries when he sees me, grinning with delight.

'It's gorgeous, Alex, you are amazing, thank you so, so much.' I kick the door closed with my foot and stand in front of it, twirling slowly.

'Very nice indeed,' he nods appreciatively and comes over to me. He kisses me tenderly, cupping my buttocks in his hands and pulling me to him.

'Very sexy, Sophie. It really suits you. Now let's see what it looks like undone.'

I slowly begin to pull the zip down, my eyes on his reaction. I pause.

'Why don't you undo the zip for me Alex?'

He does as he is asked, and his eyes widen with surprise and pleasure as my naked breasts and belly come into view. He studies me with a low whistle.

'It looks even better like this, I think.' He reaches down and kissed me gently on the lips again, one hand circling my waist and the other cupping a breast firmly, my nipple instantly hard.

'Fuck, Sophie, what are you doing to me?' he murmurs, and begins kissing me harder, pushing me back firmly against the bedroom door, pinning me there with his thigh between my legs.

I respond just as urgently, my hands pulling his face down to mine, tasting his fresh, cool mouth. My hands find their way under his shirt and I caress the smoothness of his flawless skin. We carry on kissing frantically, he slips the jacket off onto the floor, and begins tugging at my jeans so they rest lower on my hips. His hand slips inside and he finds my sweet spot instantly. I groan helplessly as his fingers expertly fuck me once more.

I come in seconds - how does he do this? - a great wave of feeling coursing uncontrollably through my body. I can feel his erect penis straining through the thin material of his sweatpants and quickly bring him to orgasm with my hand, his juices spilling out hot against my palm. We stand against each other panting, getting our breath back, before Alex leads me over to the bed and we collapse on it, side by side. He has thrown off his clothes and my breath catches in my throat as I see him naked.

'I hope none of that found its way onto my new coat!' I laugh as our breathing returns to normal.

He rolls on top of me and begins determinedly kissing me, tiny biting kisses which start at my jaw and trail to my breasts.

'I want you, Soph,' he whispers urgently, through his kisses. 'You do something to me; I can't explain it. I just know that I want you so fucking much. Be with me, please.'

His hips begin rhythmically pushing down on me and incredibly I feel his penis hardening once more against my thigh. He adjusts his position over me, moving across a fraction and resting his weight on his elbows. I can feel the velvety wet tip of his demanding erection brushing against my outer lips. The sensation is overpowering, my body is screaming at my brain to let him in.

I put a hand down to stop him.

"I'm not ready to do this with you, Alex,' I whisper back, although every single fibre of my being is frantically signalling the opposite message.

With effort, I push him off and sit up.

'Lie back.' I command, and a smile plays at the corners of his mouth as I straddle his lean thighs.

He knows what is coming and clasps both hands behind his head, relaxing back against the pillows. He smiles up at me, his eyes half closed, his breath already heavy. I lean forwards, my long straight hair falling in two heavy curtains, which I deliberately brush against his taut abdomen as I take his penis into my mouth. I begin softly, licking greedily from the base to the tip and then back down again, blowing my hot breath against his groin. He moans with desire, his hips rising to meet me. When I think he can stand the teasing no longer, I take the length of him in my mouth and suck gently, my teeth grazing his skin.

'Fuck, Sophie, that's good, so good.' He gasps and I let him push into my mouth with every roll of his hips.

I develop a smooth rhythm, sucking and grazing, and reach down to cup his balls at the same time, one finger trailing over the sensitive skin behind. I can hear his breathing becoming quicker and louder and I taste his salty release, filling my mouth, spurting into me. I'm aching to touch myself and with one hand I bring myself quickly to climax, throwing my head back, aware of his eyes transfixed on me as I masturbate.

We lie quietly afterwards, no words necessary, in each other's arms, happy and spent. It is Alex who eventually breaks the silence.

'I think I've fallen in love with you, Sophie,' he says quietly.

I don't reply, unsure how to respond.

'I still want you to be my girlfriend - I want to do this with you all day and all night. ....actually, no I don't - I want to have sex with you all day and all night, properly. Why won't you sleep with me?'

I take a while to answer, trying to think of a way to explain. It is impossible, he is impossible.

'I think I've fallen in love with you too, Alex. But I don't want to, I don't want to be in love with you. I've explained to you already. Because...because then it will be nearly over.'

I stop talking and untangling my arm from his delicious embrace, I rap my knuckles on the wooden edge of the headboard behind us.

'See this? I don't want to become another notch on this, your bedpost. Not yet, anyhow. I'm not ready, and you can say all you want that that won't happen, but I know it will, and if I'm not your girlfriend, and not always available for you and waiting for you, then I'll get to keep you little longer.'

'But I want you Sophie!' he grumbles petulantly, half rolling on top of me again and running his fingers up and down my thigh, caressing me gently.

'I need you, Sophie! I need these gorgeous legs wrapped round me every single day. I need to make love to you every single day. And I need you to leave Jasper and choose me, so we can make love every single night.'

Once again, I can feel his penis hardening against me. Surely, he isn't ready to go again, so soon. He is bloody insatiable! I take his perfect face between my hands and kiss him.

I think of Jasper upstairs, working at his desk. I think of our nights together when I'm curled up tight against his solid, rock-like, masculine presence. I think of my beautiful Alex, here with me now, and all that we have just done. He is an urgent ball of energy, pushing me, wanting me. I am no closer to choosing.

CHAPTER 22

JASPER

The next few weeks are busy. I have a block of training at City Hospital on the other side of town, so I am up early to catch two buses, and return home late. I spend every night with Sophie and look forward to our late-night intimacy.

I share my concerns about my mother, as I suspect she is turning to booze to get through the days. She phones me sometimes in tears in the middle of the afternoon, drunk and alone. My aunt tries to get her to seek help, or at least to get dressed and go for a walk, but she isn't ready. I feel impotent, such a long way from home and unable to help, and I can ill afford the journey.

It is now completely routine for me to be in Sophie's bed almost as soon as she is, and she lies with her head on my chest every night, encircled in my arms. I relish these steady moments as we talk and share our day.

She is confused, that much is clear and our closeness during our nights together only serve to make her even more so. The house is claustrophobic, and I am relieved that my life outside it is growing as my general happiness improves. I've been out a few times with the old crew from med school and Samira is pushing me for more. Her looks tempt me, her body definitely tempts me and as my sex life has been a barren desert for so long, I make my move. I compartmentalise it from my feelings for Sophie. I'm ready for some relief from my sexual frustration - I have no doubt that Alex is doing the same, whilst we wait to see who will blink first.

So, Sophie arrives home early from lectures one frosty February afternoon, to be greeted by the sound of girlish laughter coming from the direction of the kitchen. She walks in to find me sitting at the table drinking a mug of tea, and opposite me is Samira, looking as elegant and poised as ever. Samira appraises Sophie coolly as I make the introductions. Sophie offers her a friendly smile, but Samira clearly isn't inviting any sort of friendship. She puts her hand protectively on my thigh as they make small talk, claiming her territory. I'm embarrassed that Sophie has found us together, I was expecting the house to be empty, and she makes it easier for me by quickly excusing herself and going out for a run.

I talk to Samira some more, all the time wondering what Sophie is thinking whilst she pounds the streets. Maybe now she feels how I feel when I know she is with Alex. Unlike me, she has nothing to worry about. Samira is just a distraction - I know I will never have even half the feelings for her that I have for Sophie, whereas I know that she and Alex are falling heavily for each other.

I take some beers and Samira up to my room and we fool around for a while. When she's not with her mates she's not too bad, and bloody hell, she has a body to die for. But God knows why she's so determined to get her hands on me, I'm not exactly sweet talking her with my cans of Sainsbury's lager and grumpy demeanour. And she is a bit strange, I can't deny. She knows far more about me than I've ever told her, she seems to know my timetable from memory, even the day of my next rugby match.

I hear Sophie return and soon after, she is in her room next door. Samira is still waiting for what she came for, but I realise that I can't do it here, with Sophie just a few feet away, so we head over to her place.

'This doesn't mean that we're back together, Sam, it's just sex,' I warn her, as she slips my belt out of my jeans. Her hand on my dick feels great, it's been a while and I'm more than ready.

'I know, Jasper,' she replies, smiling and kneeling in front of me, looking up at me seductively through her long, long lashes.

I groan as she takes me in her mouth. I remember that she is very good at this. 'I mean it, Sam,' I warn, giving her an opportunity to back out, but either she doesn't believe me or doesn't care.

The sex is good, for me anyway. I pound into her, with my eyes closed and not kissing much, lost in the sensation of my dick inside her. I think she enjoys it too, from the noises she's making, although I don't really care, I just need the relief.

I'm not proud of myself, far from it. Is this how it is for Alex, I wonder afterwards, as we lie next to each other on her narrow bed? I'll have to ask him sometime. Does he try to make every woman feel as though she is the most sensational creature alive, or is he just getting his end away, like me? Knowing him, I suspect he gives them all his best shot, takes his performance seriously, proud that he can deliver exactly what they all need. How can I compete? I bet he's amazing, addictive even. After all, they are queueing up to have another go. I feel bad now, bad for Samira for using her, and bad for wanting to leave as soon as I'm done.

I get home sometime after midnight. The light from the TV is flickering in Alex's room and he is in there alone.

'Alright mate?' he says warmly. 'Sophie told me you had some fit bird here earlier - I wasn't expecting to see you again tonight.'

He's in his favourite chair, having a beer. He passes one to me and I sit down. 'She's that girl I was seeing before I left last year. She wants me to start up again with her, but I'm not that bothered.'

'So, did you blow her out, then?' he asks, 'Soph says she's gorgeous.'

'Nah, not exactly.' He raises his eyebrows at me, and we exchange a knowing look, recognisable to young men everywhere. It makes me smile.

'Yeah, okay I did, but to be honest, she's a bossy cow and does my head in, but my ball sacks have been bigger than a rhino's these last few weeks, lying up there with Sophie. I felt like I was going to fucking explode if I didn't get some action soon.'

He's pissing himself laughing.

'I'm not proud of myself, Al! I'm not that sort of bloke.'

He laughs again, I love his laugh, it's so free and easy. 'We're all that sort of bloke, mate, get over yourself.'

He has a swig of beer. 'So why aren't you over there now, going for round two?'

That's easy. 'Because I'd rather be here, having a decent conversation with you, instead of getting talked at non-stop by her. I've been busy and I haven't seen you for a couple of days.'

Neither of us speak for a while and we watch the darts match in a companionable silence. Did I really just tell Alex, in so many words, that I've missed him?

'Her tits are fucking magnificent, Al.'

He giggles again. 'So, when are you seeing her next?'

I shrug, 'I don't know mate, but I probably will at some point. She's barking mad, though, I'm not getting too close.'

He leans across and pats me on the thigh. 'You're even more fucked up than me over our threesome, aren't you, big boy?'

CHAPTER 22

ALEX

All three of us are fucked up actually. Jaz is spending every bloody night in bed with the girl of my dreams - and his dreams - and not grabbing her and fucking her senseless, because he's not ready and wants it to be right, blah, blah, blah. So instead, he's starting to see an unhinged old girlfriend on the side, who is by all accounts bloody gorgeous, just to give his right hand a rest. Sophie is spending every night with Jaz and yet doesn't want to make a move because he's not ready, blah, blah, blah and obviously for a much more important reason, which is that she is falling in love with me (although I think she is in love with him too.) Is that even possible? Apparently, it is. And I'm making my move on Soph, I've completely laid out my stall, but she won't have sex with me, because she thinks I'm a complete whore and will drop her from a great height. And doesn't want to lose Jaz. And Jaz and I really like each other, but ultimately, are heading for a huge fucking fall out.

Am I a complete whore? Well, I certainly have been, but I'm turning over a new leaf, starting this week. For several reasons. Number's 1and 2: my liver and my lungs. I'm going to be dead by the age of thirty at this rate. Number 3: I want Sophie to see that I'm not the complete whore she has me pegged as, and then she'll fall into my arms, kiss Jasper goodbye and live happily ever after with me in Zurich. Number 4: I'm in huge shit with the Head of English for not attending enough lectures and being behind on assignments.

I need to knuckle down and do some work if I still want to be here next year. Fortunately, Hugo and Seb are in the same boat, so we've curtailed our midweek social lives and are restricting ourselves to the weekend only. It's only week one, but it's going quite well.

And I'm also trying to do something else too, which was actually Hugo's idea. I was playing poker at his place, just me, him and Seb. I was losing every hand, which to be fair, isn't unusual, because Hugo is uber competitive and always tries his hardest, and Seb is just bloody good at poker. His dad's a prominent bishop, I still haven't worked out how he got so good. There are quite a few things about Seb that I can't work out, including why I've never seen him cop off with a bird when we go clubbing, but perhaps he's just more discerning, or discreet than me and Hugo.

So, I'm a hundred quid down and whining, but it's not the poker that I'm whining about, it's my lack of full, penetrative sex with Sophie.

'Jesus, Al, you're a bloody stuck record, mate,' says Seb, shuffling the pack like a pro. 'Get over yourself.'

'I don't want to be like this, Seb, I wish I could get over myself, but I'm totally in love, and it's killing me.'

Hugo is unusually quiet, he's generally well ahead of Seb when it comes to taking the piss.

'Stop trying to shag her then,' he says, rearranging the cards in his hand. 'Be patient and let her come to you. Okay, you might lose everything, because she might go straight to solid, dependable Jasper in tears and never look back, but at least you'll stop torturing yourself and it will help you get over her. And she will have to make a decision, won't she? Stop pleading and be cool.'

'You've obviously been dwelling on my love life more than I thought, Hugsy. I'm touched.'

He gives me the finger and we play on.

So that's what I'm trying to do. And I'm five days in and actually surviving, although my bedroom bin is overflowing with crispy tissues. And my cock is hard about ninety-five percent of the time that I'm awake, just thinking of what I'm missing. But I'm going to give it my best shot. I hope Sophie notices.

CHAPTER 23

SOPHIE

Usually when he is studying, Alex removes his hearing aids, all the better to concentrate, and so is mostly incommunicado during this time. I'm not sure whether it is my overactive imagination, but I think he is slightly cooler towards me since I refused to sleep with him. Or maybe I'm just paranoid that he is using studying and his lack of hearing as an excuse to speak to me less. After all, the house is quiet in the evenings - Jasper works diligently most nights - and being able to hear wouldn't be a barrier to useful study.

We have not kissed properly or had any further intimacy since that last afternoon together when he bought me the jacket. It is my own fault obviously – he fairly explicitly laid out his feelings for me and I have turned him down more than once, so it is not unreasonable that he has stopped trying. I miss him though.

We have collectively agreed that a big trip to Sainsbury's is long overdue. The contents of the fridge are running low and we have exhausted the meagre selection on the shelves at the corner shop.

The night before the planned mission, the three of us sit down together to make a list of student essentials. Jasper's idea of essentials is typical of hard up students everywhere: packets of bacon, vast quantities of cheap sliced bread (I have seen him toast a whole loaf in one sitting), baked beans, some cans of his horrendous Sainsbury's own brand lager and as many chocolate digestives as we can feasibly carry.

Alex, on the other hand, considers black organic olives, pickled artichoke hearts, chorizo and fresh scallops to be an absolute must, so not surprisingly, the shopping list has grown quite long by the time we set off.

It is just me and Alex on the trip, as Jasper has a full day of lectures to attend. I rarely go anywhere with Alex during the day, especially just the two of us, and as our time together recently has been less than completely comfortable, I am actually feeling slightly nervous about it.

However, I need not have worried at all, as Alex appears to be his normal cheerful self. Being out and about amongst the general public with him is a fascinating social experiment; I imagine it is not dissimilar to being with a minor celebrity. He cuts a striking figure as we wander down the aisles, with his mane of yellow hair, astoundingly handsome features and expensive clothes. I am aware of the admiring glances thrown his way from the other female, and some male customers. Alex, however, appears completely oblivious and is extremely attentive to me, he embarrassingly asks loudly which flavour condoms I prefer.

Unlike nearly all of us, money isn't a concern for him, and so, having bought far more than is on the list, the walk home turns into an arduous trek, both of us fully laden with carrier bags.

'Remind me, Sophie, why you wouldn't let me call for a taxi?' he grumbles, readjusting his grip on the five overloaded bags.

'Because I can't afford it! I can't keep on letting you pay for everything all the time,' I retort, internally regretting my decision, but determined not to let Alex know.

As we reach the *Three Wheat Sheaves* pub, with half a mile still to go, I suggest we head inside for a breather. Alex doesn't need any encouragement, and we plonk the bags down with relief at one of the nearest tables. He goes to the bar to place an order. It is four thirty in the afternoon, and unsurprisingly, the pub is nearly empty apart from a couple of shabbily dressed blokes propping up the bar, who look like they probably spend every afternoon here. A TV that no one is watching is showing a snooker match, the sound muted, and cheesy eighties music plays in the background.

We each have a pint of lager, drinking them down thirstily, and share a packet of peanuts. Returning from fetching another round, Alex leans over the table and kisses me full on the mouth. He tastes of salt and beer and my heart lurches. I have missed his kisses quite a lot recently.

'If you weren't so stubborn, and just agreed to be my girlfriend, then we could do stuff like this all the time,' he observes mildly, placing my second drink down front of me.

'If this is your idea of giving a girl a good time, then not being your girlfriend is probably quite a wise decision!' I answer, smiling at him.

'You know exactly what I mean,' he says earnestly. 'You, me, just chilling, doing ordinary stuff together. We're good at it.'

He takes a long swig from his lager. I study his perfectly symmetrical features and messy mop of thick blonde hair. Reaching over the table, I take his hand,

'I am joking Alex, I do know exactly what you mean, and I'm loving my trip to the supermarket with you.'

I put my lips to his fingertips before continuing.

'But, trust me, you would get bored. I know what you're like and this sort of mundane stuff, it's not for you, not yet anyhow. You're too young and too, well...lively.'

He rubs his chin thoughtfully.

'I still want you though, Sophie, you just don't get it do you? I'd be happy doing the mundane stuff all day every day if I could do it with you. I don't know what I have to do to convince you of that.'

God, he makes it hard for me. Maybe I should just say yes and enjoy it whilst it lasts. Being Alex's girlfriend would be wonderful. But saying yes to Alex would mean saying goodbye to Jasper, as there is no way on earth that he would tolerate that cosy relationship continuing. Which is fair enough, to be honest. And then, when Alex becomes bored and moves on, I will be left with neither of them.

But now, this afternoon, I want Alex.

This time it is me that leans over to kiss him. The level of intimacy borders on what is publicly unacceptable, but no-one is watching. I eventually break off and give him a cool serious stare, attempting a disinterested manner.

'Drinking lager during the day on an empty stomach makes me horny as hell, Alex Van-Zeller,' I state, shrugging. 'Just because I'm not your girlfriend and won't have sex with you, doesn't mean we can't have some fun when we get back home, does it? We could unpack the shopping later.'

Alex is up and out of his seat instantly, draining the last few drops from his pint.

'Jesus Sophie, you bloody know how to push my buttons. I've spent the last couple of weeks trying to wean myself off you, and it looks like I'm getting straight back on.'

The shopping doesn't feel quite so heavy after that. We dump it in the hall and are kissing before we even properly close the front door. Once in his room, I begin undoing his fly as he leans back against the desk, his hands firmly gripping my buttocks.

'You're like fucking cocaine for me, Sophie. I promise you; this is the last time.' He groans, as though in pain as I kneel in front of him and take his heavy penis in my mouth.

He claws my long hair with his hands and climaxes quickly as I suck him off, he's panting loudly as he fists the base of his penis, and silvery white semen spurts in an arc across my face and chest. There is a look in his eyes that I don't recognise, but I know he is angry with me. Recovering, he pushes me roughly backwards onto the bed and begins pulling at the buttons of my shirt, wrenching it off to reveal my pale pink lace bra.

'I'm having you one day, Soph,' he almost snarls, 'I can promise you that.'

He carelessly pulls my bra aside, exposing my breasts, kissing and nipping them severely, making me gasp with exquisite pain. I have not seen him like this before, he is taking what he wants, venting his frustration on me. It is both thrilling and frightening. I can't turn my gaze away from the angry determination on his perfect face. His busy hands are now working their way down towards my jeans, which he rips open, quickly pushing them over my hips then down to my knees. I kick them off. His tongue follows his hands down my body, and I lean back into the pillows, anticipating with pleasure what is to follow. He thrusts my thighs over his shoulders, and I am open to him, exposed. I surrender myself completely as he lies between my legs.

His mouth does not disappoint, his aggressive tongue delves deeper into me and I feel myself thrusting my hips towards him, demanding more. I am intensely aware of the pressure growing on my full bladder from the two pints of lager I have drunk earlier, but this only serves to heighten my pleasure as I strive to control my muscles, when all the time they are aching for release.

I come with a loud cry, and he throws me off and jerks his head back up towards my face, forcing me to taste myself on his lips. We kiss deeply and I reach down for his member, already standing to attention once more, but he bats my hand aside. He sits back on his heels and watches my face intently, almost defiantly, as he proceeds to masturbate himself to orgasm, his hand flying over his penis, pumping his hot semen onto my exposed belly and chest, claiming his territory.

Eventually, he collapses into me, hot and sweaty, his penis finally flaccid against my thigh, his heart rate slowing against my chest.

'I love you, Soph,' he says into my neck. 'One day you will be mine, I know you will.'

All his rage has dissipated, and he begins kissing my face tenderly, nibbling on my ear lobes and stroking my hair as if the last few minutes had never happened.

'Alex,' I murmur in a small voice, after a few minutes of enduring his heaviness on my overflowing bladder, 'If I don't go for a wee now, you are going to have very wet sheets!'

He lets out a short bark of laughter and naughtily presses his groin down harder on me. I am suddenly aware of a few drops of warm urine escaping from between my thighs.

'Ow!! Stop it Alex! Get up right now!' I command urgently and push him away from me.

He cooperates with another hoot of laughter as I quickly dodge from under him, not having time to even pull on my top as I scramble to the bathroom, one hand firmly pressed between my legs to hold back the flow. I just make it in time and sit on the loo, relief literally pouring out of me, the delicious sound of Alex's hysterical giggling loud in my ears.

CHAPTER 24

JASPER

I fly back to Kinsale for the Easter break. More money on the credit card, but I need to go. I'm dreading seeing mam and I pray that she isn't a complete mess. I pack lots of revision and, as usual, will be juggling a bar job to earn some extra cash.

Alex has disappeared off to his main home in Zurich, before spending some time in New York with his parents. He finds it amusing to send me and Sophie daily pictures, hilarious shots of him lying mostly naked in bed in tastefully provocative poses. I am speechless, I have no idea what goes on in that boy's pretty head. Sophie later tells me that she spent the whole holiday glued to her phone, never letting it out of her sight for fear that another member of her family might inadvertently come across his soft-focus photos.

I pull pints and talk sport with the regulars on automatic pilot - I've been doing it for years and they know me well. There are a few tourists now as the weather improves, middle aged walking types mostly, but most of the faces are familiar. They know my mam, my da, my aunt, uncles, cousins, grandparents, and of course they knew my brother Christian. I'm a good barman and people are nice to me.

The pub is my refuge, my mam is better than at Christmas, but we still have a long way to go. But I know that I am the only bright spot on her horizon and so I do everything I can to please her, and I think it helps. She loves my stories about med school, the patients I come across and the interesting things I have learnt about the human body.

We are close, me and my mam, we have been through a hell of a lot together and there are no secrets. She hears about Alex and our close friendship and laughs at the photos of him on my phone. He's like no-one either of us have ever met before.

'So, what shall I do about Sophie, then mam?' I ask her, as she's sorting through some washing.

'I think you and your Alex have got to let her decide what she wants to do. She's so young, I can't imagine she knows what she wants more than you two boys do.'

She lays clothes out on the airer and I know the windows in our tiny kitchen will be steamed up completely within the hour. 'But you just be careful you don't put yourself down, Jasper! This Alex boy might have all the chat and the charm and whatnot, but you are a fine boy yourself. A catch in anyone's' eyes!'

I need the confidence boost; I need to think I can compete against Alex. The term ahead will be a big one, and I'm planning on coming out on top.

CHAPTER 25

SOPHIE

The Easter holidays come and go in a blur. I fly out to Cyprus to join my family for a fortnight, and despite missing Jasper and Alex, I really enjoy the break. The sun shines and the days are warm, so I spend nearly every afternoon sunbathing by the pool, happily fantasising about my two gorgeous men.

I had hoped that the temporal and spatial distance from them both would afford me an opportunity to analyse my feelings for them, and in particular to work out in my head the direction of my relationship with Alex. Our sexual encounter after the supermarket trip had been mind-blowing, even now when I think about it, excitement flips in my belly.

Fi joins me for a week and is a much-needed sounding board. My parents are quite prim, my father in particular, and unfortunately, I have never developed the 'best friend' type relationship some girls have with their mothers. Even when I had started my periods as a twelve-year-old, my mother had just bunged me some sanitary towels and in a no-nonsense way suggested I get on with it. I have an extremely good day-to-day relationship with both my parents and we often have fun together, but there is something about them both which doesn't invite girly intimacies. I have always been envious of those girls who are able to pour all their woes onto their mothers, and no more so than now, as I would have really appreciated some sensible advice.

'I'm not sure you are being that kind to Alex,' suggests Fi as we lounge by the pool sipping cool lagers. 'I mean, from everything you say, the guy absolutely adores you. I think you should just go out with him or leave him alone, but stop teasing him like this, it's not fair.'

'Whose side are you on?' I say on a half laugh, but I can see she is serious. 'And actually, just keeping Jasper in reserve until you've made your mind up is pretty mean too, now I think about it.'

I realise I'm taking relationship advice from a girl who once drank half a bottle of Martini in the lower sixth and then held onto Nathan Longman's ankle all night as he attempted to walk around, declaring she wanted his babies. I shift on the lounger, sitting up to look at her, my voice raised in protest. 'It's easy for you to say, Fi, with your perfect Fraser and your cosy future all mapped out with him! If you had seen Alex in action, you would know how hard it is to resist him. And you would also see how horrible it would be to lose him.'

I'm cross with her now and she can tell. I'm just getting started, 'And Jasper is the one who comes to my bed, not me to his! He knows all about Alex and he still comes! And for your information, he's seeing another girl too, off and on, so don't worry about him too much. I'm your friend - I'm the one stuck between the two of them!'

I'm nearly crying with frustration and fury. I wish she hadn't come; I wish I hadn't invited her.

'Relax, Sophie,' she says, trying to calm me. 'I'm saying it for your own good! You need to choose so you can get on with your life, because at the moment, it sounds pretty toxic in your house and sooner or later, one of you is going to get fed up and walk out!'

She's right. And it's not long now before we have to decide whether we are all staying in the house next year. Alex will for sure, but if we fall out, then he might just get Hugo and Seb over, and Jasper and I will find ourselves out in the cold. The thought of not being with the boys in that house is painful, we need resolution and it needs to come from me.

Fi has a good idea. 'When I can't make a decision, my mum always says I should write a list of everything I like and dislike to help me. Why don't you tell me everything you like and dislike about the two of them now?' Fi's mum is a primary school teacher. I play the game, anyway, starting with Alex.

The list of things about Alex that I actively dislike is painfully short. 'Okay, Fi, so he doesn't empty the kitchen bin, like never, he leaves his belongings scattered all over the house, he probably has no idea how to adjust the heating, and his room, which me and Jasper call The Swamp, is full of crusty tissues and empty beer bottles.'

'Ditch him!' she jokes, 'The tissues sound gross, and as for the heating, well, I'm disgusted by his behaviour!'

'But apart from that Fi, he's fairly perfect. He smells like nothing I've ever smelt before; he kisses me like I'm the only person he's ever wanted to kiss, and did I mention that he could be Brad Pitt's much younger and more handsome brother? And, even if you attempt to dismiss from the equation the fact that he looks like a Greek God, then he's still kind and funny, thoughtful and caring....'

'I'm not sure this is helping much,' she interrupts. 'What about doing Jasper now?'

The list of things I dislike about Jasper is even shorter, I struggle to come up with a single one, and the list of things I like about him, well, pretty much everything.

I have received one enigmatic postcard from him, yet another view of Kinsale, this time it is a close up of the quaint, brightly coloured cottages that line the high street. On the back he has written, in his terrible scrawl,

'My thoughts are free to go anywhere, but it is surprising how often they head in your direction. Jx'

CHAPTER 26

ALEX

Summer term - yay! Good weather and girls in skimpy clothing - what's not to like? Good for parties too, but not so good for trying to study for year-end exams. Captain Sensible sequesters himself in a windowless cubicle of the med school library, all the better to pretend that the sun isn't shining outside and to help him forget that his rugby mates are probably sitting in a pub garden somewhere drinking cold beer.

Samira is still apparently very much on the scene, on Jasper's terms, and being a conscientious student herself, she sees revising as an opportunity to spend more time with him. Jasper mostly tolerates this - he gets a shag, in return for putting up with her weird, stalkerish behaviour. Each to their own, I suppose, and the good news is that it means he's not gagging for Sophie if he is getting his end away elsewhere. So hopefully their platonic bed sharing bizarreness will remain just that for a while longer.

I'm actually being quite a diligent reviser, with the added advantage of being able to periodically block out the rest of the world when I'm trying to concentrate. I have taken delivery of a couple of stylish wooden sun loungers for the back garden, complete with sumptuous mosaic patterned cushions, thus I am able to make the most of the unseasonably warm May weather and yet also ensure I do enough work to not get kicked out.

The added bonus for me, is that Sophie is often to be found lounging in the adjacent chair, and having hardly left the poolside in Cyprus, she has returned to uni with a good tan and a couple of bikinis in her suitcase and, praise the Lord, is making use of them whenever possible. Stuck in the library, Jasper has no idea what he is missing, although my frequent texted photos to him, of us together, go some way to helpfully keeping him updated.

I can study her body all day and never tire of it. Her legs are long and slim, her hips narrow, her arse perfect. He skin is the colour of corn and smells perfect. Her boobs are small and each one fits my hand perfectly; her nipples love my mouth. Her tummy is flat, a perfect surface on which to trail my tongue along on its way down to her pussy, which is frankly, in case there is any ambiguity, absolutely perfect. My tongue fits perfectly there too.

So, we lounge side by side, her in her teeny-weeny scrap of bikini, and me in my Calvin Klein boxers. I don't look too shabby myself. Hugo pops by and labels us Barbie and Ken.

Although this set up seems a perfect opportunity for us to continue our hitherto frequent and frenetic mutual pleasuring sessions, I am proud to report to Hugo that I have not instigated any since our return. I am happy in her quiet company, and apart from being unable to resist the odd cheeky slap of her bikini clad buttocks when she walks past me, or a hug and delicious forehead kiss before bed, we have no further physical contact.

And quiet company is good. Sex with most girls is good, amazing sometimes, it fuels my existence, it is my favourite pastime, but talking is good too, and it serves to remind me that my love is not just skin deep.

But skin deep it will have to be, as I'm weaning myself off, for my own protection, and I'm pleased with my progress.

She is pleased that she is revising an art history topic about which I am clueless, and I enjoy listening as she explains the differences between black and red figure vases from over two thousand years earlier, on which she is soon to be assessed. These delicate pots in all shapes and sizes are impressive. It is incredible to think that so much of this fragile pottery has survived for so long. Most of them illustrate tales from Greek myths, and from her photos, some potters are evidently artistic visionaries in their masterful portrayals of the whole gamut of human emotions, with only two colours in their palette at their disposal. Why am I studying English again, when this is so much more fascinating? Fuck knows.

Her favourite pot tells the sad tale of the great hero Ajax preparing for his suicide after killing a herd of Greek cattle in a fit of temper. A response which seems a little over the top, to be honest. He is pictured planting his sword in the ground, ready to impale his body upon it and take his own life. He has laid down his armour beside him and is nude and vulnerable, the silhouette of a single palm tree adds to the desolation of the scene. I can see why she likes it, although I think that maybe Ajax should have just manned up a little.

Exams finish in a week or so, and me and the boys are planning a big one. Booze and girls will feature heavily, just what I need to get this bloody gorgeous creature next to me out of my system.

CHAPTER 27

SOPHIE

Two weeks into term and Katy and Amy are planning a big night out to a club in town with all the gang from Art History. Amy is hoping that Andrew will meet her there – he has dropped hints, but his previous no-shows have seriously dented her confidence. Katy and I are still at a complete loss to identify his attractiveness.

I'm really looking forward to it; a fun reward for some seriously hard revision. We start with a couple of cocktails on the lawn outside Ancaster Hall and then move up through the Lenton pubs, stopping for a drink in each and gathering more partygoers along the way.

I spy Jasper drinking with his rugby team in the *Hand and Heart*, all of them propping up the bar and downing pints. He has come back from Ireland with his head in a much better place than since I have ever known him. His mum has finally agreed to get some professional support and has even started helping out in a local charity shop a couple of afternoons a week. I watch him for a few minutes from across the pub, before going over to say hello. He is looking very handsome, in an effortless sort of way, wearing his old grey jeans and the beautiful soft sweater that Alex bought him. I can conjure up the smell of it in my head as I've buried my nose in it so many times. His black curly hair is getting a bit too long; he has to frequently push it back off his forehead.

I observe his steady demeanour and natural grace, despite his size. He definitely has a presence about him. Not only is he physically head and shoulders above most people, but he is clearly comfortable in his own skin. I'm not the only one admiring his physique and good looks - plenty of girls are giving him the eye. Amy in particular still has a thing for him, even though he has made it quite clear some time ago, in a gentle fashion, that he isn't interested.

He eventually spots me, his eyes lighting up as he beckons me over, enveloping me briefly in his arms. We smile up at each other for a few moments, delighted to have met so unexpectedly. I reluctantly release him and say hello to everyone. I have met most of his rugby mates before, and I like them a lot; they are open and friendly. I am confident that they have absolutely no idea of the nature of my relationship with Jasper. He can't be persuaded to come clubbing - it isn't really his scene.

'Maybe I'll see you later if I'm still up?' he queries innocently as I leave, giving me a subtle wink.

'Yeah, maybe,' I replied airily, blowing him a kiss.

By the time we reach Roxy's nightclub, I feel quite pissed. After queuing to get in, I have a long drink of water at the bar to sober up. It is hot and cramped inside, the music is excruciatingly loud, and I realise too late that it isn't really my scene either. Amy has her face glued to Andrew's, and Katy is completely slaughtered and snogging a bloke who looks not too dissimilar to Alex's mate, Hot Hugo, although I can only see him from behind. It is definitely not the sort of place they would hang out, way too downmarket.

I am beginning to wish I had stayed with Jasper at the pub and then gone home with him. We could have been happily tucked up by now, whereas instead, I am standing alone at the bar watching the pissed history of art boys prancing around the dance floor.

Ben comes over to stand with me, clearly as drunk as the others. He has a girlfriend now, according to Katy, but she isn't here with him tonight. I have avoided him for most of the evening, as I don't want to have to fight off his advances for a second time. As pleasant and apparently bright as he is, reading social cues doesn't seem to be his strong point, especially after six pints of bitter. He slurs his words,

'Sophie, have you been avoiding me?' he stands closer to me and I can smell a mixture of kebab and stale beer on his breath and clothes as he sways towards me.

'Oh, hi Ben, didn't see you there, all good?'

He tries and fails to stifle a belch. I hope he's not about to vomit.
'Yeah, especially now you're here. Do you want to go someplace else?'

He places an arm heavily across my shoulders. I cringe, he is really nice when he is sober, but this is fairly grim. Where are Alex's strong arms and death stare when I need him?

'Ben, I'll be right back, can I just go to the loo first?'

I extricate myself from under his arm and swiftly head in the direction of the toilets, hoping he isn't following. It is getting really busy now and I have to push my way through groups of sweaty students. I suddenly feel hot and claustrophobic, like I'm going to pass out, and change direction, making a beeline for the door instead. Pushing through it, I make my way down the narrow stairs towards the exit.

The stairs are almost as packed as the club, crammed with students attempting to negotiate a route up or down, or in the case of one couple, inconsiderately engaging in some serious tongue and body action halfway up, and virtually preventing any movement in either direction. The bloke has his back me and is practically undressing his companion - her hands are down his jeans and clutching at his tight arse as if her life depends on it.

'Fucking get a room!' someone bellows angrily as they try to squeeze past. I attempt the same, and sickeningly, at the same moment, I realise that the devastatingly handsome blonde man who is blocking the stairs, indeed practically having full penetrative sex on the stairs, and completely unaware of whose path he is obstructing, is my beautiful, precious Alex.

I frantically push past him and almost fall through the exit, my breath coming in huge wracking sobs, tears beginning to course down my face. Hot, bitter acid burns its way up into the back of my throat and I turn to the wall, retching uncontrollably, the evening's four glasses of cheap white wine and bright orange cocktails creating an ugly puddle on the pavement. I stand leaning against the wall for a moment, catching my breath, saliva pooling in my mouth, trying to control my urge to vomit again.

Fortunately, the queue to get into the nightclub has died down, so my audience is limited, although I am dimly aware of a gaggle of clubbers pointing in my direction and laughing nearby. More in control, I begin walking, head down, in the direction of the town centre, my arm waving blindly to every taxi that passes, my vision blurred by tears.

I get lucky, and not thirty yards down the road, a black cab, its roof light indicating it is free, slows to a stop. I clamber onto the leather seat in the back and give my address.

The driver is a handsome young Sikh, his delicate features and big brown eyes framed by a huge claret turban. He smiles at me sympathetically; his eyes taking in my dishevelled state and tear stained face.

'Don't worry love,' he says kindly in the broad Nottingham accent that I have grown to love, 'I'll get you back home. These silly boys are really not worth it, you know.'

His kindness sets me off crying again and he hands me a box of tissues. He's clearly had this situation in his cab more than once before.

'They're never worth it, these young men, I'm giving you some pearls of wisdom here.'

I smile sadly at him and wipe the snot from my nose with his tissues. I take a couple of deep breaths, trying to get myself under control, distracting myself by trying to work out what language is being sung on the late-night radio. I want to stay cocooned in this taxi with this nice stranger all night, I want him to drive me away, as far away from Nottingham as it is possible to be, but all too quickly we arrive at Johnson Road and I point to my house. I fumble in my bag for some change and give him a hefty tip I can ill afford. He watches me safely through the front door before driving away, back into the Nottingham night.

The house is dark and quiet, the only obvious source of light coming from a low lamp in Alex's empty room. His door is ajar, and his delicious Chanel and coconut smell immediately assails my nose. Everything is a mess, bloody mess.

CHAPTER 28

Jasper

It's late when I hear Sophie come in. I hear her head for the bathroom - she spends an age in there with the shower running. I'm propped up in the middle of the bed reading, my head resting on several pillows. I look up with a ready smile as the door opens, concerned when I see her pale, tear-stained face. She is wearing an old baggy T-shirt.

'Sophie, sweetheart, what's wrong? What's the matter, why have you been crying?'

I hold my arms open to her as the tears start to flow.

She gets in beside me and sobs on my chest. I wrap myself around her.

'Oh Jasper, it's bloody Alex isn't it? I saw him at the club with some bird, snogging, all over her in fact, and it just upset me. The shock, I suppose. I mean, I know he's a player and has loads of girls all the time probably, I'm not an idiot, but it's pretty shit when I see him with one.'

Bloody Alex Van-Zeller. How many times have I said that over the last six months?? I should be pleased that she's seen him in action, but actually I'm not, because she's upset. I pull her a little closer. At least she's stopped crying now. She's calmed down a lot in fact. I must be good for something.

'I can't believe I'm so bothered really. And I shouldn't be,' she continues. 'I have no right to be. It's not like he's cheating on me or anything. It's me who said I wouldn't be his girlfriend. He can do what he likes, and he clearly is doing. It just hurts, that's all.'

I don't speak for a few minutes.

'I don't think you should worry about it, Soph. He's always got a string of gorgeous girls on the go. I'm surprised there are any left in Nottingham that he hasn't had a crack at. Or that you haven't seen him before. I'll tell you one thing though for sure, I don't think any of them mean anything at all. I reckon he'd give them all up tomorrow if he could have you.'

Sophie sighs. 'I don't know, Jasper, you've said that before, but I'm not convinced. I'm not going to give into him and sleep with him or agree to be his girlfriend, because it won't last, he'll move on to someone else a few months later, I know he will.' She pauses, tears are welling up again.

'It's just really hard having made that decision and knowing that it's the right decision, to then see him almost shagging some bird on the stairs of a nightclub in front of half the university. Why can't he be more normal, like everyone else?'

'We wouldn't like him so much if he was normal,' I reason, 'You love him for being Alex, not for being normal, and that's the problem.'

She wriggles into me, clearly enjoying the warmth of our embrace. Those wriggles are lethal, she has no idea what they do to my control.

'You're quite normal though, and I really like you. Maybe we should just ditch everyone else and run off together.'

I laugh, 'I think I'd probably quite enjoy that,' I agree, 'But at the moment I'm happy as things are. I've got you, I've got my studies, which I love by the way, I've got my mates and rugby and I've even got Samira (although I'm not sure I want her). My mum is on the mend, I'm feeling so much better and generally, life is not bad, not bad at all.'

Sophie is starting to look sleepy; she's had an emotional night. She rolls over and we spoon.

'Love you Jasper,' she whispers.

'Love you too, Sophie' I reply.

We stay as we are, and Sophie's breathing grows heavy. She has settled into our embrace completely, my hand wrapped across her belly like an old friend, her backside curled against my abdomen. God, this feels nice, I think to myself. Too bloody nice, in fact, I want more.

My dick is hard against her back - nothing new there, and the skin of her belly is so soft and warm under my fingers. I splay my hand from hip to hip, feeling the jut of her bones under the skin. My face is almost touching her hair, damp from the shower and the vanilla scent fills my senses. A pulse throbs wildly in my neck and my breathing quickens.

She is aware of me, her breathing pattern changes, her breath is lighter and less regular. Experimentally, she nestles her buttocks even more closely into me and they are met by my dick, hard and straight against her.

'Sophie,' I whisper in the darkness. 'Choose me?'

Without a word she rolls towards me and onto her back. I am definitely breathing more heavily now. I lean my face towards her, and my lips brush hers very gently, my elbows resting on the mattress either side of her head, steadying me. We explore each other's mouths gently, slowly. It is the lightest of touches. No other part of our bodies is touching, and I keep it this way. We have never kissed before, not properly, and I have months and months of kisses I want to share with her. I am in no hurry to move on or explore the rest of her body, my hands stay on the pillow next to her head and I am content to focus on her mouth, my eyes closed.

My body is silently starting to demand more. I wonder if I could come, just from kissing her. Probably. I pull away and smile down.

'I've decided that I'm going to make love to you, Sophie,' I whisper softly, 'I hope that's okay.'

It is more a statement of intent, not a question. I don't know how I will stop if she says no, but I can see that it is definitely more than okay. I take both of her slender wrists easily in one of my huge hands and lift them, so that her arms are pinned above her head. I shift my weight so that I am above her, my bulk supported by my elbows and knees, one hand still encircling her wrists. And even now, I don't want our bodies to touch. I lie above her like this for what seems like an eternity, gazing into her sweet eyes, drinking her in and saying nothing, her breath warm on my face. She is silently asking for more, and as I drop my head lower and begin kissing her again; the wet tip of my dick brushes tantalisingly against her lower belly. I gasp with the touch and she parts her thighs and arches upwards, so I am being teased gently against her opening.

Fuck, this is like nothing I have ever known. We are silent and slow, all those months of waiting distilled into this one moment. I am unbelievably aroused. Why on earth have I waited so long to discover that we are so good together? She thrusts her hips up towards me and I feel her growing wetness with my tip, she is willing me to enter her. But I tease us both for longer, I want this to last, because I know that when I enter her, I will struggle to hold on.

She is begging me for release, her hips are pushing up and she is straining to bring her hands down so she can guide me in, but I effortlessly continue to pin them above her head. Finally, when I know that I can bear it no longer, I ease myself inside her, all the way to the hilt. She is a perfect, tight fit and I gasp out loud in shock at the warmth and wetness enveloping me. I stay motionless, I need to gather myself before I move, so I make no effort to withdraw again or build up a rhythm. I stay inside her, filling her completely, resting my forehead against hers.

'Is this all right, Sophie?' I ask tenderly, my eyes searching hers. She nods, unable to trust herself to speak.

'You feel so good, Sophie,' I murmur, my lips soft against her ear. 'I have waited so long for this.'

I am throbbing inside her, my dick demanding that I move and her muscles clench around me, they too are willing me to start. My breathing is coming out in jerks, with the effort to withhold everything I have, and I slowly began to move, the rolls of my hips excruciatingly paced and measured - I want to feel every last bit of her, I want it to go on forever.

She begs for me to speed up and I watch her face, eyes closed, head tilted back against the pillow, her mouth half open and panting. It is the most beautiful sight I have ever seen, and I don't know how much longer I can keep this up. I think she is close, and I want to be after her, I want her to scream as she comes around me.

I torture myself by stopping again, I hold myself just outside her body and she groans, desperately trying to free her hands from my grasp, she wants to touch me, she wants to touch herself, she wants release.

I can hold back no more. I thrust into her forcefully, parting her thighs even wider, she brings her long legs around my back. I speed up, determined and urgent, a rush of heat coating my spine, belly and balls. She screams, and I feel waves of her clenching around me as I erupt, pouring my hot seed into her and outside of her, again and again, until it finally lessens, and I come to a gradual halt.

I release her arms and collapse gently on top of her, panting loudly, burying my face into her neck. She pulls at my thick hair and gently hugs me closer.

No words are necessary, we lie together in each other's arms, familiar with each other's bodies. I am spent, exhausted, done, elated, incredulous. It isn't just sex or lust, it is love making and it is meaningful, with a level of emotional intensity I didn't imagine possible. I stir again at the thought of it and wonder if I will ever reach such a peak of desire again.

I have no idea if she thinks the same. After all, she has had a taste of the Van-Zeller manhood.

I lift my head so I can study her face properly.

'I'm sorry, Soph,' I murmur, 'I probably shouldn't have done that. And ...um......I forgot about getting a condom, I think I just got carried away, I'm really sorry.'

She kisses me and holds me close again.

'Bloody hell don't apologise Jasper, that was by far the best sex I have ever had! I had no idea it could be that good. You are amazing.'

Hallelujah! I laugh out loud with delight and roll over so that she is in the crook of my shoulder. She kisses my chest, breathing me in and tracing her fingers across my abdomen. She continues,

'I've never had sex without a condom before, so at least that makes me clean I guess, and I'm on the pill, so I won't get pregnant or anything.'

I am relieved. 'Well, I've never done it without a condom either, so that must make me safe too.'

There are not many girls with whom I would feel comfortable expressing my lack of sexual experience, but Sophie is one of them, and I want her to know.

'To be honest, Sophie, I've only ever slept with Samira a few times and then once or twice with another girl, years ago back home in Ireland. We were just kids really. I'm not very experienced actually. Sorry.'

I feel my face going red and wish I hadn't admitted it. I worry she will compare me to Alex, whatever they've done together, and I'm afraid I won't measure up.

She laughs. 'Jasper, I just said that was the best sex ever! Stop apologising! I'm not surprised Samira keeps coming back for more.'

Now it is my turn to laugh.

'I shall not be seeing her again after tonight, Sophie. And I never did it like that with her, I couldn't be arsed to put in that level of effort. Which, I know, makes me a horrible person. She probably thinks I'm pretty crap in bed. I've no idea why she has put up with me really, but the less attention I seem to give her, the more she keeps coming back. But you, you're special; it was amazing for me too.'

'I've wanted to explore your body for so long, Jasper,' she says, 'Night after night when we have lain together.' Her fingers make their way across my belly and track down the trail of thick dark hair to my groin. I am hard again and she has never touched my dick before. She gently curls her palm around it, feeling the heft of it in her hand. I sigh with contentment.

'I need to be inside you again, Sophie. I want to do this with you every night and every morning.'

'You're pushing on an open door there, Jasper,' she giggles and adjusts herself so that she is lying on top of me

'I want to touch you everywhere, Jasper,' she says, and I lie back as she explores my face and neck with her lips, holding me between her hands. I let myself be loved, closing my eyes and stretching my head back, with a ridiculous, huge smile I can't conceal.

That wriggling on top of me is too much, I move my hips again and she raises herself up to take me inside her once more, before resting down again on my torso. I envelop her in my arms, pressing her body into mine as we gently rock. With the incredible intimacy I feel myself building again, my length reaching high inside her. I climax quietly, with my eyes once more open, smiling up at her with love and happiness.

She makes no effort to move and we sleep after that, her head on my chest, still wrapped in my arms. When morning comes, we are still entwined. I have never been there in bed with her when she has woken up before, it is a deliciously sweet feeling and I am in no hurry to move.

CHAPTER 29

ALEX

I get back mid-morning after a shitty night out. It starts out okay - we have some cocktails at a new gin bar in town and then we think it will be a good idea to go to Roxy's. Hugo is on a mission to drink more, and having nothing better to do, me and Seb join him.

I hate this fucking place. I've never been before, but the moment I step through the door I know I want to leave. Grimy walls, overpriced nasty beer and too many fucking pissed sweaty kids. Packed to the rafters. I'm all for turning around and going home, but by then, Hugo has spotted Sophie's goth mate, Katy, so Seb and I know it is all over. I vaguely look to see if Sophie is here too, but it's not her style, the place is heaving, and I don't see her.

I can see that Katy's fit - pixie haircut, a lot of black clothes, skinny body, lots of earrings - just not my bag. She's a bit opinionated, too earnest, too full on. Not that I have a problem with opinionated women - Christ - my mama, for starters, but there is a time and a place, and midnight on a Friday when I'm half cut isn't it. But Hugo is clearly up for something - I guess he likes a challenge, and so Seb and I retreat to the bar and count the minutes.

I am content to just have a drink with my good mate and watch Hugsy make a fool of himself, but within minutes I've got some bird giving me the once over. I've seen her before, she's eyed me up before, and she's hot, don't get me wrong - long brown hair, all tits and arse, but I'm not really in the mood, to be honest.

I wonder what Sophie is up to, whether right now her and Jasper are cosied up in that fucking enormous bed. I push that miserable thought away, thinking about him and her isn't doing me any favours and so I nod over to the girl.

It's predictably easy, and Seb fades away somewhere as I give her the Van-Zeller treatment. She's like a fucking octopus and before I know it, she's dragging me down the stairs, telling me we're going back to her place. She kisses me like she's giving CPR, her hands are down my jeans, squeezing my arse cheeks, pummelling my cock. We are only halfway down the stairs of the club, and people are pushing past, swearing at me. I feel a drink land on my shirt, a big sweaty bloke barges through me, and I realise, with perfect clarity, that I'm fucking done with this shit.

I don't want to be that Alex fucking Van-Zeller anymore, the one that drinks and fucks his way through uni, the rich boy that all the girls want a piece of, the party animal. I want to be the other Alex Van-Zeller, Sophie's boyfriend, Jasper's best mate, the one that goes to Sainsbury's with his girl, talks art history with his girl, watches football on telly with his mate, and goes to bed every night with his girl wrapped around him.

I pull away from her, I can see the astonishment in her eyes and head for the exit.

Seb is having a smoke outside, leaning up against the cold brick wall. There is a pile of sick nearby. I join him wordlessly, and he offers me one. He notices things, Seb does.

'Not your scene, mate?' he asks as he blows a perfect smoke ring up into the night sky. I watch it fade.

'Nah, not really, mate. You?'

He shakes his head. His place is close by, and we tuck into the whisky when we get back. He's calm and quiet, just what I need.

'I want her, Seb, I want her so bad, it's fucking killing me.' I rub my face with my hands. I feel like I might cry.

He doesn't speak, he's not sure what to say. He places his arm around my shoulder. I crash on his sofa.

So now I'm at my kitchen table, a cup of coffee in one hand and scrolling idly through my phone with the other. I feel like shit and I look like shit. My pale blue shirt is bunched on the table in front of me, wrinkled and torn. There is an ugly red stain on the sleeve where a drink has been spilt. Probably by somebody else trying to squeeze past me on the stairs, I think irritably. I stink of beer, whisky and fags.

I hear noises from above, the shower running, muted voices and then two pairs of footsteps on the stairs. I look up at them as they enter the kitchen, rousing myself to a half smile.

'Morning, you two.'

I take in the serious expressions on their faces, the evidence that they have both just showered, the fact that they have come downstairs together. My stomach churns, my world is caving in.

'Everything okay?' I ask, going for indifference. I study them both for a second longer, and attempt a laugh, the full realisation dawning, sickeningly.

'Oh, I get it! Still playing happy families upstairs, are we? Finally progressed to the mummy and daddy stage?'

I take a swig of my coffee, struggling to swallow the bitter nastiness of it and I stare at them both, willing one of them to say something. My hand is shaking around the mug. Neither of them speaks, a silent affirmation that I have guessed right. Sophie's face is a picture of concern and dismay, and Jaz, bless him, avoids my eye. I inhale deeply, I'm going to ride this out, dignity intact. I shrug.

'Oh well, it was bound to happen sooner or later. How come he's good enough for you, Soph, but I'm not?'

I want to hurt her, the nasty shit that I am. 'Or maybe you prefer a bit of rough, do you Sophie?'

'Shut up, Alex, and don't be horrible. It doesn't suit you.' Sophie retorts sharply and she is right to tell me off. Jaz doesn't deserve that.

She sinks into the chair opposite me and reaches across for my hand.

'It's not like that, Alex, it's not like that at all.'

I want to take that hand and hold it up against my cheek, I want to drag her onto my lap and bury my face in her neck and never let go. But I do none of those things. I snatch my hand away immediately and Sophie makes no effort to get it back.

'I saw you last night, Alex,' she says. 'I was at Roxy's, and I saw you on the stairs with that girl, you were virtually shagging her on the bloody stairs.'

Tears form in her eyes at the memory. 'I was really upset and so I went home early and then.......and then....it just happened,' she finishes lamely. My eyes are lasering into her.

'We didn't mean it to happen, honestly, that's the truth. But it just did.'

I look away from her and up at Jasper, who is standing in the doorway behind Sophie, and I say spitefully, 'Well done mate, you win, so well done. I reckon you've been planning this for ages. Was this your game all along? Tell her all of your sob stories, cry on her shoulder, let her rock you to sleep and then have your wicked way with her? Some fucking friend you've turned out to be.'

I'm shaking with anger now and I push my mug away, spilling coffee all over the table.

'Fuck off mate,' responds Jasper without raising his voice, but I can see him squaring up in the doorway. Filling the doorway.

'It's not like that and you fucking well know it. Sophie's absolutely right. It just happened, we didn't plan for it to happen, and now I wish it hadn't, but it just did. You're going to have to deal with it.'

I continue to stare at him, my fists clench. I don't do anger; I don't do hatred. I'm never vile and I certainly don't do violence, but right now, I want to strangle the man in front of me, who I consider my closest friend.

And if he wasn't so fucking enormous, then I probably would. So, I do nothing, and we are silent, all contemplating what happens next. I exhale deeply and lean back in my chair, rubbing my unshaven face with my hands. I'm crumbling, all the fight is leaving me, and my eyes are wet with tears, threatening to spill over. I don't want to fucking cry in front of them, I never cry, please don't let them see me cry.

'Fuck, fuck, fuck.'

I take a deep breath and look up at Jasper. 'Sorry for being such a shit, I shouldn't have said all that. I'd have done the same myself. I don't mean what I just said, I'm just...'

My voice breaks and I pause, trying to regain control of my emotions. 'I don't want to fall out with you, you're great, and my best mate, in fact. Please, forget everything I just said.'

I'm so fucking weak, I should hit him, like I know he would if it were the other way around.

I turn to gaze sadly at Sophie and shake my head regretfully.

'You can't say I didn't try, Sophie. I've wanted you for so long. All I've ever done is show you how much I've wanted you, but you've turned me down again and again and again. I get the message now, loud and clear, but I want you to know that I gave it my best shot.'

Tears run unchecked down my cheeks. I'm broken and they can see it. I'm Ajax, falling on my fucking sword. Sophie leans over and tries to take me in her arms. I don't want their pity and I gently push her away and wipe my eyes with the back of my hand.

'That girl last night, Sophie, I can scarcely remember her name,' I say softly, 'She's nobody. I love you, Soph, I love you so much. The whole world knows that. The girls...the drinking, that's just me trying to get over you. And I've tried so bloody hard to forget about you, believe me.'

I'm in physical pain, a tight band of pain is burning through my chest wall. Even breathing hurts.

'It's a bit tricky to forget you though, when we're in the same house and I see you every fucking day.'

I can't stand it anymore and I rise, pushing my chair back from the table, signifying the end of the conversation.

'Alex, please don't go,' begs Sophie, standing up too. 'Stay here a while and let's talk about it, I don't want us to be like this.'

I stand in front of her, memorising every feature of that perfect face, as if I will never see her again. I step forward and plant a firm kiss on her forehead.

'I'm not sure we've got anything left to talk about anymore, Sophie,' I say, and make no attempt to brush away the tears I can feel trickling down my cheeks. 'It's simple, sweetheart. The best man has won.'

I reach up behind each ear and remove my hearing aids. I head towards Jasper who moves from the doorway, his head bowed. I walk to my room and close the door.

CHAPTER 30

SOPHIE

There is absolute silence after that. Jasper and I look at each other despairingly. I make the first move.

'I'm going to go out for a bit,' I say, picking up my house keys from the table.

'I'll come with you if you like?' he offers, but I shake my head.

'No. Thanks, but I think I need to be on my own for a while; I need to clear my head. Stay here and keep an eye on him. I'll be alright.' He gives me a quick hug as I leave the kitchen.

I walk the streets of Lenton for over an hour, aimlessly selecting roads at random, trudging with my head down, the scene in the kitchen playing out on an endless loop in my brain. I feel sick to my stomach when I picture Alex's anguished face; his brief burst of anger and nastiness just a shield against his desperate sadness. I notice that I have unknowingly walked in a huge circle as I recognise the entrance gate to Lenton Park. I sit on the same bench that I sat on with Alex before. The park is busier than it was then, the weather has improved.

A group of lads are half-heartedly kicking a tired football between them, some with a can of beer in one hand. Probably students, I think. A gaggle of girls lie on the grass, laughing and watching the boys, discordant rap music blaring from a tinny speaker next to them. The swings and slides are busy too, a toddler is screeching with delight as the swing is pushed higher and higher by his mum, another is wailing and refusing to get back in his pushchair.

I sit on the bench for ages, not wanting to go back to Johnson Road and the horrible atmosphere that is all my fault. How the hell has everything got so screwed up?

I think fondly of Jasper, so solid and safe. I realise how important he is to me, always the same, never questioning me, making no demands on me. He loves me and I love him, uncomplicated, straightforward and as simple as that. Our love has grown from a deep friendship, born of Jasper's misery and now based on a mutual respect and care for each other.

I adore having him with me at night, of course I do, I can't imagine it any other way. Yes, the sex had been mind-blowing, but what is more important to me is our wonderful friendship and I am determined not to lose that.

He hadn't been ready for a serious relationship with me, or with anyone else. He had been happy just keeping his life on track, watching his mum get better, passing his exams and planning a career. So, he had asked nothing of me and got everything in return. In idle moments, I have often imagined us together one day in the future, happily married and living in a cosy cottage in the Irish countryside, kids and a Labrador playing outside, the whole package.

Funnily enough, that is never an image I conjure up when I think of Alex, and certainly now it is less of a future reality than ever. I have really blown it this time, I think, tears welling- yet again! - behind my eyes. It is not until now, until I truly believe that I have lost him forever, that I fully understand what he means to me.

Where Jasper is safe, solid, dependable, Alex is exciting and noisy, unpredictable, bursting with life and energy. It is Alex that makes Johnson Road into a true home, not just a student house share, but a real home. Who cares if he is untidy and chaotic and drinks too much? He is warm, welcoming and hilariously funny; even Jasper in his most despairing early days of grief, could temporarily put his problems aside when Alex was around.

I realise with growing dismay how wrong I have been about him. He has only ever shown me kindness, patience and generosity; his complete and utter respect and love for me shining through, the only constants about him. Even when I refuse to sleep with him, when he knows that Jasper shares my bed. But I have been too stupid to notice. I have been blinded by my own assumptions based on his looks, background and party lifestyle. I'd never stopped to consider how insignificant all of this has been to him, if only I'd bloody noticed.

He had loved me; he had truly loved me. He wasn't wasting his energy thinking anxiously about the future and whether the relationship would last; he was living in the here and now, asking to be trusted, asking to be given a chance. But I haven't been brave enough, I have been too short-sighted, too bloody parochial in fact, too worried about getting my heart broken on some unknown day that might never come, and now I've blown it forever, too scared to love him back. And now it is too late. I'd seen it in his eyes, he'd admitted total defeat.

CHAPTER 31

JASPER

It is the dog days of the summer term, and for most students, exams are over, and everyone is winding down, skiving afternoon lectures to sit in the sunshine and while away their time drinking beer and listening to music with friends. I'm beginning to think that I can't wait for it all to end, to disappear back to Kinsale and escape the depressing, claustrophobic atmosphere of Johnson Road.

Alex is virtually absent the entire time, it seems he comes home only to shower, change clothes and go out again. From time to time I come across him in the kitchen and he makes small talk, but the matey sessions in front of the TV are a thing of the past. I really miss him. It appears that he bears me no ill will, for which I am grateful.

He struggles more with Sophie. Whenever she bumps into him, passing on the stairs or in the hallway, he will greet her with a half-smile and then indicate that he isn't wearing his hearing aids. She doesn't believe him of course, no doubt it is sometimes true, but it is also an excellent method of avoiding a difficult conversation.

It would appear there are three losers in this relationship, not just one. We sleep in the same bed every night, but we are not together, we just share a space and a comfortable mattress. She makes no attempt to be anything other than companionable, for which I am grateful. It would feel wrong.

To add to our woes, a typed letter has appeared on the kitchen table, addressed to all three of us. It is from SLA, the agency letting the house. It is time to sign the lease renewal for the next academic year. The letter sits there, being ignored, the elephant in the room. We have ten more days to reply; otherwise the house will be automatically assigned to one of the many groups of students no doubt queuing up to take it over.

I have made no efforts to seek alternative accommodation for September, and I am confident that Sophie hasn't either, as up until a few days ago, we had all assumed our current idyll would continue indefinitely. That was until we'd blown it all, I think gloomily. Katy and Amy had asked Sophie to join them ages ago, but when she declined, they had gone ahead and sorted out a house with another couple of girls. The two of us are probably going to end up in a dump somewhere next year, miles from anyone, with goodness knows whom.

I have a sickening feeling that Alex may not come back to Nottingham at all and will no longer be a part of our lives. I don't know much about his background, apart from the fact that there is more money than I can imagine, and I don't think a university degree is necessary or important to him.

I pluck up the courage to phone Hugo. I don't think he cares for me very much - we are not natural bedfellows, but he cares for Alex, and agrees to meet. We select the *Wheatsheaves* where we won't know anyone. He is at the bar, a tumbler of whisky in his hand.

'All right mate?'

We shake hands. He coolly appraises my old jeans and charity shop sweater. And this is where he and Alex differ - I would never know if Alex notices my poorness or not. Except of course he does notice, because he never allows me to pay for beers, and shares everything that he has with me.

Maybe I'm being hard on Hugo, as he is more pleasant to me than I thought he would be.

'Sort it out, Jaz. He's about to get a train out of Nottingham and never come back. I'm guessing none of us, Sophie included, wants that to happen.'

'So, what do you suggest, Hugo? Because if you tell me to give up Sophie, it's not going to happen. She made the choice, not me.'

'Yeah, but she's made the wrong choice, hasn't she? Nothing against you, mate, but he was right for her, he would have done anything for her, and between you both, you've fucked everything up big time.'

I'm revising my opinion of him downwards. He's not being pleasant at all. 'Actually, Jaz, I say I've got nothing against you, but fuck knows what she sees in you, when she could have bloody had Alex.'

I'm up next to him, in his face. He's tall and broad, he's a poncy rower, but I reckon I could have him. I've got a mad Irish temper that none of these southern pussies have seen yet. Alex senses it's there, that's why he backs down every time, but Hugo doesn't know me well enough.

'Do you want to repeat that, Hugo?' I ask him softly, and he stares at me for a moment, calculating his odds. He decides it's not worth it.

Tipping his head back, he crunches the ice from his drink. 'You and Alex need to talk. I don't know why you can't just bloody share her like before. Alex whinged a bit, but at least everyone was happy-ish.'

Alex and I do need to talk, I'll accept that from him.

'I'll meet him in town, he won't talk to me at home. Set up a place and pretend it's you, he won't come otherwise.'

He agrees and gets up to go. As he walks away, I add, 'And if it's any consolation for Alex, I think she's thinking she's chosen the wrong one too. Let's just say, our relationship is now platonic, and that's a fucking understatement.'

CHAPTER 32

SOPHIE

I've been spending most of my lunch breaks with Katy, either in the small café in the Humanities block, or taking our food out onto the grass and lying in the sunshine. Amy is nowhere to be seen. Having finally given up on Jasper, she has been determined to succeed in her quest to win over Andrew, the Scottish engineering student. She has gone to the extreme length of joining the university mountain hiking club, of which she had discovered he is an avid member. Spending the last of her money on a shiny new pair of sturdy walking boots, she had signed up for an arduous weekend camping and hiking trip in the Peak District.

Apparently, according to Katy, from the moment Andrew had nailed his final tent peg into the ground, then he had nailed Amy into the ground too, and needless to say, not much walking had been done by either of them, then or since. The new boots had been returned to the camping shop, still in the box.

So, it is just the two of us most days, and eventually, after having been asked almost every day if everything is okay, I confide my problems to Katy. She is a good listener and hardly interrupts as, over the course of an afternoon, I relate the whole sorry tale.

'So, let me get this straight,' says Katy slowly, picking her jaw up from the ground.

'You have been sleeping in the same bed as Jasper from pretty much the second week of the first term, but just in the friend zone, although you think he has an erection nearly every night and possibly touches you in rude places when you are asleep. And you've had sex with him on one night only, which was beyond amazing, but until then not really even kissed him properly. And he had a sort of girlfriend, who is absolutely stunning and clearly hates you. But is not going to see her again since he slept with you.

'The gorgeous, God-like Alex, you've been frequently snogging and having some slap and tickle with also since the first term. But you have not slept with him at all, even though he declared undying love for you and has begged you to be his girlfriend. How the fuck you turned him down, Sophie, I have absolutely no idea. So, he has been drowning his sorrows in booze and getting his end away elsewhere.

'The lovely Jasper is completely in the know about you and the sex-god but doesn't seem to mind at all. Really? Unfortunately, the sex-god is completely in the know about hunky Jasper and minds very much indeed, so much so that he hasn't spoken to you since you admitted the one occasion of hanky-panky with Jasper. And now, you and Jasper are miserable, Alex isn't talking to either of you, and all three of you are massively fucked up in the head.'

I nod, close to tears. Katy passes me a tissue and finishes her succinct summary by adding, 'And you're really upset, because you think you love the both of them, but have chosen Jasper, and Alex will now leave Nottingham.' I nod again, tears trickling down my face.

'I don't just think, I know I love both of them, but that about sums the situation up, yes. I know I have to choose one of them, but I don't think I'm ready to choose yet.'

Katy hands her me whole packet of tissues and contemplates the sorry tale for a few moments. She grins mischievously.

'And there was me and Amy, and even Ben come to that, thinking that you were a lesbian and just hadn't come out yet! And all the time, you've been embroiled in a love triangle with two of the sexiest blokes I know. Wow, that's some problem to have, Sophie, I almost envy you!'

I smile at her and dry my eyes. Katy carries on, more seriously, 'If you really want my opinion, Sophie, I think that you've got to try and get over Alex and make a go of it with Jasper, which from what I know of him, I'd suggest is a fairly tolerable outcome, all things considered. Have a normal relationship with him. You know, maybe live in separate houses, with friends, like normal students do, see each other a few times a week, not be cooped up in this toxic household, where the three of you are watching each other all the time, to see what happens next.'

'It doesn't feel like that when we are all there, or it never used to,' I protest. 'It was great, the three of us had an amazing time together. Until I messed it all up, we were going to stay together next year too.'

'Well, you need to face the fact that it's over and Alex will move on, so you and Jasper will have to try and have a normal boyfriend/girlfriend thing, otherwise, you will lose both of them.'

CHAPTER 32

JASPER

I think Hugo has done it deliberately to piss me off, he has chosen the fanciest gin bar in the East Midlands, and possibly the country, for me to have my *rendezvous* with Alex, who will of course think he's meeting Hugo. Not in a million years would he expect to find me in here. The place isn't that big and is fairly full, with lots of muted, no doubt sophisticated conversations taking place, between small of groups of mostly women. I go to the bar and am presented with a menu, which more accurately could be described as a small novel. I have read thinner textbooks. There are over two hundred combinations of gin-based drinks and no beer. It is a foreign language, and I pick number twenty-seven at random.

The young lad behind the bar makes a performance of mixing it up, shaking liquid from one metal jug to another, then adding pretty much an entire fruit salad. I'm paying twelve bloody quid for the pleasure of this.

I know what I am going to say to Alex, but I'm apprehensive about saying it. It might just mess things up even more, or it might put us back on an even footing. And make Sophie love me again, because at the moment, she's giving me the cold shoulder.

Even if I hadn't been watching the door, I would have known the moment that Alex walks in, because approximately twenty-five women pause mid drink, mid chat, mid-life, to watch him saunter up to the bar. He is a wearing a pair of light-coloured chinos and a petrol blue Ralph Lauren shirt. His hair is its usual messy blond birds' nest. I have never seen a better-looking bloke in my entire life, and judging by the nudges and whispers around me, neither has anyone else in here.

He spots me, looks surprised and not totally happy and comes over.

'Where's Hugo?' he asks, puzzled and not unreasonably, looking around for his friend.

'He's not coming,' I reply. 'Look, Al, I wanted to see you alone, and away from the house, and this was the only way. Hugo's worried about you too, we came up with a plan. Sorry.'

He stands in front of me, contemplating his options. He looks down at my drink.

'What the fuck are you drinking, mate?'

I glance at my goblet and its pink concoction. 'Number twenty-seven. I panicked and picked one at random.'

He sniggers and turns towards the bar. 'You should have gone for number sixty-nine - it's much better.' He's staying then, I realise, which is a good start.

'Aren't we a bit too old to be making number sixty-nine jokes, Al?'

He looks at me like I'm mad. 'Jaz mate, you are never too old to make number sixty-nine jokes. But seriously, it's the best one on the menu.'

He returns a few minutes later with a normal looking, clear gin and tonic in a straight glass. I'm nervous, I feel like I'm on a first date – how the fuck does he do this to me? I regard him more closely. He is pale, his blue eyes lacking something I can't put my finger on.

'I'm so sorry, Al,' I begin, but he waves me off.

'I don't want to hear it, Jaz. You got the fucking girl and that's all there is to say.' He half empties his drink and leans back in his seat, looking around the bar abstractedly.

'I'm saying it anyway, Al, so just shut up and bloody listen. When I say I'm sorry, I truly am. It's wrong, she's chosen wrong, any least I think she has.'

'It's what she thinks that matters, Jaz,' he replies, 'And she's chosen you. But thanks for not gloating. Unless that's what you've come here to do.' He's folded his arms now, challenging me.

I'm irritated by him. 'Of course, it's not what I've come here to do.' I take a swig from my pink drink and wince as, with another gulp, I drain the entire goblet. 'Fuck, that's disgusting.'

He smirks. 'Can I get you another?' Standing, he drains the remainder of his too.

I shake my head. 'Why not? Get me a number at random, without looking at the menu. I'm going to need about five of them before I say what I really want to say.'

He gives me a curious look and heads for the bar, returning a couple of minutes later with a repeat of his own elegant drink and another paler pink goblet, mercifully minus the fruit.

'Coconut gin, apparently,' he states, placing it on a coaster. 'With ginger ale. Number one hundred and thirty-one. I've had a taste, it's like Pina Colada but marginally less sweet.'

We drink in silence for a few moments. The first gin is beginning to have an effect on me.

'I'm not sure I've won her actually, Al. She's really upset and well, let's just say, she's not exactly gagging for me to fill the Van-Zeller sized hole in her life.'

'Is she sleeping with you?' he asks sharply, and I shake my head.

'Not in the biblical sense, no.'

He lets out a short laugh, but there is no humour in it. 'Well, this has turned out well for everybody then, hasn't it?'

We both think about this for a moment. It's not just Sophie, I realise that is struggling to pretend everything is hunky dory between the two of us. It's me, too. I wonder if there is a Van-Zeller sized hole in my life as well. My gin has come with a straw, which I discard. It's even worse than the first one. Christ, how do people drink this stuff for pleasure?

'So, what did you want to talk about then, Jaz? This is very pleasant, don't get me wrong but I could probably find something else to do this afternoon, rather than talk about the girl who turned me down for my best mate'

Hearing him say that, the bit about being his best mate is pretty special actually. I had no idea, although I hadn't really thought about it until now. Him and Hugo and Seb are obviously very close, but me and him, well, we couldn't be any more different. He's standing up again. 'Come on, Jaz, drink up. Choose a number.'

He waits whilst I slug it down. This is like the worst post-rugby drinking game I've ever experienced. His glass is empty. I stand up too.

'It's my shout, Al, I'll get the next round.'

He looks at me like I've just said the most ridiculous thing. 'Jaz listen to me. Don't ever for a moment think that you have to buy me a drink. Especially not in somewhere like this. It probably hasn't escaped your notice by now, that I have more money than I know what to do with. And you are very obviously skint. So, sit down and pick a bloody number.'

Number fifty-six is a clear liquid, thank goodness, and in a more manly glass, but very strong. By the time I'm halfway through it, I've got a warm glow and I am ready to talk.

'What are your plans for next year, Al?' I ask. 'I'm guessing you've seen the letter from SLA in the kitchen.'

He nods and stares at me. 'Yeah, I have. I'm not sure, to be honest Jaz. I thought we'd just carry on, but obviously that's not on the agenda anymore. Hugo's mum is buying a house for him, and he wants me to share with him and Seb.'

'That sounds all right, Al,' I say, thinking exactly the opposite. I know us being together is clearly not going to happen now, but even so, hearing it out loud is depressing me. He drinks and then continues,

'But I don't think I will. I'm not sure I want to stay in Nottingham at all after all this.' He sighs miserably and looks away. 'I don't know, Jaz, a big part of me just wants to fuck off back to Zurich and pretend none of this ever happened. I'll chalk it up as an interesting social experiment that went wrong.'

He's aiming for humour, but it falls flat. And suddenly him living with Hugo sounds like a really good option. I need to get my proposal out there. I just need to polish off this horrendous drink first, I still haven't got the balls to say it.

My glass is empty and as he goes to get number one hundred and seventy-four, I go for a slash. As I weave my way through the tables, I realise I'm quite pissed now. I reckon there were at least two measures in the last glass. And I'm realising a little late in the day that I didn't bother with lunch or breakfast.

On my return, Al is still at the bar. An attractive young woman has engaged him in conversation, and he is listening politely. But he's not giving her the usual Van-Zeller charm and he makes his excuses to her as he sees me return. Another bloody goblet, and he smirks at me as he places it down. He's spent more on gin in an hour than I spend in a month on food.

'Come on Jaz, then. Spit it out,' he says, and I dive in. This could go one of two ways.

'Okay, Al, but if this goes wrong, can you just forget we ever had this conversation?'

He's looking at me curiously. 'Why?'

I take a big breath. 'Well, first of all, I want us to live together next year, all three of us.' He is shaking his head and raising his palm towards me. 'No, Alex, just hear me out. Please.' I carry on.

'What has happened between us all has ended badly, not just for you, but for me and Sophie too. We've both lost you, you've lost us, and I think Sophie and I will lose each other.'

'You and Sophie are not my problem anymore, Jaz,' he says with a shrug. 'Forgive me for not giving a shit how that turns out.'

'Yeah, I know, but if you could, you'd have her back, wouldn't you? Tell me honestly, Al, I need to know.'

'You know I would,' he replies, without hesitation. 'And what pisses me off, more than anything, is that I actually believe that she wants me, too. And I don't think that's just my huge ego talking. She told me she's in love with me, for Christs sake! I don't think she was making it up!'

'I know she wasn't making it up,' I say, although it pains me to say it. 'This is all my fault, Al. I pushed her to choose. After she saw in you in the club with that girl. She was upset and I took advantage, even though I knew that girl would have meant nothing to you. I told her to choose me.'

His eyes narrow at that, but I still haven't got it out, the bit I'm finding hard to say. I'm feeling pissed and stressed. He's waiting patiently.

'I need a number three, Al, go and get me a number three, for fucks sake.'

Number three is Gordons gin with plain tonic water and a slice of lemon. Hallelujah, this I can just about tolerate.

'I think we could both love her, Al,' I say, with the glass at my mouth, slurring into the drink.

'We do both love her, Jaz,' he says, confused. 'That's the fucking problem.'

'I mean, we could both have a relationship with her,' I repeat more loudly, 'If she'll let us, or have us, obviously.'

'You what?' he says. He's looking at me strangely. I knock the whole lot back.

There, I've said it and I lean back with my hands clasped behind my head, my eyes closed. He is stunned, I know he is, because he doesn't answer and I'm too scared to open my eyes and see the expression on his face. Or maybe he's upped and gone, that would be a reasonable response too. And then he speaks.

'What, you mean like sperm brothers?'

The gin is churning in my stomach, I think I'm going to be sick.

'I'm going to be sick,' I blurt, and push my chair back quickly. I stumble to the toilets and make it into the cubicle. Gin tastes even worse on the way up than it does on the way down, and it burns. I will never touch the stuff again; I haven't been sick with booze since I was about sixteen.

I stand panting over the toilet bowl, my forehead flat on the wall above. A warm hand lands on my back and rubs me gently. He's surely taking the piss.

'You all right, big boy?' he asks. I can tell he's trying not to laugh.

'Fuck off, Al.' I groan, as another loud retch courses through me. He steps away and I can hear him giggling.

'You know I'm not one of life's natural sharers, don't you, Jaz?' he says from somewhere behind me. Saliva is dripping from my mouth into the toilet bowl.

'I'm a spoilt brat, an only child,' he adds helpfully, as if I hadn't already worked that out for myself.

'It's a one-time fucking offer, Al!' I shout back and then retch again. This time it's dry, and I grab a stretch of bog roll and wipe my mouth.

'What makes you think she'll go for it? It's a bit bloody weird,' he asks, and I push myself away from the wall and stand facing him. The room is spinning.

'I know it's weird,' I say, 'And I don't know if she'll go for it, but it's better than what we've all got going on now, isn't it?'

'Well, Jaz, I suppose it couldn't be any fucking worse, could it? But how would it work - is it like a timeshare, you know, you have three weeks and I have three weeks?'

I turn away and vomit again, painful bile now. God, I'm sophisticated.

'I have no idea how timeshares work, Al, but, no, probably not like a timeshare.' Why the hell are we discussing bloody timeshares? I try again.

'What I'm trying to say is, shall we just give us all a bit more time, to give her a bit more time, and we'll see how it all pans out? Carry on the three of us, like before? Because, I don't think that she is ready to choose.'

He's stewing on this, I can tell.

'There would have to be ground rules,' I croak, standing to face him again. He looks so amazing, and I look so horrendous. And he's the one who didn't get the girl! But he needs to hear the lot.

'Number one: you don't set foot in that fucking bedroom. That's mine, I'll kill you if you do.' How I can possibly think that I'm in a position to be dictating rules, I can barely fucking stand.

'Number two:' Christ, what was number two? I can't think straight anymore.

'Yeah, the sperm brother thing, I haven't worked that one out yet, but you know, maybe not in the same day, or something?'

He's looking at me like I've just stepped off another planet. Why did I think this might be good idea? It's a lot to take in, I'll give him that. I don't expect him to leap at the idea, that's for sure. Nor Sophie. Christ I'm dumb.

My colour must have returned to my usual Irish pallor instead of a sickly green as he indicates to the door. 'Finished?'

I nod weakly and we head outside. I still feel pissed, but the fresh air helps my stomach. I look across at him, he appears to be stone cold sober. 'How come you don't feel so shit? I must have had nearly an entire bottle of gin in there.'

He gives me a wicked look; the old mischievous Van-Zeller look that has been missing from my life.

'Sparkling water, mate,' he grins, 'I've turned over a new leaf.'

CHAPTER 33

SOPHIE

I am recalling my conversation with Katy whilst slouched on the back row in one of Prof Mackie's final lectures of the year. The last few weeks have been hellish, there is no other word for it. Alex is refusing to speak to me, and Jasper is behaving differently too. We are tiptoeing around each other, unsure of what the other is really thinking. Sex with him was unbelievable, but we haven't had a repeat performance - neither of us know what to do next. The end of term can't come quickly enough, even though I still have nowhere to live next year. I could always get a room in halls, which would be ironic, seeing as all my friends are moving into houses.

We have been concentrating on the Hellenic period, the final period of sculptural antiquity to be studied this year. With everything else going on at home, my studies have been the only constant, straightforward and pleasurable aspect of my life and I have been throwing myself into them.

I have really begun to appreciate the Hellenics; artists were competing with each other and surpassing themselves in their technically confident approach to realism. Indeed, some of the sculptures were so life-like, I feel that if I could reach out and touch them, they would still be warm.

Because the Greek originals had often been destroyed, many still in existence today are ancient Roman copies, often made of marble, which adds to their lifelikeness. One of these is The Dying Gaul, which we had studied the week before in our smaller tutorial groups. The pathos of this heroic gladiators' final death scene as he lay dying from the bleeding wound in his chest, perfectly captured by the unknown sculptor, was almost too much for me in my state of emotional turmoil. Tears welled in my eyes as we analysed the depth of feeling portrayed and I had to quickly excuse myself on the pretext of needing to make an urgent phone call.

So competent and prolific had Hellenic artists become, that they had then abandoned depicting heroes and warriors and begun sculptures of everyday scenes and people. Not only that, but they had also turned their hands and chisels to more pagan themes, and today, Prof Mackie was concentrating on portrayals of satyrs, or fauns as the Romans referred to them.

These mischievous woodland sprites were the faithful companions of Dionysus, the naughty God of song, dance and wine. He told us how they were portrayed less and less as the half man-half goat creatures of popular myth, but took on increasingly human attributes, and sculptors liked to show them in comedic form, with ridiculous great phalluses and foolishly drunk.

It is hot and stuffy in the auditorium and, unusually, the Prof isn't captivating me as he normally does. Maybe I am failing to concentrate because the only faun I know about is Mr Tumnus in the Narnia books, and I'd never really enjoyed those as a child. More likely, it is because my mind keeps straying back to Alex and the misery of our last argument and my regret for how I had misread him for so long. I hadn't slept well last night, even with Jasper's solid, safe presence beside me, and so I lean back in the seat, my eyes closing.

'Now ladies and gentlemen, I'm going to finish today with what some say is a mere footnote in Hellenic pagan sculpture, but for me, it is probably the most intriguing work of all the Hellenic pieces, and possibly one of the western world's earliest examples of overtly sexual art to boot. Now I see I've captured your attention!'

He pauses and raises his eyebrows slightly, noting with satisfaction his audience suddenly becoming more alert. My ears also prick up, and I sit forward in my seat, intrigued.

'Feast your eyes, boys and girls, prepare yourselves to drink in the most perfect specimen of manhood you are ever likely to see.'

He makes a theatrical show of extravagantly clicking the remote control for the enormous white board behind him. The previous slide, of a humorous black and red figure vase displaying a laughing, goblin-like character pointing to his donkey sized obscene phallus is replaced with, well...what could only be described, as a smooth, whitish-grey, two-thousand-year-old marble version of the one and only Alexander Gottfried Wilhelm Van-Zeller.

I gasp involuntarily, causing the lads on the row in front of me to turn around and snigger. Prof Mackie continues, blissfully unaware of the effect the blown-up photograph of the sculpture is having on me. I am frozen in my seat, transfixed by the image in front of me.

It is a life-sized model of a naked man, sprawled on a chair-shaped jagged lump of rock or tree stump, his flawless skin protected from the rough surface by the most delicately carved animal skin. The young man's head is thrown back, his eyes shut tight, his full lips slightly parted. His tousled hair falls in curly waves and frames the perfectly symmetrical chiselled beauty of his face in repose. His torso is exquisite, every line of every muscle beautifully defined, tapering to his narrow hips.

I feel an irresistible urge to reach out and run my fingers down the perfectly sculpted musculature of his chest and shoulders. One arm is flung carelessly above his head, the other hangs loosely at his side. His long, strong left leg is stretched out in front of him, the other bent up at the knee, his heel resting on the rock underneath. No dainty prick here, his extremely provocative open pose draws the eye to a normal-sized flaccid human penis and balls, nestled softly in his lap.

'This man is in his prime, he knows his sexuality is irresistible, his body utterly captivating. He is sound asleep, dead drunk, sated with wine and love. It is a picture of wild abandonment; he has seduced, violated, imbibed, cursed and danced and now he rests, content and exhausted.'

I can scarcely listen. My heart is pounding, and a light sheen of sweat has broken out on my forehead. The Prof is describing Alex, my wonderful Alex, with his joy of life, his mischievousness, his determination to live everyday as though it is his last day on earth, as if tomorrow he would be no more and would never be able to laugh, cry or love ever again.

I am suddenly overwhelmed with an intense desire for him, like a bolt of lightning striking me, and I know, with all my heart, with every fibre of my being, that I can't, and won't let him go without a fight. I stand a little dizzily, sweating profusely, and begin pushing my way past the other seated students. The row is long and full, Prof Mackie starts speaking again as I make my way across, whispering repeated apologies to the others in my row as I squeeze through. Katy sees my no doubt pale, anguished face and starts to rise to join me, but I motion to her to stay put.

'I'm fine, I just need some fresh air,' I mouth, as I make my escape.

The Prof continues, thoroughly enjoying the role of ringmaster, knowing his audience is hanging on his every word. His voice is booming, I can't shut it out.

'But beware, ladies and gentlemen, that is not the end of the story! A word of warning! Love this man at your peril! His magnetic beauty will pull you towards him, his air of sleeping sweet vulnerability will entice you into his warm embrace, you will crave to be the sole object of all his affections, you will fight to be the one leaving him in this sated state.

'Yet, I beseech you to tread very carefully my friends. Look closer, and you will see, almost hidden from your feasting eyes, a curled wispy tail, snaking out from his perfectly toned derrière. Caress his locks of silken wavy hair and your hand will come away torn and bleeding from the spiked leaves of ivy growing wantonly in there. For this is no mere mortal seducing you, this is a wolf in sheep's clothing, this is Dionysus's finest weapon! Class of 2018, I present to you, the peerless, magnificent Barberini Faun!'

I almost fall through the fire doors in my rush to leave, the Prof's strident, preaching tones echoing in my ears. I don't want to hear any more. He's wrong, the Prof is wrong! My Alex is none of those things, is he?

My breathing has slowed, and my pulse rate has just about returned to an acceptable count by the time I reach the corner of Johnson Road. I push open the front door with relief and stand over the kitchen sink, gulping down cold, refreshing water straight from the tap. It is several minutes before I feel a semblance of my normal self and am no longer the mad bewitched creature that has just run as quickly away from an overheated lecture theatre as I possibly can.

The house is quiet, there is no one home, and I strip off my damp clothes and stand for an age under a cool shower until the jet spray renders me clean and somewhat revived. In the quiet of my room, with shaking hands, I nervously type the words 'Barberini Faun' into the search engine on my laptop.

My search is instantly met with hundreds of images taken from every angle, of this beautiful ancient masterpiece. Just looking at the small screen, filled with this fantastical creation, wrought by an anonymous hand so many, many years ago, brings back my intense feelings of desire for Alex, my very own flawed, drunken satyr, my very own Barberini Faun. Knowing with absolute clarity, what I have to do, I dress quickly, put a comb hastily through my damp hair, stuff a few things I think I might need into my shoulder bag, and leave the house.

CHAPTER 34

ALEX

I'm confused, bloody confused. Apparently, it would seem that without me, a constant thorn in his side, Jasper's relationship with Sophie has taken a downturn. I don't understand it. She chose him, she chose him, she chose him, and now, apparently, there is no happy ever after for any of us.

So, it would seem that there is hope for me, after all. But how can I be sure? The Jasper who vomits gin and can scarcely string a coherent sentence together seems to believe that we can go back to how we were, wilfully trying to ignore that the other is playing the same game, that we both want the same girl. I don't know how happy those times were. I think I was happy, but knowing he's up there with her, fucking her, can I lie alone at night in my bed downstairs and block out that image? I'm not so sure. Or will it be him, sitting in lectures mid-afternoon, imagining my mouth sucking on his girl's pussy, and not feel a desire to come charging home and pummel me senseless?

I stumble through the last weeks of term. I turn up to everything, much to my tutor's surprise, mostly because I don't want to be at home. Do people really go to every lecture every day? It appears that they do. But now, the last one of today is over, and I have the choice of going to Hugo's and getting rat arsed, or going home and sneaking into my room, hoping I am unseen. I plan the former as I leave the Modern Languages building, my laptop and a textbook under one arm. I hold the door open for an older man, on his way in as I go out, and then my heart lurches as I see her, waiting for me on the bench outside, her graceful beauty catching me unawares as usual. I halt, unsure what to do next.

'Alex, hi' she says hesitantly. 'I've been waiting for you - can we talk? Please?'

I detect a pleading note in her voice as she stands a few feet from me, waiting nervously for my reply. I try to think of something cool and smart, but my brain fails me. I should decline graciously and walk away.

'Yeah, ok. I suppose so. Er......let's head up to that grassy bit around Hu Stu, I feel like some fresh air.'

We fall into step together as we stroll up to leafy Hugh Stewart Hall, careful to maintain a distance between us. It is unusually quiet; we see hardly anyone else as we walk purposefully through the verdant parkland. Neither of us speaks. When we get closer, Sophie pulls a small woollen throw out of her bag.

'We can sit on this if you like.'

We sit side by side in an uncomfortable silence, both unsure how to begin. I pick restlessly at a few blades of grass. Finally, I break the silence, not facing her, studying my hands.

'So, what can I do for you, Sophie?'

My heart has started beating faster again, with nerves this time. I am terrified; knowing that the next few minutes could possibly change my life forever. I have no idea how this will end.

'The last few weeks have been horrible, Alex. I don't think I've ever felt so miserable. I don't know how you feel now, but.... I've missed you. Jasper's missed you too and we want you back - we need you back.'

She pauses, waiting for my reaction. None is forthcoming, I continue to stare down at my hands, and start to pick at a loose piece of skin on my nail.

'You make it sound so simple, Sophie,' I eventually state, in what is hopefully an even, adult tone. She interrupts me.

'It is simple, Alex! I've been a bloody idiot and I know it. You have only ever been lovely to me - you are always thoughtful and generous and funny and well, lovely is the right word. And all I've done is mistrust you and think the worst of you and assume you are going to drop me from a great height if I let you know how I feel about you. But I've realised that's not you at all. You're actually the sweetest, kindest person I know. I've been in love with you for ages, but I've been too scared to show you.'

She stops speaking and waits for me to fill the void. I remain silent, her words are the ones I've been wanting to hear, the apology I feel I am due, but I'm no longer sure that I want. Zurich next year, it could be fun, I love my Swiss life, I can try to forget about her there.

She reaches into her bag, turning away from me with embarrassment at having said all those things out loud.

'Oh and....I've got something for you, although you may not want it now. I brought it back after the Easter holidays as a present, but somehow, what with everything going on, the time wasn't right to give it to you, so you might as well have it now.'

In her hands is a small glass whiskey bottle, the cheap flattened rectangular type with a narrow neck and broad shoulders. Inside is a dark red liquid, which sloshes against the sides as her hands shake slightly. She passes the bottle to me and I examine the homemade label on the front, unable to hide my smile. With a green fountain pen, she has carefully printed the words,

"Sophie's Sloe Gin. For Alexander Van-Zeller, with love. January 2018."

'I made it for you in the Christmas holidays,' she explains. 'I went sloe picking over Hampstead Heath one afternoon, and then looked up a recipe. I've never made it before, I hope you like it.'

She watches anxiously as I carefully unscrew the metal cap. I sniff the neck of the bottle, and then take a swig. It's good, and I savour the underlying taste of bitter gin mixed with the sugary tartness of the sloes. I swallow appreciatively, passing the bottle back to her.

'It's delicious Sophie, you try some.' She takes it from me and has a sip.

'It tastes of you, Alex,' she whispers, miserably, and my heart breaks.

'Thank you, Sophie, it's really thoughtful, I love it.'

She hands the bottle back to me and I sip some more.

'We're in a bit of a mess, aren't we?' I say, smiling sadly at her. I lift my free hand to her face and tuck a loose strand of hair behind her ear. It is an intimate thing to do, and I wonder why I did it.

'We don't have to be, Alex. We can be how we were; I want to start again with you. I said I'm in love with you, and it's true.'

'What about Jasper?' I ask, aiming for neutrality. 'Aren't you in love with him too?'

Now it is her turn to look pained. This is the question she is dreading, the crux of our problem.

'I don't know, Alex. I didn't think it would be possible to feel like this about two people at the same time, two people who are so different. He's very special, amazing really. He still needs me, he needs us both, I don't think you realise how much he appreciates what you do for him - we are like a family to him. I know that you are very fond of him too, despite what happened. I'm not prepared to let him down, no matter what.'

'But you want him too,' I reply, 'You want to have him as well as me. Am I right? Because I'm not sure I can do that.'

She thinks for a moment. 'Yes, Alex, yes I do. I can't help it, it's just how it is, and maybe I wish it wasn't. But I do know one thing for sure, above anything else, Alex. Right here, right now, on this blanket and under this hot sun, I'm in love with you. In fact, I'm not just in love with you, Alex, I love you.'

She takes my hand from my lap and squeezes it tight; I don't pull away. Emboldened, she leans towards me and kisses my lips gently. Her hand and her lips are too much for me, everything that has gone before condenses into this one moment, Jasper retching and asking me to stay with him next year, Sophie telling me she loves me. The three of us together.

For a brief moment I can't respond, and I feel her hesitate, then I let go of her hand and put both of mine on her face and I return the kiss. I am smiling into the kiss, I am coming home, and we lie back now, facing each other, kissing deeply in the hot sunshine, my hands cupping her face, her arms around my waist, holding onto me as if she would never let go. And I never want her to let go, not ever.

We stay kissing, cuddling, drinking sweet sloe gin, and talking, so much talking, until it is late, when the sun is starting to fall behind the trees and our blanket is in shadow.

'Let's go home, Alex,' Sophie says gently, 'Let's go home.'

We walk slowly through campus, arm in arm now, I'm feeling tipsy from the effects of the gin, the hot sun and Sophie's love. I know she feels the same way, and I hail a cab once we reach

University Hospital, too weary for the slog back up the hill towards Lenton.

We start kissing again in the back of the cab, the journey takes longer than normal in the stop-start evening traffic. I don't care, I would be happy if the journey lasted forever as long as she is holding me.

She is wearing a short denim skirt - her long tanned legs are bare, and my hand feels its way to the top of her thighs and even now, my long fingers are teasing her, probing their way inside. She stifles a moan as I begin bringing her to climax, my body covering her from the taxi driver's gaze should he happen to glance in his rear-view mirror. It is unlikely; he has sport radio turned up very high and is clearly engrossed in the final overs of a test match. So, she orgasms to the unlikely applause of a cheering crowd at Lords and me, Alex Van-Zeller, giggling into her shoulder.

We make it through the front door and into my bedroom, picking up where we have left off moments before. She pulls off my T-shirt and then wrenches off her own, and bra too, so I can feel the full heat of her glorious skin pressed against me.

Putting a hand down the front of my jeans she is instantly met by my hard cock; I am naked underneath. She undoes the button fly and as my jeans fall to the floor, I step out of them. She wriggles out of her skirt and knickers and I begin to lead her over to the bed.

'No Alex,' she whispers, 'I've got a better idea.'

She takes my hand and pushes me back across the room, towards my favourite low easy chair.

'Sit.' she commands, and I lower into it, leaning back and openly taking in her nakedness.

'You're gorgeous, Sophie' I murmur, and she smiles down at me impishly.

'I want to make this really special for you, Alex.'

She leans forwards to kiss me, and with a hand either side of my head, puts her fingers through my hair and gently unclips both hearing aids, placing them carefully down on the desk. No-one has ever done this before, I wouldn't have let them, it is far too intimate, I feel exposed and vulnerable when it is not on my terms. But I trust her, and clasping both hands behind my head, close my eyes and surrender completely, now aware only of the sensations she is creating for me, the rest of the world completely shut out.

I am aware of her kneeling down before me, between my parted legs and she resumes kissing my face and neck, her hands caressing the muscles of my chest, encircling each nipple firmly between finger and thumb. Her lips move lower, down onto to my chest. I begin involuntarily rolling my hips up towards her, my pulsing cock vying for her attention. She ignores it, her mouth continuing its teasingly slow journey down my body. She cups my balls lightly in her warm, dry hands, squeezing each one softly in turn and tickles the soft skin behind. Her thick mane of hair falls onto my body and it moves with her, creating a light, teasing caress of its own. She follows the path of blond hair trailing from my navel with her tongue and skimming her lips over the end of my cock, she pauses briefly, lapping at the salty wetness that is growing there. I groan as she continues on lower and she begins kissing the soft tender skin of my upper inside thighs.

'Come on, Sophie, you're killing me, it's so good.' I moan, panting heavily now.

She's tortured me enough; her lips return to my cock and she firmly takes me in her mouth. My hip grinding increases with intensity, I'm fucking into her mouth. I open my eyes briefly to look down at her and she is watching me through her lashes - her shiny red mouth round my cock looks fucking fantastic. I am swelling even more; my balls are tensing; I am about to come, and she takes me out of her mouth.

'Jesus, Sophie, don't stop, please.... don't stop,' I pant, I hear the panic entering my voice.

She ignores my pleas and lifts herself off the floor. She straddles my lap and the whole length of my cock is inside her tight, hot pussy. She cries out with pleasure and I am growling incomprehensible things to her, it is too much, I can only think in my mother tongue. I thrust up to meet her and she climaxes within a couple of thrusts, crying out again and again as waves of tightness squeeze my cock. My hands are now firmly grasping her hips as she rides me, the tempo is becoming faster and faster and I am seconds from my own climax. I can hold on no longer and I come, in an explosion which goes on and on, hot jets of semen flooding her as she collapses forwards onto me, utterly, utterly spent. With her arms tightly around my neck, she buries her face in my hair, sobbing uncontrollably.

'Don't cry, babe,' I whisper softly, kissing away her tears. I repeat it in Swiss-German, I declare my love to her over and over in my first language.

We stay like that, me inside her, for a very long time, until Sophie rouses herself.

'Was that okay, Alex?' she asks anxiously, looking directly at me as she speaks.

I lip-read the simple sentence easily. She has no idea how I feel right now.

'It was more than okay, Sophie, it was out of this world! Why were you crying?'

'Because I'm happy,' she answers simply, and I see the tears once more. 'Because I have got you back again.'

I kiss her, gently this time, on her forehead.

'I love you Sophie Ashworth.'

She rests her head down on my shoulder. Everything is going to be fine, I have her again and she loves me. And the Jasper thing? We'll work something out.

CHAPTER 35

SOPHIE

'Stay there a minute, I'm parched. I'll get us some water.'
I mime a drinking action as I speak and he nods, blowing me a kiss. Pulling on his wonderful-smelling T-shirt, I disappear out to the kitchen. Returning a few minutes later with two glasses of water, I pause at the door and study him. He hasn't moved from the chair, he remains sprawled out, legs apart, his now flaccid penis lying long against his thigh. He has one arm across the back of the chair, as a pillow for his head, his other arm loosely hangs at his side. His magnificent blue eyes are firmly closed, his full lips slightly parted and I can hear his slow regular breathing pattern. And so, he lies there, my very own unblemished, flawless, immaculate Barberini Faun - fast asleep, sated, vulnerable and thoroughly at peace.

Later that night, much later, I hear the front door closing softly and Jasper's familiar tread on the stairs. He has exams again all week and has been working hard. I listen as he runs a brief shower, and then five minutes later, he joins me in bed, snuggling up behind me as usual. I lie still, contemplating what to say.
'All good?' he queries, sensing my uneasiness.
'Er...yes, I think so.' I reply.
I shift slightly, still facing away from him.
'Alex and I made up today, well......a bit more than made up actually,' I feel his body stiffen slightly, but he doesn't immediately pull away from me.
'It doesn't change us, Jasper, well this anyway. He knows that now. Can we make it work somehow?'

Jasper doesn't answer for a few minutes, and then he kissed the top of my head through my hair.

'It's okay Sophie, I'm cool with it. Honestly, I really am. It's all good.'

I roll over towards him, taking his big hands in mine, our faces inches away from each other on the pillow.

'I want you for myself, Sophie, but I won't make you choose. You have to do that all on your own.'

He exhales deeply. 'I love you, you know that, but I'm not going to make any demands on you or anything, or weep and wail. We'll just see what happens. I'm okay with Alex too; he's a great guy. I'd be shagging him myself if I was that way inclined.'

I giggle and kiss his hands, holding them up to my lips.

'Jasper Coutts, I don't deserve you, you are truly fabulous.'

He shakes his head. 'I wouldn't say that, Soph. I'm just playing a long game that's all. We're very young; we've got a lot of living to do before with think about the future, our future. I'll get you in the end, when I'm ready and when you become tired of that pretty boy downstairs. There's no rush.'

He kisses me hard on the lips, suddenly serious, his mouth closed, looking straight into my eyes as he does so. He is affirming his words, stamping his mark on me.

There is one shadow hanging over our newfound peace. The letter on the kitchen table, reminding us about the lease renewal. Today is Thursday and we have until five pm on Monday to inform the agency of our decision. I desperately want the three of us to sit down and have a frank discussion, but what with Jasper's final day of exams tomorrow and Alex sleeping or out with his friends all weekend, I don't know how I can casually engineer it. Finally, I come up with a plan and send them both a short text:

Boys, we need to talk about the lease. How about we have a day out somewhere on Saturday? Weather forecast looks good xx

Alex replies instantly: Cool gorgeous, where shall we go?

Then Jasper: I'm in, what about a day in Skeggy?

Alex again: What, or where, is Skeggy?

Jasper: Skegness, mate, Riviera of the North, it's unreal.

Alex again: Ooh, I love the Riviera! Count me in!

If only he knew, I think, chuckling to myself. Jasper is being a bugger. I conclude the texting by suggesting we would need to hire a car; which Alex immediately offers to organise and pay for. I am relieved, as neither myself nor Jasper have the funds to cover this extravagance. We also quickly establish that I am too young to drive a hire car and that Alex has never bothered to learn to drive, as his family employ a chauffeur, who is apparently an excellent driver. Thus, it is Jasper who has the pleasure of getting into the driving seat of the sleek blue Mercedes that Alex has arranged to be delivered to the house at 9.30 am sharp on Saturday morning.

Armed with food, picnic blankets, spare hearing aid batteries, some booze and a spare coat for Alex (he is only wearing a sweater as he still assumes clearly that he is heading towards the British equivalent of Monaco), we clamber in excitedly. I elect to sit in the back and be in charge of the satnav, Alex is DJ. This soon turns out to be a huge mistake, as he seems to have a never-ending playlist of German hits, which Jasper scathingly and repeatedly refers to as shite Eurotrash.

I sit alone on the back seat, luxuriating in the sumptuous buttery leather. Jasper is a smooth steady driver, one hand resting on the steering wheel, the other loosely on the gear stick. Unlike virtually every other young man alive, he manages to resist the temptation of putting his foot to the floor on the open stretches of road, content to cruise comfortably.

I am completely relaxed and utterly happy, seeing the two of them together; one head of thick dark curls, and the other golden waves. They are laughing and joking with each other, Alex repeatedly fondling Jasper's thigh or resting his hand over Jasper's on the gear stick to wind him up. He is such a flirt.

Eventually, Jasper gets his own back at a set of busy traffic lights, secretly attaching his phone to the in-car sound system and having complete control of the music selection via the steering wheel buttons. Thus, the remainder of the journey passed to a soothing soundtrack of Elliot Smith, who incredibly, manages to make Morrissey sound positively upbeat.

It may have been shaping up to be a barmy June in the rest of the U.K., but in a sunny Skegness, there is still a stiff northerly breeze. The tide is out, and the long sandy beach stretches ahead of us, sparsely populated despite the time of year. Monster seagulls screech overhead and I breathe in the salty, seaweed smell of the British seaside, instantly evoking happy memories of early childhood bucket and spade holidays. I am toasty inside my new flying jacket.

'It smells just like Kinsale,' comments Jasper, adjusting his coat collar in an attempt to keep his ears warm, and sniffing the air appreciatively.

'Christian loved being taken to the beach. Mam and I took him down most weekends if it were dry, which isn't that often in southern Ireland to be honest. We'd leave his wheelchair at the car and I'd carry him over the sand. I think it was the sensation of the dry sand that he liked the best. We used to pour it over his fingers and toes. He couldn't really laugh properly or anything, but it seemed to calm him, he hardly ever used to have a fit on those days. I suppose it was smells like this that he liked too. Shit, I'm not sure I should have come now.'

He wipes the back of his hand across his eyes and turns away from us. Alex glances at me worriedly, I can see the cogs of his mind whirring, we are both unsure what to say or do. He steps forwards and thankfully takes charge.

'Right mate, here's what we're going to do.' he says breezily.

'It's fucking freezing - whoever said that this was the Riviera was fucking having a laugh. We are going to march as quickly as we can to the far side of this ridiculously long beach and pray that there is a Michelin starred restaurant at the other end, where we will spend the afternoon dining on the finest oysters and quaffing pink champagne. Failing that, we will turn around, march back again and sit in the car with a picnic and a blanket on our laps.'

He retrieves his hip flask from the inner pocket of his padded Moncler skiing jacket and takes a gulp. Screwing the lid tightly on and tenderly placing it back in the lining, he grabs us both by the hand and we set off.

Needless to say, there is no fine dining experience at the other end of the beach. But the brisk walk certainly cheers Jasper up, and the boys even have a race over the last few hundred metres. Jasper wins easily or maybe Alex lets him win, I'm not sure. There is, however, a shabby cafe with one or two people already inside, huddled around the small Formica tables. I politely ask for three cups of tea. A dumpy, sullen looking girl, not much older than ourselves waddles over with our order. Steaming mugs of unappetising dark brown liquid are plonked unceremoniously in front of us, accompanied by a chipped plate holding three slices of cheap white bread, slathered in margarine. Alex raises his eyebrows questioningly, takes a sip of his tea and grimaces. Jasper grins at him,

'You're living the dream, mate, living the dream.'

Jasper swallows down an entire mugful of hot tea in two mouthfuls and then proceeds to wolf his own share of the bread. We motion to him to have our slices too.

He watches Alex contemplating his mug. 'I hope you're going to drink that, Alex, I don't want to see it go to waste.'

Alex slides the mug over wordlessly and reaches again for his hip flask.

'So, Sophie, you wanted to talk about the lease?' says Jasper in between mouthfuls.

I open my mouth to speak. Before I can, Alex interrupts.

'Do you know what? We can make this very simple.' He pauses and fiddles with a teaspoon.

'Jaz, you just said that I'm living the dream and I can tell you something: I absolutely am. I've got everything I need and everything I want right here with me. Okay, so I seem to have found myself as part of a little *ménage à trois*, which to be fair, I didn't see coming. I'm not sure any of us did, and it's taken me a while to get my head around it. But, it's happened, and as my Grandpa Gottfried is fond of saying, it is what it is. I don't know what's going to happen next year, but I'm game for anything. So, as far as the lease is concerned, I'm in.'

He sits back in the cheap plastic chair, studying us both, waiting for a response. We are stunned. Neither of us had expected this. Even though me and Alex had made up in spectacular style, I would have bet any amount of money that he wasn't going to tolerate the situation long term. He is too used to getting his own way.

'I'm in too.' Jasper blurts. 'This is the best family I've got. Whatever happens with any of this weird shit that we've got going on,' He makes a sort of triangle shape with his fingers, 'You've both been the best mates ever and I don't want it to end.'

They both look expectantly at me, waiting to hear what I am going to say. I take a deep breath.

'You're both amazing and I've had the best year of my life, honestly. I'm sorry I've got us into this mess. Part of me wishes I'd just kept my distance from both of you and that we'd just stayed as housemates, maybe cooking together and watching telly a bit, but basically, no more than that.'

Jasper interrupts. 'Don't blame yourself Sophie, it's not your fault that you and I got close, it's mine. You were so kind to me when I really hit rock bottom and then I couldn't help myself from wanting a bit more.'

He looks away, embarrassed. Alex fills the pause.

'However, Sophie, I can completely assure you that it is one hundred percent your fault that I've turned into a complete sap,' he says, smiling at me. 'I cannot believe that I am practically agreeing to sharing you with this bloody Irish oaf.'

Now it is my turn to blush. Alex leans over and kisses me full on the lips. Jasper gives him a withering look.

'Simmer down, big man,' says Alex, flashing him a smile, 'You'll get your turn, I'm coming to you in a minute.'

Jasper reaches for one of my hands and holds it in his own, smirking at Alex.

I shake my head at them both.

'I do know one thing, though, you two. I'm not going to choose. I can't choose, I love you both. Equally, I think, just differently. I didn't know that was possible, but I've discovered this year that apparently it is. So, I'm saying yes to the lease, as long as you both know how I feel and are cool with it.'

Now it was my turn to sit back and I stare at them both defiantly.

Jasper winks at Alex. 'That's a fiver you owe me, mate, I told you she'd say yes! And you know I'm happy with that, I've told you already.'

We look at Alex.

'I'm okay with it too, bring it on. But promise me one thing: can you let me know if he's in the room next time you wank me off?'

We are still laughing as we leave the cafe. Alex hands the very surprised waitress a crisp fifty-pound note on the way out.

'Best tea ever, darling' he says, and she is rewarded with one of his most charming smiles.

The wind has died down and we can finally feel a bit of warmth. Grabbing our things from the boot of the car, we settle into a spot on the beach, looking out to sea. Time passes quickly, as the best times always do. We eat some of the picnic, listen to music for a while, but mostly just enjoy doing very little in each other's company. Later in the afternoon, Jasper spies an ice cream van and goes off in search of 99 Flakes, just to complete Alex's British seaside education.

I lie back on the rug and close my eyes, opening them again seconds later, when Alex kisses me gently on the lips.

'Love you babe,' he whispers.

'I know,' I reply, 'And I love you too.'

He kisses me more fully; I feel the familiar stirrings of arousal.

'I meant it when I said I'm not choosing, you know.' I say, between kisses.

'I do know,' he replies, 'And I'm not going to ask you to, I'm happy just as we are.'

He lies back next to me, fiddles behind his ears briefly, and then closes his eyes.

'He's powered down,' I announce apologetically when Jasper returns bearing ice cream, 'Too much sloe gin and not enough food.'

'Never mind,' says Jasper contentedly, 'It leaves more for me.'

We polish off our ice creams in silence, Jasper eating both his and Alex's, gazing out at the endless brown-grey sea. Jasper puts his arm around me and holds me close.

'I don't know what's going to happen with us, Soph. I love you though, and that's not going to change.'

'I love you too, Jasper,' I reply, meaning it just as much as when I had told Alex a few minutes earlier. He leans down and brushes his lips lightly against mine, like he had done the first and only night we had made love. I fervently hope it isn't the last. I rest my head on his shoulder for a while.

'For some bloody reason, I think I love him too,' says Jasper sighing, indicating down to the reclining Alex with a turn of his head. We both watch him sleeping, his long lashes fanned across his cheek.

'God knows how he manages to keep that body in such good shape though,' he muses, continuing to study him as he sleeps on. 'He doesn't seem to do any exercise or gym work, he's either out drinking or sleeping.'

I laugh. 'As far as I can tell, he's just pickled in gin and olives all day!'

Jasper nods in agreement. 'Does seem to be working for him, though, doesn't' it? Maybe he should patent it as a diet, he would make a fortune. I mean, he is without doubt the most fanciable bloke I've ever seen, Soph.'

Alex snorts, opens one eye and explodes with a fit of giggles. 'I didn't realise you cared that much big boy, but thanks for the compliments, just keep them coming, babe.'

I shriek with delight. 'You absolute bugger! You just pretended to take your hearing aids out, and I was sure I saw you do it!'

I punch his arm playfully and Jasper pins him onto the ground whilst I start tickling him. Soon all three of us are rolling in the sand, squealing with laughter. Eventually we calm down, Alex admitting defeat as Jasper holds him in an arm lock. He will always submit, and Jasper will always be stronger, I think, and I wonder if that is the key to our future happiness. I get my breath back, smiling down at them, my beautiful boys, still intertwined on the sand.

'Come on you two, it's time to go home, back to Johnson Road and sign that lease.'

And with that, we gather up our things, and arm in arm, the three of us walk back to the car.

CHAPTER 36

SOPHIE

I can hardly contain my excitement as I wait for Alex and Jasper to arrive back at Johnson Road for the beginning of the new academic year. I haven't seen either of them for eight whole weeks, and at times, it has seemed like the longest eight weeks of my life, even though I have spent a perfectly lovely summer in Cyprus with my family. Fi flew out to visit for a couple of weeks, the young officers on the army base were as fun as ever and the weather divine, but even so, it had not been enough to distract my thoughts from the two of them for any significant length of time.

Frustratingly, I have hardly had any contact with them either and inevitably, doubt is starting to creep in as to whether they have really meant all those declarations of love at the end of last term.

Jasper has spent the summer working on a building site in Cork, and as reluctant as ever to engage with any form of electronic communication, he has intermittently sent me some marvellously enigmatic postcards, which are now treasured amongst my most precious possessions. My particular favourite expressed only one heartfelt sentiment:

'I love you more than bacon sandwiches, Jx'

Knowing Jasper, and his love of all thing's bacon, I feel somewhat reassured - this is a declaration of a hell of a lot of love. My mother picked this one up from the doormat before me, and she had read it with puzzlement on her face.

'Gosh, Sophie, you seem to have a rather strange admirer.'

I now have so many postcards, that if I line them all up, side by side, I reckon they add up to a complete map of Kinsale.

Naturally, Alex has not endured a summer of manual labour, but has spent most of the time at the family's summer holiday residence in Mykonos and has evidently not been too lonely, judging by his occasional Instagram posts. He sent me flowers every week, over-the-top bouquets of stunning orange and yellow roses, ordered from what seems to be a very exclusive florist based in Zurich.

Now my mother is even more confused. Fortunately, she was spared the horror of reading any of the explicit messages on the notes that accompanied the roses; I can't begin to imagine what was going through the florist's mind as she carefully transposed them and added them to the delivery. For the final week of the holidays, Alex demonstrated his usual generosity and paid for Jasper to fly out and join him for a week of Greek sunshine.

I need not have doubted for one minute their feelings for me. I am busy in the kitchen, putting together all the ingredients for a chicken stir-fry when Jasper quietly steps into the hallway. I run to greet him and am rewarded with a huge smile and an enormous hug. I bury my face in his solid chest, breathing in his wonderful Jasper smell.

'I've missed you, Soph, God I've missed you.'

That soft voice, turning my legs to jelly as usual. I stand back, holding his big hands so I can take a good look at him. A summer spent working on a building site has done his physique no harm at all, and he has a light tan too, courtesy of his time in Mykonos. And best of all, he is smiling from ear to ear. I compare this radiant version of Jasper to the haunted and pale shell of a man I'd met almost exactly one year ago, in this very hallway.

'You look amazing, Jasper, it's so good to have you back.'

I put my arms round his neck and reach up, kissing him squarely on the lips. Gosh, he tastes good too, wonderful in fact, and I kiss him again, my tongue exploring, our bodies pressed close.

'Easy, tiger!' he laughs, disentangling himself gently. 'That can wait, I've got something to show you.'

He takes my hand and leads me through the front door. A gleaming silver Vauxhall Corsa sits neatly on the driveway.

'It's a few years old,' he says proudly, wiping a small mark from the bonnet with his thumb. 'That's what I've spent most of my building work money on. I'm going to be doing so many placements in different hospitals this year - Mansfield, Derby, Lincoln - that it's almost impossible to manage without a car, so I've treated myself to one. Goes like a dream. My mam even plucked up the nerve to go around to my dad's house and demand he stump up some cash towards the insurance.'

'Very cool!' I exclaim. 'It's fantastic! I can't wait to go for a ride. Where are you taking me?'

Jasper checks his phone.

'Well, his lordship is currently on a train due to get into Nottingham in about.... um... twenty-five minutes, so why don't we go and surprise him?'

The afternoon traffic is as bad as ever as we approach the town centre. I don't care, I am very happily ensconced in the front seat next to Jasper, holding his hand in between the gear changes. I examine his strong face in profile as he drives. The change in him over the last year is extraordinary.

'Why do you keep on staring at me?' he asks eventually, smiling down at me.

I blush. 'I don't know, I can't help it. I'm just so pleased to be back with you. I can't wait to see Alex either.'

Jasper sighs. 'Alex bloody Van-Zeller. How often do I say that? And how much easier would my life be if he didn't exist?'

He is still smiling. I squeeze his hand.

'I know, mine too probably, but he does exist, so that's that. I'd be lying if I said I wasn't worried about how this year is going to work, but we'll find out, won't we?'

We arrive at the station only a couple of minutes before the train is due. All of the parking spaces are taken, so I hop out whilst Jasper stays in the car, hovering on double yellow lines with the engine running. I run into the station and quickly scan the arrivals board. Platform 7, arriving from London St Pancras. I make my way over the concourse and stand next to the barrier, excitement mounting.

A squeal of brakes announces the train's arrival into the station, and seconds later, people start pushing through the barrier. I search eagerly for the familiar figure of my beloved Alex and do a double take when a tall, slim, deeply tanned man, dressed in jeans and a blue polo shirt casually strolls towards the gate, fiddling with his ticket. It is Alex.

I gasp with shock - he has shaved off all of his golden locks and now sports an extremely short, blonde crew cut. Blimey, he somehow manages to look even better! Alex glances up and sees me at the same time as I recognise him, and a huge grin spreads across his face.

'Sophie!' he yells delightedly and sweeps me up in his arms. 'What are you doing here? This is a fantastic surprise!'

I return his bear hug. He smells wonderful and my legs become wobbly for the second time in the space of an hour. He pulls me to one side, out of the path of the streams of commuters heading out of the station. Placing his hands either side of my face, he leans down and kisses my mouth, before squeezing me tightly to him again.

'You have no idea how much I've wanted this all summer,' he murmurs and kisses me again, deeply this time, not caring about the hordes of people around us.

'Your hair, Alex, it's all gone!'

He laughs and rubs the back of his head slightly self-consciously. 'Long story Sophie, it can wait. Do you like it? I'm still getting used to it.'

'I love it. And I love you.' I reply and kiss him back. Reluctantly I pull out of his embrace. 'We need to go, Jasper's waiting in the car.'

'Hey, big boy, missed you,' says Alex as he manoeuvres his long legs into the back of the Corsa. He leans forward and ruffles Jasper's hair.

'It's only been three days, mate,' replies Jasper. 'I'm still recovering to be honest!'

Alex looks around the interior appreciatively. 'Nice wheels, Jaz. A bit more basic than I'm used to, but hey, we can do the biggest shop ever at Sainsbury's now!'

Jasper laughs. 'I haven't bought this car in order to ferry you to Sainsbury's, mate. Or for picking you up from the pub, before you ask, for that matter.'

I rest back in my seat, happy to listen to them bickering, obviously picking up where they'd left off. Alex nuzzles into the back of Jasper's neck as he drives – he tries to ignore him, struggling to keep a straight face. Mykonos has undoubtedly been a riotous week.

'You should have seen Jaz in the beach bar, Sophie. Night after night! The man's a love machine! We picked up a couple of Aussie birds one night and they couldn't get enough of him. It's the sexy Irish accent thing he's got going, they absolutely love it, and the beer belly - for some reason they couldn't get enough of that either. He was having to shake them off with a shit......'

'Alright, I get it thank you,' I interrupt, giving him an acidic look.

Jasper puts his hand on my thigh reassuringly. 'Alex is obviously not telling you the whole story, Soph,' he says, throwing Alex a dirty look through the rear-view mirror. I wait for him to elaborate.

'I think you'll find that it was the other way around most of the time. There's a fair amount of exaggeration going on here, Van-Zeller. What I realised in Mykonos, Soph, is that Alex fundamentally believes that he's the spawn of one of the Greek Gods themselves - Adonis, that's the one. He spends his entire holidays in Mykonos attempting to live up to that persona as far as I can tell. He's got girls eating out of his hand everywhere he goes. And just for the record, I haven't got a beer belly? I think it's my perfectly sculpted abs that you're referring to?'

Alex laughs with glee, clearly enjoying winding Jasper up. 'Hey Jaz, remember that Spanish girl with the absolutely enormous tits who came onto you in the sea? Mind you, her sister Xantha was pretty fit too, even though she looked about thirty. Didn't feel thirty though, felt about eighteen. By the way, he's definitely a boob man, Soph.'

I make the V sign at him from the front of the car and pretend to concentrate on looking out of the window. Jasper shakes his head.

'He's talking bollocks, Soph, he's just teasing you.'

'I know,' I say haughtily, 'and I'm refusing to rise to it. Seems the Barberini Faun has been living up to his reputation! He hasn't missed me that much after all. I'll get my own back, don't worry, I just need to work out how.'

I can see Alex looking puzzled as I watch him through the rear-view mirror. He is a thorough pain in the arse sometimes, even though I utterly adore him. 'What did you just call me?' he questions.

'Never you mind.'

CHAPTER 36

ALEX

Why was I such a dick in the car? Jaz didn't rise to it at all, but Sophie is riled, I can see that. Of course, Jaz didn't cop off with any girls in Mykonos - if anyone is the definition of a one-woman man, then Jasper Coutts is it. Not that he didn't get plenty of opportunity with that accent and that six pack, not to mention his sad brown eyes and that world-weary running of his hands through his hair, he could have picked any out from the crowd.

I've been chilled all summer about the whole *ménage à trois* thing. Jaz and I talked about it in Mykonos too, and I convinced myself that this loose arrangement we seem to have fallen into will be cool. And then I see her at the station, and the thought of her being in his bed tonight pierces my heart. Hence the dickish behaviour, although I have no idea what I am trying to achieve.

Back at home, I immediately crack open a bottle of champagne. I know in any other student household tonight they will be supping cheap tinnies and nasty white wine, but I'm not a normal student and I've never pretended to be. The other two are used to me by now, and anyway, I need a bloody drink - I need to anaesthetise myself by bedtime.

We are soon settled around the kitchen table, talking and eating Sophie's chicken stir fry. It is great to have them both here, I think, even though Sophie hasn't yet forgiven me for being a complete tit earlier. Looking at her now, smiling at Jasper, her blue-green eyes dancing with happiness, her elegant collar bones and tits looking fucking amazing in a little red top I've not seen before, I know without a shadow of doubt that if I want to keep her, then I need to suck up this arrangement and just get my head around it.

She's looking at me now, eyeing up my short hair. My hearing aids are obviously completely on display now, she's never been able to see them actually attached to my head properly before. Mama thinks it makes me look younger and innocent. Butter wouldn't melt, apparently.

'So, Alex, talk me through the new hairstyle?'

I awkwardly run my hand over my bristly head.

'Oh, it's nothing really. Mama is a trustee of a charity - well, I am as well actually - involved in helping kids with hearing loss. Especially the older school age kids and teenagers. Just being a teenager is hard enough for some people, I suppose. As well as dealing with normal teenage stuff, some of these kids then go to school and get bullied or whatever for wearing hearing aids or signing. That's just too crap for words. Some kids feel really self-conscious too - you know, the last thing you want at that age is to be different to all your classmates.'

I am warming to my theme; I've been brought up with this stuff for as long as I can remember. 'The charity does all sorts of things - provides counselling, raises awareness, pays for extra speech therapists, you get the idea. So, I go along sometimes when I can and chat to some of the kids - apparently, it's good for them to see how other deaf people don't see their hearing loss as a disability or a barrier to getting on in life. So, they can talk to someone like me, who actually loves being deaf most of the time and, as you know, I wouldn't want to be any other way. I usually go and help out at some point during every holiday.'

I pause and take another sip of my drink. 'Anyway, I suddenly realised that I was probably being a bit hypocritical. After all, on the one hand I'm saying that I'm proud to be deaf, but at the same time covering up my hearing aids. Some kids have bigger aids, with wires attached, or not as much hair as me, so they don't have the option to hide them like I can. It's not hiding them as such really, it's just that I don't want the hearing thing to define me when I meet people for the first time. So, long story short, I had all my hair shaved off, for the first time ever.'

I sit back, speech over. I hope they don't ask me the name of the charity - although from seeing our place in Mykonos, I think the cat is out of the bag as far as Jasper is concerned.

'Well done, mate,' he says, leaning across and patting me on the arm. 'I'm proud of you.'

Sophie smiles gently at me and says nothing. I confuse them sometimes. One minute they see the spoilt rich kid bragging about his holiday exploits, and the next, casually and hopefully modestly outlining my charitable good deeds, which I would not have mentioned if I hadn't been prompted.

I turn to Sophie, 'Sorry I was an arse in the car, I'm just anxious I think, about how it's all going to work out with the three of us this year.'

She reaches over and holds my hand across the table.

'You're forgiven, particularly as it would seem that you are apparently a saint during your spare time.'

'It's going to work out great,' affirms Jasper, helping himself to more fizz, 'Particularly if you keep providing us with this calibre of booze. I'd never had posh champagne before I met you.'

Easy for you to say it's going to work out great, I think, you're the one warming her bed later, whilst I'll be wanking onto my belly on my own downstairs. I don't say this out loud.

'You're supposed to sip it elegantly, Jaz, not neck it like a can of Stella!' I retort. 'Especially as I'm treating you to one of my favourites.'

Sophie picks up the bottle and reads the label out loud.

'Georges Vesselle. Never heard of it.'

I top their glasses up and begin opening another bottle. 'Let me educate you, philistines. It's a tiny champagne house in Bouzy. My father visits once every year if he can, has a gargantuan meal with the ancient owner, which lasts well into the night, and is then driven home again, laden with cases. It's nowhere near the most expensive, fairly cheap compared to some, but I think it tastes delicious.'

Jasper drains his glass and reluctantly stands up. 'I'm going to have to call it a night, I'm afraid. I've got to sort out my stuff for tomorrow. I'm starting a surgical placement at the hospital in Mansfield in the morning, so I've got an early start.'

He puts his hand on my shoulder and ruffles my hair fondly on his way out. There is a lot unsaid in that gesture, I sense he is apologising for the new world order, which is going to begin unfolding soon, apologising for laying out the ground rules which don't appear to work in my favour. I appreciate his thoughtfulness.

After that it is just the two of us left in the kitchen. Sophie seems a bit tiddly, although the alcohol unfortunately seems to have done nothing for me. She puts her hand out to feel my spiky hair and runs her fingers over my hearing aids.

'It's funny to see these on display. I forget about them most of the time when I'm talking to you.'

I take her hand and kiss it. 'It's funny having them on display, it definitely takes a bit of getting used to. I was on the Tube yesterday and some random woman started asking me about them and telling me all about her grandson and his hearing aids. It was quite sweet really, we ended up having a good old chin wag. Mind you, I do feel stared at sometimes too. I was stared at by a couple of young women for the whole journey coming up on the train this afternoon.'

Sophie shuffles over so she is sitting on my lap. She puts her arm round my neck, studying me. 'Your eyes are the most beautiful blue, Alex, did I ever tell you that? And young women always stare at you, because you're so bloody gorgeous.'

'I know,' I reply, amused. 'I just added that bit of information to try to make you feel sorry for me.'

I grin and kiss her, my hand instantly making its way up the inside of her thin red top. Her skin feels wonderful after so many weeks without it. She shifts on my lap so that she is straddling me and becomes immediately aware of my cock, hard as steel, pushing against our layers of clothing.

'That feels rather lovely, Sophie,' I murmur, and she doesn't disagree, the weight of her breasts cupped in my hands is too delicious for words. 'I've really missed these,' I add, just in case she hasn't noticed.

We kiss some more, and I forget about Jasper upstairs, waiting for her. But she hasn't and puts her hands over mine as I reach for her jeans.

'Trust me, Alex, our time will come to do this, but it's not now. Not tonight, not with Jasper in the house.'

I stop and pull away from her, rubbing across my chin with my hand. So, this is how it will be, him calling the shots, me playing second fiddle.

'Am I second best, Sophie?' I ask softly. I instantly feel pathetic asking her, where is my fucking dignity? The Alex who seeks constant reassurance isn't the one she fell in love with. But I have to ask, just this once. She is irritated by me.

'Don't be ridiculous, Alex. My God, never in a million years could I describe you as second best. When I saw you at the station today, I felt like crying you looked so good. I love you so much, you know that.'

I'm mollified, a bit. 'Come on, Alex,' she says, stroking my blunted hair. 'We can do this; we've been through it so many times. It's the only way forward at the moment. And I'll make it up to you, it will be worth the wait.'

She stands up and I nod my agreement. If I don't like it, I can find myself another girl. I know that, she knows that. At least I won't be able to hear them - being deaf has to have some advantages.

I can do this, I tell myself. I can't throw in the towel on the first night, it was always going to be the worst. It will get easier. I will show her that I am more than a match for Jasper, even if he is making all the fucking rules. But I'm going to wait until she's begging for it.

CHAPTER 37

JASPER

I am freshly showered and sitting on the side of the bed, a small white towel hanging loosely from my hips.

'Those weeks spent on the building site paid off,' says Sophie, openly admiring my chest and arms. 'I'm not surprised you gave Alex a run for his money in Greece.'

I'm nervous - we have actually only ever had sex one night; her praise is good for my ego.

'So how was Mykonos really?' she asks, curiously, probably not entirely sure she wants to hear the truth, but unable to bear the not knowing at the same time. I put her mind at rest.

'Trust me, Soph, we both wished you had been there with us. But oh my God, Sophie, his house is unbelievable. They own an estate essentially, that is absolutely out of this world, like something off a film set. It's a huge white villa - a collection of villas really - all joined together and each within their own grounds, set high in the hills. They've got acres and acres of land. The views are probably the best on the island. They've got staff that cook and clean and drive them around. Basically, as far as I could tell, the household staff do everything, it was like being the only guests in the world's most exclusive hotel.'

I shake my head in wonder at the memory. 'And I met his parents briefly, although they were flying somewhere else the day after I arrived, but they couldn't have been nicer to me. They are extremely glamorous, and they clearly adore Alex - they're a really close family, you can tell.

We had a meal together on my first night and they already knew all about Christian and med school. They were properly interested, you know, exactly like Alex is, not just polite interested? I can see from where he gets his kindness. And of course, Alex insisted he paid for everything the whole time I was there, he wouldn't even let me buy him a drink, not once.'

'Gosh, it sounds fantastic.' Sophie replies, undressing. 'Aren't you getting into bed?' she adds, noticing that I haven't moved.

I turn to her. 'Only if you want me to, Sophie. I'm obviously much happier now and I'm sleeping fine. I don't want you to think I'm just taking the piss, and if you want to be on your own sometimes, especially now you and Alex are close again, then I'd understand, and I'll go next door.'

Sophie has finished removing her clothes and stands in front of me, completely naked. She is a vision of loveliness; I can't leave the room now even if she asks me to.

'Listen to me, Jasper Coutts. I'm going to have a quick shower, and if you're not in that bed by the time I get back then I'll be bloody furious. We've got a lot of catching up to do. You might not think you need me anymore, but I know for sure that I definitely need you, so do what you're told!'

She pauses at the door, whispering, 'And Google the Van-Zellers whilst I'm in the shower! I'm nosy, and I'm interested to see where all that money comes from.'

Twenty minutes later and we are cuddled up next to each other in a mountain of deep pillows, my laptop open and propped on my knees. We are increasingly incredulous as she quietly reads out an article from an American financial website, entitled 'Switzerland's top ten financial institutions and who owns them.'

'*Sacharet & Co*, dating from 1802, is one of the oldest private banks in Switzerland and more than 200 years later, it remains in the hands of the same family. Established in Zurich at the beginning of the nineteenth century by Siegfried Van-Zeller, the current CEO is 56-year-old Wilhelm Van-Zeller, who is worth an estimated 8.5 billion Swiss francs. He married British born socialite Helena Samuel-Charles in 1993 and they have one son, Alexander. Famously private, the family devote much of their time to philanthropic pursuits.'

'And a lot of shagging,' I add with a smirk, 'Well, at least one of them does anyway.'

Sophie giggles and nudges me in the ribs. 'Blimey, Jasper, I'd guessed his dad probably wasn't manning the counter down at the Lenton branch of Barclays, but even so......what's Alex doing here with us two?'

'God knows,' I reply, frowning slightly, 'Maybe getting away from it all for a few years? Being anonymous before he has to take over the reins? His name is probably fairly well known in Switzerland. Jesus, can you image Alex running a bank? He can scarcely make a cup of tea!'

'For someone who is going to inherit billions one day, he is very low key, isn't he?' remarks Sophie. 'I mean, it's obvious he's got plenty of money, but he certainly doesn't live a flash life here. He spends his days with us two, for God's sake!'

'I like him all the more for it,' I say. 'The fact that he keeps it all quiet, I mean, not the fact that he has all this dosh - I couldn't give a fuck about that.'

We re-read the article and several others below, which more or less tell the same story. He was being modest about the charitable works too - the Van-Zeller Foundation, established by his parents around the time when Alex was born, performs a huge amount of good works, all around the globe.

'No wonder the house in Mykonos is so amazing,' I say, putting the laptop to one side. 'Oh, and I meant to tell you, I've found out how he keeps that body in such good shape. I met his personal trainer Carlos, this skinny Italian guy, who basically follows him wherever he is in the world and beasts him for two hours every morning. Apart from when he's in Nottingham obviously. Carlos has without a doubt landed his dream job, as he fancies the pants off Alex, so getting that body perfectly honed is a labour of love as far as I can tell.'

Sophie giggles again. It's a beautiful, throaty sound.

'How's your mum?' she asks, turning to face me.

'Much, much better, thank you for asking.' I reply, with satisfaction. And this is a real good news story. 'She's doing a back-to-nursing training course, which she's really enjoying. And she's even been out for a drink a couple of times with the boss of the building site I was working on. He's recently come through a divorce and he saw her drop me off a few times and got me to introduce him. He's a nice bloke, actually.'

'I'm so pleased for you Jasper, that things are working out.'

I'm glad we are talking for a while, like we used to. This is us, the talking, we did this way before sex got in the way. I'm feeling more relaxed now. I brush some of her hair back from her face and kiss her softly. 'I still wake up every morning and immediately think about Christian,' I say, 'But it's not like it used to be. I feel sad when I think of him, of course I do, but it doesn't define me anymore? I can just accept now, that a part of me is carrying around this sadness, but I'm okay with it. To be honest, I have an inner dialogue going on with him all the time. I tell him about my day and what I think about stuff. I suppose that it's like having an imaginary friend. Sorry, that makes me sound a bit weird; I don't think I'm probably explaining it very well.'

I've surprised myself by telling her this, it is extremely personal, I haven't even told my mam. Sophie kisses my mouth tenderly. 'You've explained it beautifully, Jasper.'

We make love after that. Side by side and with the utmost gentleness; our kissing deepens as we became more wrapped up in each other's arms. There is no urgency to our lovemaking as we gently reacquaint ourselves with each other's bodies.

'Slow and controlled is definitely your style, Jasper,' she whispers to me, 'And you are so damn good at it.' When the time comes, she pushes me onto my back and straddles me, softly crying out as I penetrate her deeply. We climax together and both fall asleep within minutes afterwards, Sophie lying exactly where she is, in one of my favourite places for her; on top of my warm body, her head on my chest and totally at peace in my loving embrace.

CHAPTER 38

SOPHIE

The next fortnight passes very quickly. Jasper is completing an obstetric placement in Mansfield. His days are long - babies don't keep office hours - and so he frequently stays overnight in hospital accommodation. Alex seems to have slightly curbed his nocturnal lifestyle and is attending most of his lectures.

I am disappointed to discover that I no longer have weekly teaching from Prof Mackie, and I miss his brash Scottish intonation as he shares his boundless enthusiasm for antiquity.

A younger, elegant female professor named Prof Harding has replaced him, with a very different teaching style altogether. On first impressions, I decide that Prof Harding is thoroughly miserable, and unfortunately, nothing changes my viewpoint over the course of the term. Her depressed but cultured and modulated tones explain that studies this year will focus on the broad theme of Women in Art, with a choice of modules ranging from examining interpretations of the Madonna and Child, to deliberating non-Western portrayals of the female nude.

'That sounds like a hell of a lot of work,' groans Amy, as we open our texts.

'I want my beautiful, naked, marble men back,' agrees Katy.

'And our lovely, cuddly professor,' I add, 'Not this grumpy cow.'

The first painting we examine is one that I recognise from visiting the Uffizi with my mother several years earlier. It is a dark and shockingly violent image of the chaste young widow, Judith, viciously decapitating the Assyrian leader Holofernes after he tries to rape her, ably assisted by her loyal female servant, Abra. The Prof's upper-class drawl echoes around the auditorium.

'Judith Slaying Holofernes was painted by Artemesia Gentileschi, the first female artist ever to be recognised by the *Accademia di Arti del Disegno* in Florence. It was thought to be painted in revenge for the artist's own humiliation of being raped by Agostino Tassi, one of her father's friends, and himself a renowned landscape artist.'

Prof Harding gives the distinct impression that she isn't particularly fond of this piece of art. She almost spits out the name of the rapist, Tassi, although she clearly takes pleasure in repeating the flowery Artemesia Gentileschi, rolling it around her tongue in an irritating pseudo Italian accent as often as possible.

I miss Jasper hugely whilst he works in Mansfield, especially at night. The vast expanse of bed is very cold and empty without him, and even with him safely in another town fifteen miles away, Alex is not going to cross the line and venture upstairs. But being alone in the house with him certainly has its upsides. He has a deadline for a significant piece of coursework, and so is to be found almost every afternoon, half naked of course, with his books and papers spread out over the kitchen table. The golden torso, with a hint of fine blond hair below his navel is slouched over the kitchen table. He taps a pen against his sensual lips as he thinks, the pen held in his long elegant fingers, I could watch him all day and never become tired. Mostly he doesn't bother with his hearing aids, thus is completely absorbed in his task, occasionally picking his way through a bowl of fat black olives as he types.

Since the first day of term, I am convinced that he is waiting for me to make the first move, intentionally pretending to have no sexual interest in me, yet at the same time is undoubtedly taunting me with continually displaying his finest assets, which only serves to make me crave his touch even more. If we are going to do this properly, this ménage à trois, then it will be up to me to initiate something.

I carry my laptop and a couple of books down to the kitchen and take the seat next to him. He looks up and smiles briefly, before returning to his essay. To my satisfaction, he is wearing his hearing aids. The late September weather is still fine, and I have carefully dressed in an off the shoulder long floaty maxi dress, which I know Alex likes.

I pull out a second wooden chair for myself and prop my bare feet high upon the back rest, letting the thin material of the dress ride up to my mid thighs. I sense Alex giving my legs a sideways glance before settling down again. Ten minutes pass in a comfortable silence before I shift in the chair and cross my legs at the ankle, deliberately allowing the dress to fall even higher on my tanned limbs. I leave my hand trailing loosely on my inner thigh, continuing to appear thoroughly engrossed in my work.

Alex wriggles slightly in his chair, and out of the corner of my eye I think I spot a tell-tale bulge in his sweatpants as he discreetly adjusts himself. I stifle a smirk, now starting to feel more than just a little turned on myself. More minutes pass in silence, the only sound the endless ticking of the kitchen clock. Slowly, I inch my hand higher up my thigh, until the tips of my fingers are hidden under the rucked-up hem of my dress and just touching my wetness. I sense Alex stiffen beside me; his hands have ceased tapping on the keyboard. The tension between us is palpable. I go for it.

'Gosh' I say at last, stretching languorously, 'I seem to have forgotten to wear any knickers today.'

Alex stands up quickly, forcefully slamming down the lid of his laptop. 'You, Sophie, are about to find out exactly what this fucking agreement is really all about.'

Roughly lifting me out of the chair, he easily pins me against the kitchen wall, his thigh wedged between my spread legs, my dress bunched up around my waist. He is determinedly kissing my mouth, neck and bare shoulders, nipping and biting, his face flushed, clear blue eyes wide open. There is nothing sweet or tender about it, he is taking me, taking his pleasure, staking his claim. His wondrous fingers immediately take over from where my own had been moments before, and with his other hand he pushes down the loose straps of my dress, exposing my bare breasts. I come within seconds of his fingers fucking inside me, I cry out loudly.

'Jesus, Alex, don't stop, don't stop!'

He pauses, licking his fingers, sucking my juices from each one before leaning forwards and whispering breathlessly in my ear, 'I can do this all day long Sophie, just say the word, sweetheart. Now, be a good girl and bend that skinny arse of yours over the kitchen table for me so I can fuck you from behind.'

I follow his command wordlessly, gripping the edge of the wooden surface with both hands to steady myself against the onslaught. It is a wise decision, as without preamble, he thrusts deeply inside me, making me gasp with shock and delight. He withdraws almost completely before slamming into me again and again, his balls slapping loudly against my buttocks with every forward thrust. The pain of it is exquisite, my head is shooting stars and I am almost screaming when he finally climaxes, shuddering as his penis pulsates inside, pumping every last drop into me.

As soon as he finishes, he turns me around, helping me up, kissing me more gently this time, on my cheeks, my eyes, my nose, his hands stroking my hair. Loving, sweet, tender Alex is back.

'And now Sophie, my gorgeous, I'm going to make love to you properly.'

He carries me into his room, my legs wrapped around his waist. Gently laying me on the bed, he quickly removes our clothing, before joining me under the covers. He places his hearing aids on the bedside table, affirmation that he does his best work in deaf mode is about to follow.

For the next few hours, I am convinced that I have entered a parallel universe. Alex is an incredibly skilful lover. He is passionate, inventive, and not afraid to be forceful, but focussed wholly on my pleasure, entirely in tune with my every sensation and emotion. And bloody insatiable - he wasn't joking when he had said earlier that he could keep going all day, that was for sure. There is not an inch of my body that he doesn't explore or stimulate with his fingers, tongue or penis; I find myself blushing, days later, when I think about all of the things that we have done to each other during those hours. I have been truly and thoroughly fucked.

I know I will remember this afternoon for the rest of my life. It is growing dark by the time he finally lies back, sweaty and exhausted, sated at last and utterly, utterly content. I am aching, swollen and sore, but if he asked for more, I would say yes. When I am sufficiently recovered, I reach across him, turning on the bedside lamp so he can lip read.

'How's this all going to end, Alex? What are we going to do, the three of us?'

He studies me intently, his eyes following the movement of my lips. He nods his understanding.

'Maybe it's not going to end, Sophie. It doesn't need to end. Jaz and I, we've talked about this in Mykonos. I'd be lying through my teeth if I said I didn't mind when you're up there with him, and he'd be lying if he said he was okay when we're being together down here. We both want you for only ourselves, but we know it's not going to happen, not unless you want to choose one of us, so that's that. Are you about to choose?'

I shake my head no. Of course, I am not going to choose. How can I? He is speaking again.

'And anyway, I've come to realise that he's like the brother I've never had. I love him, and I want to try to be a second-rate replacement for the brother that he used to have. I wouldn't hurt him ever, not for anything. The three of us, we're a team now and that's how it's going to stay.'

I kiss him lightly on the end of his nose. He is saying the words I need to hear.

'Won't everyone think we are a bit strange, or think I'm a bit strange at least? It's not normal to have two boyfriends on the go at the same time, especially when they both know about each other. Just because you and Jasper have made a decision that you can live with, it doesn't mean everyone else will understand.'

Alex nods his comprehension again. He is definitely modest about his lip-reading talents - I have yet to have a conversation with him that he hasn't grasped.

'I don't care if it's weird and it doesn't matter what anyone else thinks. No one really knows and we don't need to tell them – not yet anyway.'

He pauses before adding mischievously, 'Of course, I know I'm a much better lover than him.'

I laugh. 'You're both so different, Alex. I can't compare and I don't want to. He makes me feel safe and warm, like nothing can touch me ever. Sometimes, when I'm not with either of you, I see me and Jasper married, with jobs and kids, the whole works, it would be so easy. But then there's you and me, I need this too - you do something to me that I can't explain. When I'm with you, I feel like I could rule the world. It's exciting and unpredictable and I wouldn't want it any other way. Have you understood all that?'

'I think so,' he replies. 'When it's your luscious lips I'm staring at, I could probably lip read in mandarin! So basically, to paraphrase, you said that Jasper is shit in bed and that I'm the world's greatest lover, yes?'

I giggle and clamber across him out of bed. 'I'm bloody starving.' I announce. 'Don't go anywhere.'

I slip out of the room naked and return minutes later with a mountain of buttered toast, and we wordlessly munch our way through our midnight feast.

It is two days later when I return from afternoon lectures to find a small package on my bed, beautifully wrapped in soft black tissue and tied in a satin bow. An unsigned note, written in green ink, in a familiar, beautiful loopy hand, accompanies it.

'I am worried that you seem to be running low on underwear, maybe these can be of help. Thank you for the best afternoon of my life, AV-Z x.'

Inside the parcel are five sets of matching bras and the teeniest of knickers, all in different shades of the finest silk. An Agent Provocateur tag is attached.

It's going to work out, I think. It's actually going to work.

CHAPTER 39

SOPHIE

Jasper finally returns home to us on Sunday evening, slamming the front door heavily behind him and plonking his bag noisily on the parquet floor. Alex and I are watching a film, cuddled up together in his comfy bed, and we look at each other questioningly. It isn't like him at all to slam doors. Alex flicks off the television and we both follow him upstairs to see what the problem is.

'Bloody Samira!' he grumbles crossly, as he starts putting away his books and clothes. He looks really fed up.

'I ended it with her ages ago, at the beginning of the summer holidays, obviously, when we all, you know....'

Alex and I know exactly what he means, 'But Jesus, she's making it difficult. She's been on a placement at Mansfield hospital too, so I've seen her nearly every fucking day. I found out that she swapped with someone so she could be there the same time as me – bloody stalker. She's barking mad - we had a huge row and she threatened to top herself at one point, but it's just bloody manipulation, I know it is. I don't get it, it's not like we had much of a relationship anyway! It was only sex and was never going anywhere, I always thought I made that pretty clear to her.'

He sits down heavily on the bed with a sigh. Alex sits next to him and puts his arm round him in a consoling manner.

'Well mate, sounds like you are well shot of her. She'll move on soon enough.'

'That's what I thought!' responds Jasper, running his hand through his thick curls, 'But it's been more than ten weeks now and she still tries to phone and text me at least three times every day.

Most of the time I don't pick up, but when I do, well, bloody hell, she's obsessed.'

He turns to look at me. 'And it's you she's obsessed with Soph. She's convinced that it's all your fault that I'm not going out with her, she's convinced that you have deliberately poisoned me against her over the last twelve months. I tell her until I'm blue in the face that it's got nothing to do with you - not strictly true obviously- but it's like I'm talking to a brick wall, she just doesn't hear it. I think I'm going to have to change my phone number or something at this rate.'

'Have you finished at Mansfield now?' I ask him.

'Yes, thank goodness,' he replies, with a grimace, and wrinkles his nose in disgust.

'And that was pretty crap too. Delivering babies is not going to be my future career, that's for sure. Bloody horrendous business.'

He shudders at the memory, and Alex and I laugh. He carries on, 'I remember reading some magazine interview with a pop star, now who was it? That guy out of Take That who my mam likes.'

'Er, Robbie Williams?' I supply, and he nods. 'Yeah, him. He said that being at the business end of his wife giving birth was like watching his favourite pub burn down, and do you know what? He was absolutely right; I couldn't have put it better myself.'

He's smiling again now, and I give him a kiss and a hug too.

'It's great to have you back. We really missed you. Don't worry too much about Samira, she can't hurt you. Alex is right, she'll move on eventually.'

Women in Art proves to be fascinating, even though Prof Harding's dry delivery of the subject drives us to distraction. The more lectures we attend, the more we become convinced that the Prof disapproves of just about every male artist ever to apply paint to a canvas. Not a single genius is spared, from the sublime Sandro Botticelli to the magnificent Pierre-Auguste Renoir. At first, I try to give her the benefit of the doubt, thinking that it is maybe all down to her slightly bored, superior tone, but as the weeks progress, I conclude that the Prof is in fact, a total man hater. She is obsessed with what she terms 'the male gaze' and how nearly all depictions of women in western art (apart from the Virgin Mary), have been painted by randy male artists for the sole purpose of titillating other randy men.

As she explains one afternoon, 'In the eighteenth and nineteenth centuries, the gentlemen disguised their lust by admiring paintings of mythological women – Venus, woodland nymphs and such-like. This was permissible of course, because those ladies were unattainable, unworldly and completely unreal. I believe however, that this style of art, was merely the acceptable face of pornography for the well-heeled gent. And this has led us to the state we are in today, where women are endlessly judged by how they look and how they dress.'

Her voice is rising steadily through this monologue, it is now almost at a shriek.

'For example, if a woman is to put on just the tiniest bit of weight, and I mean the tiniest bit of weight, compared to how she was, say one year earlier, then she would be castigated, thrown out, flung onto the scrap heap!'

There is a pause and Prof Harding appears to collect herself by shuffling some papers on the lectern in front of her and blowing her nose loudly. The students raise our eyebrows at each other. Blimey, which unpleasant, unreconstructed cad had broken her heart? Whoever it was, it seems that all the male artists of the last five hundred years are going to be expected to atone for the behaviour of this one primitive man. I note the absence of a wedding band.

By Friday night, Katy and I feel we've earned a night out. Amy is otherwise indisposed. Her relationship with Andrew the mountain climber has gone from strength to strength, and even Katy, who house-shares with her, scarcely bumps into her these days.

'I still think it's going to end in tears,' she warns. 'There is something about him that I really don't care for. I can't put my finger on it, but he's not very good for her.'

We have met up in the *Hand in Heart* pub and then are planning to go on to the *Wheatsheaves*, where the rest of the Art History set are likely already settled in for the night. This suits me perfectly, as Alex is out on the town with Seb and Hugo, and I can predict that Jasper will be watching the rugby in the *Wheatsheaves* with his mates. We grab a table in the *Hand in Heart* and catch up on the gossip. Katy doesn't believe in wasting time with small talk, so she comes straight to the point.

'So, how's life in the love nest going?' she half jokes.

'Very well, thank you,' I reply. I sound prim, defensive. 'We are all just getting along fine.'

But Katy isn't anywhere near finished with the inquisition. 'How does it work then; do you have a roster printed out and stuck to the fridge? Or am I being really naive and the three of you are all at it together?'

I laugh and redden. 'Of course not, you idiot, it just, well......it just works. I can't explain how, really.'

Katy shakes her head, fascinated and determined to find out more. 'But, to put it bluntly, doesn't one of them mind when you are humping the other?'

My face is scarlet. 'Jesus, Katy, probably, yes, I don't know! I didn't plan for this to happen, you know! I've no idea what I'm doing. I'm just making it up as I go along!'

'Yeah, but come on Soph, two hot blokes like that, surely they can't be happy with the situation?'

I'm getting the third degree. I take a gulp of lager. 'I know, Katy, but I said I couldn't choose between them and they came up with a solution. Honestly, I have no idea how it's going to pan out, but so far, we all seem okay, so watch this space.'

'So, if Alex decides to find himself a girl out on the town tonight, will that be okay? Because, I'm guessing you and Jasper will be cosying up later.'

'No, Katy,' I reply, 'Of course it's not okay. This isn't an open relationship, it's just the three of us, and I happen to be the only girl, that's all.'

She still hasn't finished. 'So, they must hate each other, really.'

'No,' I protest, 'And that's probably why we are managing to make it work. They are extremely close, to be honest I've never heard a cross word between them, apart from ages ago, when Alex first found out about Jasper and me. They went on holiday together in the summer, just the two of them and had a fantastic time. Sometimes it's me that actually feels like a spare part when they're together, particularly when the sport is on the TV. We're just really careful to be respectful of each other, I suppose. Jasper is usually out all day at med school, and so Alex and I get a lot of time alone, and then at night, well, Jasper always shares my bed. I'm very happy actually.'

'I bet you bloody are!' Katy smirks, swigging her wine.

I am aware that I am sounding extremely defensive and realise that even confiding to my close friend makes it all sound a little, well, sordid.

'Honestly, Katy, it's not just about sex, there is a lot of love between the three of us. Alex says we're a team and I think he's right. You are the only person who knows about the sex bit really, I think. It's not exactly something you go around bragging about, not as the woman in the relationship anyway. It makes me sound like a right tart. And I know Jasper wouldn't discuss it with anyone either, he's very private. Alex might have told Seb and Hugo, I suppose, but they would just give him a congratulatory pat him on the back, say well done and then forget about it. They're complete airheads.'

Katy nods pensively, 'Good looking airheads, though, especially Hugo. He's hot. If he wasn't so damn ex-public school, then I'd be all over him. Unfortunately, he stands for everything my leftie principles despise!'

I laugh. 'You don't have to cross him off your list just because he doesn't vote labour and subscribe to the Socialist Worker, Katy! And maybe he secretly does? You won't find out if you just stereotype him out of hand. Just because his mother chose to send him to public school, doesn't mean he's automatically not a nice guy. And he's still young free and single as far as I know....'

'And very posh!' Katy sighs, 'Never mind, Sophie, and don't steer the subject away from the love triangle. If ever you tire of one of them, there are plenty of girls happy to take them off your hands!'

We meander around the corner to the *Wheatsheaves* and join the others. As predicted, Jasper is indeed leaning against the bar, with what seems like half of the med school, and his face lights up as I head over through the packed pub.

'Hi, beautiful, I was hoping you'd turn up.'

He puts his arm around my waist and kisses me long and hard. I am aware of his mates watching us with interest, the sport on the overhead television temporarily forgotten. One of them wolf whistles and Jasper good-naturedly flicks him the V sign over my shoulder.

'They're just jealous,' he says, in a voice loud enough for them all to hear and kisses me again, nuzzling my neck. Although I am blushing furiously, I am delighted with this very un-Jasperlike public display of affection.

'So, Jaz, is this your new bird?' asks the bloke nearest to us. Jasper winks down at me, giving a brief flash of his small, even teeth.

'I suppose you could say that, after a fashion.'

I smile back at him, loving the way he is looking at me, as though no-one else in the room matters. He continues to hold me close against his broad chest, frequently kissing the top of my head as he resumes watching the remainder of the game, ignoring the occasional sniggers of his mates. At half time, he downs the rest of his pint, says his goodbyes and we make our way out, to more whistles and lewd suggestions.

'Mates before dates, Jaz!' one of them cries to further heckling. 'Bro's before ho's!'

They make so much noise, that I am convinced that there isn't a single person in the pub who hasn't seen us leave together. He waits for me by the door as I nip into the ladies for a wee. His old girlfriend Samira is in there, applying lipstick in the mirror. Her expression is one of concentration, but it changes to hatred as she spies me coming out of the cubicle behind her. Trying to pretend that I haven't seen her, I begin to wash my hands, but she is not letting me escape that lightly. No doubt she saw Jasper and I together at the bar.

'Sophie isn't it?' she says, looking at me through the mirror. Her voice is harsh, 'You are a fucking bitch.' She returns to her lipstick and I hurriedly exit.

'All right, sweetheart?' asks Jasper. I nod, shaken up from my encounter. We kiss again in the cool air, Jasper's warm hands held tightly in my own.

'Did you mind me kissing you in front of everyone?' he asks, slightly nervously, 'I couldn't help it, I just needed to touch you.'

God, this man is sweet. 'Of course, I didn't mind, Jasper! I loved it, and trust me, there wasn't a single girl in that pub who wouldn't have changed places with me given the chance.' Especially Samira.

He really doesn't have a clue as to how handsome he is, I think, shaking my head again in disbelief. It is just one of the many things about him that I adore, and I am not surprised that Samira is struggling to get over him. Once home, I grab a towel and head for the shower. Jasper hovers outside the door.

'Can I join you?' he shyly asks. I smile to myself. The contrast between him and Alex could hardly be greater. Alex wouldn't have asked - he would have slung me over his shoulder and marched me straight in, ripping my clothes off along the way.

Without answering, I pull him into the bathroom and slowly begin undressing him, planting hard kisses on his firm chest and stomach as I work my way down the buttons of his shirt. He's letting me undress him, making no move to join in, his hands rest lightly at my waist, letting me love him. And I so want to love him. I kneel on the hard tiles and undo the buttons of his fly, continuing the path of my kisses as I wriggle his jeans and boxers over his hips. I skate my lips over the crown of his erect penis, licking off the bead of juice that is waiting there, causing him to take a sharp intake of breath. Standing up again, I slowly remove my own clothes, before dragging him under the powerful hot jets of water. I throw my arms around his neck, loving the feeling of his hardness pressing into my lower stomach as we embrace.

'I've never had a shower with a girl before,' he whispers.

I kiss him. 'Stand still and let me wash you.'

Filling my hands with liquid soap, I marvel at the taut muscles of his pale shoulders, arms and chest as I massage it all over his smooth flesh. God, I love this man, his solidity, the absolute masculinity of him. Filling my hands again, I take my time to soap the muscles of his strong thighs and calves, before finally I bring my hands back up to his heavy balls. I take his hard penis into my mouth, my slippery hands circling the base, and I suck gently. His hands are in my hair, and after a few moments, he stops me.

'It's too good, Soph, I'll come too quickly,' he pants and brings me to my feet, before effortlessly lifting me up. With my back pressed against the tiled wall for support, my legs clasped firmly around his waist, he enters me gently, inch by inch, until he fills me completely.

'I love being inside you, Sophie,' he murmurs, 'Shit, this feels so, so good.' He moans, I love the sound of his pleasure, his low groans, his heavier breathing as he gets close, his penis swelling inside me. He is so strong that I ride him easily, our bodies slippery, bathed in a rainfall of hot water. I close my eyes, my head falling back, feeling utterly safe, and surrender myself to the moment.

Afterwards, we sit opposite each other, cross-legged on the floor of the shower cubicle. I reach for the shampoo and Jasper takes it out of my hand.

'It's my turn. Let me wash your hair for you,' he says, 'I'm good at it.'

He begins massaging the shampoo carefully into my long hair, his big hands surprising delicate. He certainly has a practised touch.

'I used to shower with Christian,' he explains, smiling slightly at the memory. 'We had one of those plastic shower chairs, and I would sit him in that, and wash his hair. It was shorter than yours, obviously. After a few times, I realised that it was easier if I got in the shower with him; I'd just end up getting soaked anyhow. So, after I'd washed his hair, I would pick him up out of the chair, kick the chair away and hold him against me to rinse out the shampoo. He was light as a feather, and I think he loved the skin-to-skin contact, you know? I certainly did, I loved cuddling his little soft body. I used to sing to him too, all sorts of daft Irish folk songs. My mam thought I was crazy. And then, when we'd done, I'd wrap him in a big fluffy towel and lean against the bathroom radiator with him cuddled on my lap until he was warm and dry. Although, usually he'd wee all over me at some point and I'd have to shower again straight afterwards.' He laughs softly and shakes his head.

I love this story; I love how he thinks nothing of his utter selflessness and how he feels comfortable enough to share such intimate memories with me. I stand up, turning off the shower. 'Okay, Jasper, I'm ready for my big fluffy towel now and a cuddle against the radiator, and I promise that I won't wee on you.'

CHAPTER 41

ALEX

The following week gets off to a shitty start. Jaz comes back from med school whilst Soph and I are preparing supper. He uncharacteristically slams the front door, for the second time in the space of a month.

'Someone has bloody keyed the side of my car this afternoon, whilst I was parked up at the hospital. It's definitely deliberate - you can tell whoever did it has just started at one end and made sure they scratched all the way down the whole side.'

Sophie and I are appalled. 'Didn't anyone see? They must have CCTV down there.'

'They have,' he answers. 'I went to the Security Office; the bloke in there was really helpful. But when I told him where I'd parked, he said that we'd never spot who it was. He showed me on the CCTV. The car was near the bus stop for the med school, and he reckons about four hundred people will have walked past that bus stop just this afternoon alone. And the damage was on the far side, so anyone of them could have casually strolled along with a key sticking out of their hand and you wouldn't pick it up on the camera. Bastard, whoever it was.'

Sophie stops what she's doing and puts her arms around him. I realise that I don't mind this natural display of affection, to be honest, I want to do the same, he is so fed up. 'I can't believe it was targeted at you personally; you haven't got an enemy in the world. It will have been some random git with nothing better to do.'

'Yeah, probably,' he says gloomily, 'But it's still bloody irritating. I'm going to have to fix it myself I think - it's not very deep, but it goes across three panels, which will cost a bloody fortune to get done properly.'

'I'll pay to get it repaired for you, Jaz,' I offer immediately.

He shakes his head as I knew he would. He's proud, and I understand. Fuck though, I'd buy him a new car if I had to.

'Cheers, mate, but you give me enough help as it is. Nah, I'll work out how to fix it myself sometime, maybe in the holidays when I get around to it.' He stomps off upstairs.

It is the following morning. I am woken by Sophie shaking me vigorously by the shoulder. Not my favourite type of wake-up call. It looks like I'm being shouted at too. Now what have I done? I can see her saying my name over and over and tears are running down her beautiful face. She is wearing a little white T-shirt, knickers and nothing else. Very tasty.

'Hey, babe, what's up?'

She thrusts my hearing aids into my hand. I would normally find this a little rude, but clearly, she has been traumatised by something.

'Put these on, Alex, I need to talk to you.'

I do as I am told and lever myself up against the pillows. She's sobbing now. 'Hey, Soph, I'm here, it's okay. What's wrong?'

She puts a piece of paper and a crumpled white envelope into my hand. 'Look at this! It's come through the post this morning. It is addressed to me and it's horrible.'

I study the note with puzzlement, turn it over and then check the envelope, just as she no doubt did minutes earlier. The envelope is addressed to Sophie Ashworth, with our address written in neat print, and sent first class post. In the middle of the plain white sheet there is one word, written in black felt tip, in capital letters: "SLUT." I now understand why she is so upset.

'Come on Soph, don't cry.' I say. 'It's just some twat playing a joke on you, not a very nice one though. Get in.'

I scrunch up the paper and hurl it across the bedroom floor towards the wastepaper bin, then lift the duvet back and shuffle over. She lies with her head on my chest, and I stroke her hair. My cock is twitching at the feel of her silky hair under my fingers and her smooth long legs intertwined with mine. Possibly not a good moment to suggest some morning sex, I think wisely. God, I'm maturing.

'Who the hell would do this to you?' I muse aloud. 'It doesn't make sense; you haven't hurt anyone.'

My anger is building on her behalf - it will be nothing compared to when Jasper finds out.

'I know!' she sobs.

I kiss her through her hair. 'Sshh, Sophie come on, perhaps whoever sent it has got the wrong person, maybe it was meant for someone else.'

'Yeah, maybe.' But she isn't convinced, and neither am I. Is this something to do with our cosy *ménage à trois*? But no-one knows about it, apart from Hugo and Seb, and they don't care. I guess Sophie has probably filled Katy and Amy in on some of the details (hopefully not my pathetic whining), but again, they have no axe to grind.

I am sweetness and concern personified. I catch the bus with her onto campus and am waiting outside the lecture theatre for her when she comes out of the building a few hours later. I even finished an overdue essay in the interim. Sophie has recovered somewhat from her earlier shock, and as we walk together arm in arm back towards Lenton, she almost seems back to normal. I make her laugh by stopping at the exact spot where we had first kissed over a year ago, when I had walked home with her from the Cripps party. So much has happened since then. I pull her close and kiss her again. It is as wonderful as the first time.

'It's going to be fine, Sophie, let's just forget you ever received that stupid note.'

CHAPTER 42

SOPHIE

But it isn't fine at all, in fact it is going to get a whole lot worse. A few days later and I am with Katy and Amy, we are treating ourselves to a coffee and sharing a huge slice of chocolate cake at the small café in the Art History building. We have just finished a tutorial covering the extraordinary life of the tragic Mexican artist Frieda Kahlo. Katy and Amy are having a heated debate as to whether her work is somehow damaged by the twenty-first century commercialisation of her image.

'The question is,' says Katy earnestly, 'Is her face now a shorthand illustration for modern feminism, or is the omnipresent Kahlo branding an affront to her socialist ideals? I think it completely is.'

Amy disagrees vehemently. 'I think that if she were alive today, she would love it! She would see her fame as an inspiration to disenfranchised women everywhere. At the end of the day, she was a disabled, mono-browed Mexican from the back of beyond, who managed to take the art world by storm!'

Katy is shaking her head. 'No way, Amy! How could a woman who had a communist flag draped on her coffin rest easy in her grave if she knew how her name had been exploited by today's capitalist society?'

I can't muster an opinion either way, and stay out of the argument, absent-mindedly sipping my drink. I struggled to concentrate on the tutorial and its complex themes, as my mind had refused to let go of the image of that horrible, crude word. I haven't told either of my two friends about the anonymous note - it is embarrassing somehow, so I have endeavoured, (and when I have been distracted by Alex) almost succeeded in pushing it to the back of my mind. But no matter how I try, the memory of it still lingers, and my stomach lurches for the hundredth time as I mentally relive the moment of opening that awful envelope.

The girls have reached an impasse regarding the true status of Frieda Kahlo in modern western society, and move on to other topics of conversation, namely the ups and downs of Amy's tempestuous relationship with Andrew. He is currently giving her the cold shoulder and she has no idea why. When she excuses herself to nip to the loo, Katy turns to me and says mildly,

'You're very quiet today. All good in the love nest?'

I smile at her, shaking my head slightly. 'Never better, Katy, never better.' And it is true. We have found a rhythm, the boys have resumed their cosy beer and Sky Sports sessions, and the three of us have discovered a level of contentment that we hadn't anticipated possible. I know it's weird set up, we all know it's weird, but it is our own private weirdness and it works.

We are gathering our bags together when Amy comes rushing back, all colour drained from her face. She is almost shaking as she sits down. We look at her in alarm.

'Are you alright Amy? What's wrong?'

Amy puts her hand over mine. 'Oh, my goodness, Sophie, you need to come and see. Someone's written something horrible about you in the toilets.'

I feel sick, I can taste the chocolate cake rising in my throat as I get to my feet. My legs are leaden, and Amy puts her arm around me as we file into the ladies loos. I can see her throwing Katy an anxious look. It is there, writ large on the big mirror above the hand basins. Scrawled across the entire width of it, in bright pink lipstick, are the words: 'SOPHIE ASHWORTH IS A SLUT'.

I gasp in horror and clamp my hand over my mouth. I run into one of the cubicles retching, all of the chocolate cake coming straight back up.

'Quick, Katy! Let's wipe it off before anyone else comes in.' I hear Amy saying urgently.

My two friends frantically start pulling out paper towels from the dispenser and rubbing at the mirror. Thankfully, it doesn't take long for all traces of the bright pink lipstick to be removed. I stagger out of the stall and lean weakly against one of the sinks.

'I bet hardly anyone has seen it,' says Katy kindly, trying to reassure me whilst I swill my mouth out under the tap. 'It definitely wasn't there when I came in here about an hour ago.' she confirms.

'What's going on, Sophie?' asks Amy, in a worried tone. 'Who the hell wrote that?'

I'm crying again now. 'I don't know,' I sob. 'It's the second time this week. It's obviously someone who doesn't like what I'm doing with Alex and Jasper, but I didn't think anyone really knew, to be honest.'

Katy puts her arm round my shoulders. 'Come on, let's get you home.'

We walk back through the café and out into the fresh air. Amy pauses.

'Hang on a sec,' she says, and she turns, jogging back into the building. She returns a minute later, disappointed.

'I just went in and asked the woman behind the counter if she'd seen anyone she didn't recognise come in earlier, but she doesn't think so. Sorry Sophie.'

They see me safely onto the bus. It is nearly empty, and I close my eyes and rest my head back against the plastic seat. Who is doing this? Me and Alex and Jasper, we're good, we're not hurting anyone.

I am still shaking when I unlock the front door. I lock it behind me, suddenly I feel paranoid, like maybe someone is watching me, ready to send me another note, or worse. The house is quiet, I had guessed that Jasper would still be at med school but had hoped that Alex would be back. Still feeling nauseous, I take a very long shower, brush my teeth and climb into bed, bunching the duvet up around my neck in an attempt to block out the rest of the world. With relief, I hear the front door opening not long afterwards. Alex calls up to me.

'Hey Sophie, it's me, I'm home.'

He bounds up the stairs, two at a time. 'Katy phoned me, Soph - she was worried about you. I came as soon as I could. I'm so sorry, sweetheart.'

He strips off and slips under the covers next to me. Burying my face in his neck, I cling to him sobbing.

'It's really scary, Alex. I don't know what to do. Someone's got it in for me. I'm frightened. What are they going to do next? What if I get attacked or something, or someone breaks into the house when you or Jasper aren't here?'

Alex tries his best to reassure me, but I am unconvinced. Eventually I fall asleep, exhausted from the emotional turmoil, firmly cocooned in Alex's arms.

CHAPTER 43

JASPER

Alex wakes up with a yell as I haul him out of bed by his leg and he's crashed down unceremoniously onto the bedroom floor.

'Fuck, Jaz, let go of me! That fucking hurt!' He's rubbing his arse through his Calvin Klein's with one hand and reaching for his hearing aids with the other. I'm standing over him, desperately trying to control my urge to kick him.

'Jasper!' says Sophie with alarm, also wide awake now, 'What the hell are you doing?'

I am tired and hungry. It is after ten at night and I've had a long day shadowing junior doctors on the wards and then I've been in the library since five. And I've come home to this.

'I told you the fucking rules, Alex!' I roar furiously, 'And you Sophie! Not in this fucking bed!'

Sophie is sitting up now and I can see she is unhappy with me. She looks like she's been crying too. Alex is watching me apprehensively from the floor. 'If you stop behaving like such a bloody caveman, Jaz, I can tell you why I'm here.'

So, he succinctly fills me in on the episode and I feel like a complete idiot. I put out my hand to Alex and haul him up off the floor, bringing him in close. Sophie is right, he does always smell good.

'Sorry, Al, I thought...'

'You are such a knob sometimes, Jaz.'

He's forgiven me already, the kind, gentle soul that he is. My anger at Alex turns to anger at whoever is upsetting Sophie. I'm furious.

'If I find out who's doing this to you, they're going to wish they had never fucking been born,' I rage. 'How dare they?'

Alex is much more measured; he doesn't possess my temper. 'We'll sort it out, Soph, you're safe here with us two.'

'Maybe that's just the problem,' she argues, tearfully. 'Perhaps there's someone out there who doesn't like the three of us being.... the three of us.'

'Well, if that's the case, then they can fuck off,' I respond swiftly. 'It's no one else's business what we get up to! We're not hurting anyone. And who knows anyway?'

'I'm not so sure it is about the three of us,' interjects Alex reasonably. 'It's only Sophie that's been targeted. I mean, no one's sent you or me any nasty messages, have they?'

I yawn and run my hands through my hair. 'I'm knackered. I need a shower.'

'You get in the shower and I'll sort us some food out,' says Alex, kindly. Now I feel even worse for dumping him onto the floor.

Twenty minutes later, he is back with three pizzas, glasses and a bottle of red wine. Sophie and I are already sat up in bed and he hovers next to us, uncertain what to do. I indicate to the place he was previously occupying with a jerk of my head. He doesn't need asking twice and soon we are peacefully chewing pizza and drinking wine. Sophie has brightened up considerably. Alex is being mischievous, fondling my thigh under the covers and then trying to pretend that it is Sophie.

'Stop bloody flirting with me, Alex!' I laugh, pushing him away, 'Remember mate, you're just a temporary visitor here, we'll kick you out if don't behave.' I deliver this warning with a grin. Him being here with us is nice, the three of us are good together.

Alex looks round the cosy room appreciatively. 'I think I could get used to it, though,' he decides, giving Sophie a kiss. 'And this comfy bed is easily big enough for all of us, you know.'

His voice takes on a fake pleading note, 'And I do get very lonely downstairs on my own sometimes. Honestly, Jaz, I'll be as quiet as a mouse, you won't know I'm even here.'

Sophie giggles and snuggles up to me. We both know that is extremely unlikely. Alex's presence can fill a room. 'Shall we let him stay, Jasper? Just this once?'

I can't be arsed to argue, and the fact that Sophie is happier is enough for me. The evening ends with the floor strewn with empty plates and me with Sophie in my favourite position, firmly on my side of the bed. I'm cuddling her from behind with my warm hand solidly resting flat on her stomach. She and Alex face each other, one of her own hands is tightly held in his. I'm not completely sure how I feel about this, but it is not triggering my caveman response.

CHAPTER 44

ALEX

Next day is Saturday. Jasper wakes first, and I'm dimly aware of him putting on his gym kit and slipping out the door. Sophie snuggles closer to me and I encircle her with my arm, my hand straying down her smooth back to her perfect arse. Christ, I could really get used to this every morning.

'Morning, gorgeous,' I murmur without opening my eyes.

I fumble under the covers for her hand and draw it down onto my rock-hard cock. I smile to myself as she begins stroking it. Jasper would have a fucking fit if he knew. Serve him right for throwing me out of bed yesterday.

'Does Jaz get this special treatment in the mornings?' I ask with a happy sigh.

I sense her shaking her head and look down to see her lips. 'No, he's usually up and out the door before I wake up.'

I stretch and roll my hips up towards her hand. It is an absolutely fucking marvellous start to the day. 'He doesn't know what he's missing. I definitely need to sleep here more often,' I whisper.

Another plain white envelope greets Sophie at breakfast. She is making a pancake mixture, and I'm squeezing oranges. We have become very sophisticated in our domestic bliss. Jaz has picked up the post from the mat on his return from the gym and he silently hands it over.

'You could just chuck it in the bin and forget about it, Sophie.'

She thrusts it back at him and flops into a chair.

'You can open it; I don't want to.'

He takes it and I place my arm protectively around her shoulders whilst Jasper rips open the envelope. He scans it and then angrily throws it down onto the table.

'WHAT'S COMING NEXT, SLUT?'

No one speaks. Sophie turns and hides her face in my chest as I hold her close. Jasper paces the floor, fuming.

We don't have to wait long to find out what is coming next. Amy calls to say that she has received an anonymous note through the letterbox, informing her that Sophie is sleeping with her boyfriend. Thankfully, Amy is completely dismissive of the idea - Andrew has hardly been out of her sight in the last month and frankly, wouldn't have any energy left to sleep with anyone else by the time she's finished with him. And the fact that Sophie wouldn't touch him with a barge pole, we keep to ourselves. Sophie is at her wits' end though.

'Do you think we should report it to the police?' she asks us tearfully that evening as, for the second night running, I make myself extremely comfortable upstairs. 'I mean, I feel really safe here with you two, but I'm going to have to leave the house at some point, aren't I?'

'I don't know what to think about the police,' admits Jasper. 'I'm not sure they would be able to do anything?'

On Sunday morning, we discover that Jasper's car has two flat tyres. On closer inspection, there is a sharp tack lying on the drive next to the car. He is absolutely livid.

'I'm going to kill this fucking bastard when I find out who it is.'

He is pacing the kitchen again, fists clenched and his face white with anger.

'It's a bit odd that it's only you two being attacked, don't you think?' I muse, rubbing my chin. 'No one has done anything to me yet, unless I've just been too dim to notice. I'm still not convinced that this is someone who's unhappy with the three of us, otherwise I'd be getting shit too.'

Jasper suddenly bangs his fist against the kitchen wall.

'I am such a fuckwit!' he says breaking the silence.

'You two, listen, I know who's doing this. Alex is absolutely right; it's nothing to do with the three of us at all. It's all about me. It's bloody Samira isn't it? I told you that she was obsessed with Sophie, all she ever used to do was quiz me over where Sophie was, what she was doing, who her friends were, what we did together. She was jealous as hell. And the texts and phone calls stopped about a week ago - actually at about the time I had my car scratched at the hospital! It's bloody her, I know it is, she's a fucking psychopath.'

He takes his phone out of his pocket and starts angrily punching in numbers.

'Hi Samira, it's me.' A short pause, his brow furrowed. 'You don't sound very surprised to hear from me. What are you playing at?' Another brief pause then, 'Don't give me that crap, Samira, I know it's you who scratched my car (thanks for that extra expense, I could have done without by the way), and you can stop with the bloody notes too. How dare you do this to someone who hasn't done anything to you?'

A longer pause. 'I've told you for the millionth time, it's got nothing to do with her! And this isn't exactly going to win me back, is it? Just fuck off out of my life and leave my friend alone, okay?'

He cuts her off and throws the phone onto the table.

'Yep, it's her. She didn't admit it of course, but I didn't exactly get the impression that she was surprised to hear from me. And she just laughed about my car.'

He takes Sophie's hand. 'Sorry Soph, sorry that I went out with a complete psycho and got you involved in it. You don't deserve any of this.'

'It's okay, Jasper. It's not your fault. I just want it to stop. It was horrendous having all that writing on the mirror - I don't know who's seen it or read it, it's awful.'

'Yep, I'm convinced it's her,' repeats Jasper, even more certain, 'I remember now that she once told me how, years ago, she deliberately broke a window at her friend's house because she had invited some other girl on holiday with her family instead of Samira. She was really pleased with herself. I thought it was a bit fucked up at the time, but you know, you forget this stuff. Until something like this happens.'

'Well,' I say, 'hopefully she will just stop now you've called her out on it. The only other way we are going to get her stop is either to catch her in the act or to get her to admit to it. We can't just go to the police and accuse her, without any proof.'

I pause, lost in thought. 'I've never even seen her. Presumably she doesn't know who I am?'

Jasper shakes his head. 'Nah, I don't think so. I've never mentioned you either. You're not the sort of bloke you tell your girlfriends about, not if you want to keep them anyhow. We didn't have that sort of relationship really. It was just sex to be honest - well, it certainly was for me anyhow. Obviously for her it was something much more.'

I nod, processing this information. These sorts of relationships are my area of expertise or were until recently. 'Can I see a picture of her? Have you got one on your phone?'

I wolf-whistle when Jasper pulls up her Instagram profile. She's pretty bloody tasty. I'm so glad that Jaz has no idea how attractive he is to the opposite sex, he would be unbearable to live with, and I'd be a nervous wreck. 'Not bad at all, Jaz. You've got good taste in women - looks-wise anyway. Clearly on the inside she's as mad as a cut snake. Where does she hang out at night?'

'The same place as most of the other female med students of course,' replies Jasper easily. 'In the *Grove Tavern*, because it's usually filled with male junior doctors.'

I stand up, smiling to myself. 'Cool. I've got a plan. She's going to wish she'd never started her little campaign by this time next week. Oh, I'll help you do those tyres later - just give me a shout when you're ready.'

Sophie endures another horrible week. I feel so sorry for her. Even though there aren't any further nasty comments written on mirrors, or any poison pen letters through the letterbox, her anxiety that there will be, or that everyone in her tutor group has seen it and is talking about it without her knowing is turning her into a bag of nerves. Katy and Amy are incredibly supportive, they have gone up massively in my estimation, and I report back to Hugo, who is maintaining a discreet interest in Katy's movements. He copped off with her once, on that fateful night, but I don't think Katy told Sophie, and the new mature me decides it's not my place to stir things up.

Scoring massive brownie points, I escort her to and from every lecture, leaving her and then greeting her again each time with a passionate kiss in front of whoever happens to be passing by. I'd be doing more than that if I could get away with it in public, her distress is bringing out my protective side and I seem to have a natural flair for it.

'Katy told me ages ago that you were in love with me,' she says one day as I'm about to leave her for a few hours, 'And I didn't believe her.'

'Do you believe her now?' I ask, searching her eyes. 'This is the real deal for me, Soph, you know that don't you? Whatever happens with Jaz.'

She smiles at me. 'Yes, I do, particularly as you tell me just about every morning and night. It's almost worth having this awful poison pen writer just to have this special time with you.'

Jasper is equally supportive, but Sophie and I both agree that he should carry on with his intensive programme of studies. On the pretext of supporting Sophie, I am insisting on joining them in bed every night. I am planning on stringing this out indefinitely, the bed is plenty big enough, and well, I like it. A lot. I don't know what Jaz is thinking, but he hasn't kicked me out again, and of course, I don't dare touch her when he's within kicking distance, that would really be pushing it. He's out of the house early every morning, though, so it's not too bad.

He's still asserting his dominance, by almost ignoring my presence in Sophie's room entirely. He waits until I remove my hearing aids, and then he carries on as before, talking and kissing and cuddling her as if they are completely alone. If I sense it ramping up any more than that, I turn away from them and block it out. I'm torturing myself unnecessarily, knowing that barely two feet away, his cock is pushing inside her, his massive hands are squeezing her arse, caressing her tits. There is no question that I'm in deep, and fucked in the head, because in the dead of night, these thoughts make me hard.

CHAPTER 45

SOPHIE

The weekend comes around at last. On Saturday evening, Alex showers, smartens himself up and disappears out early, leaving a heady aroma of Chanel and coconut shampoo behind him. Alone for the first time in a week, Jasper and I take some crisps and a bottle of red wine up to bed and watch a film together on his laptop. Afterwards, we make sweet, slow Jasper-love and then sleep, happily curled up against each other.

We are woken at midnight when Alex barges into the room and turns on the light.

'Good news boys and girls, Uncle Alex has solved our Samira problem!'

He stands at the end of the bed, looking triumphant as we both blink, adjusting to the bright light, Jasper swears at him. He waits until he has our full attention.

'Okay, so Plan A was to seduce Samira and then somehow get her to confess to everything, and for me to record it on my phone. Then I could confront her with the evidence and suggest she stopped, or I would threaten her with the police. If that didn't work, then I had Plan B, which was to seduce her and then get her in some compromising positions, possibly with handcuffs, maybe a cucumber or something, and then take photos on my phone and threaten her with those. I didn't really have a Plan C, but it doesn't matter, because fortunately for me, she came up with one all of her own, without any prompting, and it was even better than Plan A or Plan B!'

We are sitting up straighter now, completely focused on his story.

'So, I'll tell you what happened. I went to the *Grove Tavern* and had a drink at the bar. The beer was shit, so I was glad she turned up the first night, as I didn't want to have to keep going back. Anyway, after about half an hour of shit beer, Samira came in with a noisy group of girls, and I had the impression that they had already been drinking elsewhere.

'I kept my eye on her and when she went to the ladies, I followed and then waited for her to come out again. It is a very good place to pick up girls, I discovered. I may send Hugo in that direction. There was a big queue; she took ages and I got propositioned twice by the way, both nice girls. I have their numbers now in my phone.

'Ok, so when Samira came out, I tapped her on the arm and gave her my best 'blue steel' face'.'

At this point in the narrative, we fall about laughing at his ridiculously over the top seductive expression. He ignores us.

'And I asked her if there was a cigarette machine anywhere. She told me, but then I pointed to my hearing aids and asked her again, explaining that it was too noisy for me to hear the answer. Of course, now she was completely hooked, and I steered her towards the outside so we could talk somewhere quieter. I have used this approach on many previous occasions and it never lets me down. She then told me my accent was cute - I know it is anyway, but I like hearing it - and we got onto talking about different things. I said I was from abroad, new to the university, just starting a year here, didn't have any friends yet, blah blah blah. To cut a long story short, she not surprisingly fell for all my charms - I have been doing this stuff on autopilot for years, so it was easy enough.'

'Very modest of you Alex,' interrupts Jasper, laughing.

I shush him, 'Don't interrupt! I want to know what happened next. And whether cucumbers were involved.'

'No Sophie, sadly no cucumbers, but I can arrange for you and me to try cucumbers if you like. Now, keep on listening, this is the good bit. I asked if I could walk her home and naturally, she said yes. On the way, she was telling me how she had been alone since her ex-boyfriend dumped her, how she had seen him kissing his ugly housemate in the pub and that it was so embarrassing as everyone knew he had dropped her for this other girl - she called this other girl a slut several times, which made me certain we had the right person. Oh, my goodness, she seemed so, so angry.

'When we got to her house, we started kissing (cover your ears, Sophie, it made me feel terribly sick, honestly, she's very, very unattractive close up.)'

'That is such a lie, Alex, but carry on anyway,' I reply, giggling.

'So, we kiss, we do all sorts of other things to each other, she was very, very keen to do everything with me of course, but I manfully held back. By the way, Jasper, you were right, she really does have the most magnificent breasts. Anyway, I digress. After we do all that and have more drinks, she asked me if I wanted to do some coke. Coke! A student doctor too! I was shocked to be honest. I had spent the previous five minutes working out how to get the conversation back round to the subject of you two, or failing that, how to introduce fruit-based sex into the conversation, so this was a complete gift to me. I said yes please to the coke, and whilst she was lining it up, I pretended I was just texting to cancel my taxi, which I explained I had arranged to pick me up from the pub.'

He takes a big breath, before continuing. Jasper and I are riveted.

'So, when she took the line of coke first, I filmed her doing it whilst pretending to text. I also put the voice memo on and asked her whether she did coke a lot. It's all there clearly on the recording - quite a lot of coke recently is the answer, since that horrible, horrible Jasper broke up with her. She even offered to sell me some - said she could get me a good price!'

Jasper is shaking his head in disbelief. 'Bloody hell, Alex, I had no idea she was interested in that stuff! I can't believe she used drugs when I was with her, I'd have known, surely. I feel really bad that she's ended up doing that. It is a crazy thing to do as a med student - she'll get kicked out of med school for sure if anyone finds out.'

'Oh, don't waste your time feeling too bad, Jaz,' responds Alex, 'She really, really hates you; she wants to see you both dead, that was extremely clear to me. I totally get that she is upset, but seriously, she has a screw loose.'

He carries on, clearly enjoying himself. We are ready for the next instalment.

'So, she has the coke and then offers some to me. I put my phone back in my pocket and then I say that, actually, I think I will go home after all. She is disappointed, obviously, and then cheers up again when I ask her if she wants my address. Of course, the answer is yes, and as I say the magic words '5, Johnson Road' I could see complete confusion crossing her face, and then confusion turning to very cross indeed as she realised what is happening. I then said, very innocently, oh I'm so sorry Samira, did I not explain who my housemates were? And then I told her that I now have a video of her doing coke and talking about doing coke and talking about selling coke. And that if she sends one more message to either of you two, then the Dean of the medical school would also see the video too. And then I legged it, because she looked like she would have killed me there and then if a suitable weapon were handy. So, now I am here, and knackered from running away so fast. And I love you both, did I mention that?'

I leap out of bed and give him a massive hug. 'I can't believe you did all that for us! You're the bestest friend ever.'

I forget that I am naked under my T-shirt. Alex fondles my buttocks lovingly, and exceptionally bravely. He is watching Jasper warily over my shoulder. Jasper raises his eyebrows but says nothing. I have no idea how he will react.

'And I'm coming to join you both in there, so make room for me, big boy.' He's really pushing it now.

Stripping quickly, he dives into bed, wriggling into the middle before I get there first. Leaning over, he gives Jasper a sloppy forehead kiss and gets roughly pushed away for his troubles.

'Fuck off! Stop bloody flirting with me, Alex! I've told you before! You will get kicked out! Wow, I can't believe it, Al. I owe you, big time. I had no idea you were doing this for us.'

'Well,' said Alex, making space for me, so that I am in between them once more. 'Let's just hope it works.'

CHAPTER 46

SOPHIE

I feel as if an enormous weight has been lifted from my shoulders. I'm almost skipping into lectures on Monday morning and throw myself wholeheartedly into the tutorial session. The debate this week is entitled 'Photographic art degrades its female subjects.' Prof Harding evidently agrees wholeheartedly with this statement, as with great disdain she shows slide after slide of black and white images of erotica, beautiful women in provocative poses, crafted by the likes of Helmut Newton and Robert Mapplethorpe. I have the distinct impression that this is the Prof's least favourite part of the syllabus.

'These voyeuristic, perverted men claimed they were challenging the conventions of a post war western society, breaking boundaries, would you believe,' she drawls in a withering tone. 'Or, as I am more inclined to believe, they were just fulfilling their own fetishist fantasies and delivering them to a wider audience; it's up to you to decide.'

Personally, I mostly find myself disagreeing with the premise of the debate and with Prof. Harding's eminent opinions. In particular, Newton's elegant and decadently stylised women are cool and confident, sometimes even menacing as they revel in their perfect bodies. They mock the male gaze, by enticing them into their urban homes, allowing them to listen in on their phone calls, or to join them in sleazy hotel rooms; titillating them but never relinquishing control and always, always in on the joke.

Mapplethorpe's works also celebrate the female form, but in a different way. He often sections up a woman's body, focusing on immaculately staged silhouettes of sleek rib cages or outlines of perfectly plump breasts or a long, shapely leg. I wonder idly about

Prof Harding's sex life. Absent or very conservative, is my conclusion.

The only downside to no longer having vile messages lurking around every corner is, of course, that Alex is no longer waiting for me after each lecture. So, I am pleased to find that when I let myself back into the house later the same day, that he is already there, in his favourite chair in The Swamp, idly watching football in his sweatpants. I leave him to it, as he is speaking in Swiss-German on the phone, most likely to his dearest papa. I hear my own name mentioned several times and smile as I head upstairs.

An idea has been forming in my mind on the bus home. The erotic images we have been studying turn me on. Showering quickly, I change into my new black silk Agent Provocateur bra and knickers and complete the outfit by adding my only pair of high heels. They are black strappy things, the last time I had worn them had been at Fi's New Year's Eve party. Alex's phone call has ended, and so letting my hair fall around my face and donning a slash of bright red lipstick, I make my way down to his room. I stand in the doorway, leaning casually against the frame, waiting for him to notice.

'Hi, beautiful.' He gives a low whistle. 'Very Helmut Newton, darling.'

I am amazed. 'How the hell did you know?'

He laughs. 'Mama and papa are avid art collectors. My papa has a couple of framed originals in his home office in Zurich. Helmut was an old family friend of ours, actually. I don't remember him of course - I was too young when he died. But I've been secretly wanking to those images for years - I suspect papa has too, the dirty bugger. His photos are every man's secret fantasies, Sophie, and it looks like mine are about to be played out.'

He drains his beer can. 'Come over here and sit on my lap, I need to take a much closer examination of this beautiful new underwear and the delightful person modelling it.'

He runs his hands appreciatively over my body.

'Do you think it demeans me, Alex, dressing up in sexy underwear and high heels, for the sole purpose of giving you pleasure?'

Alex grins and guides my hand down onto his erect penis. 'I think that if anyone is being demeaned around here, it's me, sweetheart – I couldn't walk away from you now if the bedroom was burning down around my ears.'

His beautiful fingers begin tracing around the elastic of my knickers before resting lightly on my hips. My groin is tingling with anticipation of what is to follow. I dream sometimes of Alex's hands, there is something about his slim, elegant tanned fingers that intrudes into my thoughts at the most unlikely moments. We kiss, his tongue tenderly exploring my mouth. Every time I kiss Alex, it feels like the first time, he somehow manages to be familiar and yet so new and unfamiliar at the same time.

After what seems an age, his hands leave my hips and explore lower, I close my eyes and surrender to the touch of his fingers as they slip inside my knickers, exploring every inch of me before expertly bringing me to climax. I know he's watching my face as I come, loving what he can do to me. He wriggles out of his sweatpants and I adjust my position, so I am straddling him. His penis is inside me, hot and hard, and I ride him slowly, exquisitely slowly, resisting all his efforts to speed up. I look down at him thrusting in and out of me, taking his pleasure. He shudders as he comes, swearing in his own language, when he can stand it no longer. I keep him inside me as I collapse against him, our bodies slippery with sweat.

'I love you, Alex, I really do.'

He gazes into my eyes, searching for answers. 'You know how much I love you too, Soph. I love you so much I can't explain it, you are like cocaine to me.'

He laughs quietly, 'I told Mama about you, she thinks I'm crazy. Alexi, she says, you are too young to be so in love, you should still be meeting lots of girls, like you used to. I tell her that I don't want anyone else, I only want Sophie. She is worried that I will have my heart broken, I think. Are you going to break my heart, Sophie?'

'Never,' I reply vehemently, without a second of hesitation. 'I can't ever imagine a life without you in it, Alex.'

We kiss again and I feel the beginning of him stiffening once more inside me. He lifts me up and carries me to the bed where he makes love simply and tenderly, with me underneath him, completely coated in his luscious smooth body and his clear blue eyes never once leaving mine.

CHAPTER 47

ALEX

It is a Friday evening a couple of weeks before Christmas. As far as Jaz is concerned, Friday nights were invented for the sole purpose of drinking beer in a pub with some uncomplicated and like-minded mates. Thus, he is invariably found propping up the bar in the *Wheatsheaves* with his med school chums. Sophie and I have started to join him later on in the evening, and then the three of us all go home together. Pubs like this are completely not my bag, but I try not to dwell on the complete sap I have become. Hugo is confused beyond measure.

Whether Jasper's mates ever wonder why his odd, deaf housemate seems equally as tactile with his girlfriend as Jaz is himself, then they never show it and always make me feel welcome. For this I am grateful.

On this particular Friday, we have finished our drinks and signal to Jasper that we are leaving. The pub is especially packed and rowdy, and my hearing and lip-reading abilities are being tested to the limit.

'Two seconds and I'll join you,' mimes Jaz, indicating to his remaining half full pint glass.

Outside, the evening has turned cold and Sophie huddles next to me for warmth whilst we wait for him. The only other people around are a noisy crowd of students waiting for a cab on the other side of the road. Sophie hovers from foot to foot in an effort to keep warm.

A scrawny looking man, appearing as if from thin air out of the darkness a few feet away from us catches our attention. His eyes are darting around feverishly, and I realise it is me that he is aggressively staring at. He sidles closer to us. He is older than most students and clad in a scruffy denim jacket and dirty grey jeans. My first impression is that he is likely homeless and about to ask for money. He is pale and jittery. Without warning, he suddenly pokes a grubby finger in my face,

'Hey, you, you posh wanker, are you Alex?'

He has a strong local accent. I step back, pushing his hand away, my heart rate picking up.

'Sorry,' I say, confused and edging away slightly, 'I don't know who you are.'

The man is breathing heavily now and sweating profusely.

'I've got a message for you from a pal of mine, you fucking deaf cunt.'

He swings a punch out of nowhere, a surprisingly swift upper cut at my face. I see it at the last second and manage to partially dodge the blow, a sudden pain over my left eyebrow. I feel blood and stagger back against the wall, more from the shock than the injury, putting my hand up to my face. 'Hey!' I hear myself protest angrily and Sophie screams. It all happens so quickly - he follows through with a fast knee in my groin. 'Fuck!' I shout, winded and stagger backwards again. I am no fighter, that's for sure, my instinct is to run, but my bollocks hurt too fucking much.

I am dimly aware of the absence of noise from the crowd of students over the road – they have fallen silent and are observing the events unfolding. Time has slowed, and I see the man homing in on me again, readying himself for a third attempt. He is panting and sweating even more now, despite the cool air.

'How do you feel now, you deaf cunt?' he taunts and somewhere in my mind I recognise that his name calling hurts me more than my bollocks. He is about to take another swing, and I brace myself to fend him off. He is halted mid strike, and I see the surprise on his face as two strong arms are grabbing him and hurling him roughly against the brick wall of the pub. A giant of a man, in so many ways, has arrived on the scene, and he is not at all happy.

'Who are you calling a deaf cunt, then, you fucking piece of shit?' Jaz spits furiously, bringing his face up close and almost touching the nose of my assailant.

He has both of his enormous hands round the man's neck, virtually lifting him off the ground, only the toes of his shoes barely touching the tarmac.

'You fucking mess with my mate, you fucking mess with me, cunt,' he growls.

Jasper's beautiful soft Irish lilt has gone, replaced with a much harsher tone that I would never have believed possible. The man's cocky swagger has disappeared, his pale face is turning red with the relentless pressure of Jasper's huge hands squeezing harder and harder around his neck. A dark stain begins to spread at his groin as his bladder loosens with fear.

'Jasper, stop!' shouts Sophie panicking, 'You're going to kill him!'

Somewhere within his red mist, Jasper hears her, and lets go of him. The man falls to the ground, clutching at his neck, retching and coughing. Jasper gives him an unnecessarily sharp kick.

'What's your game then?'

The man is whimpering now, and his voice is hoarse. He is petrified and I would be too, this version of Jasper is fucking evil.

'Some fucking bird that I deal to sent me, she paid me fifty quid to beat the shit out of that posh twat. She didn't fucking mention you though, the fucking bitch.'

Jasper stands over him, catching his breath. He looks like he is about to lay into him again. His attention is diverted by a siren blasting through the cold air, extremely close by, making us all jump.

'Shit,' he says, looking around, 'Someone's called the fucking police.'

Sure enough, a police car pulls up with a screech of brakes and two burly male officers step out. The next ten minutes pass in a blur of taking names and asking questions. Both of the officers are a smooth mixture of firmness and politeness, clearly practiced at handling Friday night altercations. Sophie and I each explain several times what has happened; one of the girls over the road, who had phoned 999 even comes over and corroborates the story. But it is no use; the officers are almost apologetic as they explain that Jasper and the man are both being arrested and taken to the nearest station for formal statements.

I can't believe what is happening; the whole thing has escalated so bloody quickly. Sophie is crying as she hugs Jasper. I'm still in a state of shock, blood is running down my cheek and I'm dazed as I too embrace him.

'Fuck, I'm sorry Jaz, I'm so sorry. It should be me, not you mate, you don't deserve this.' I mean every word; I would change places with him if I could. Basically, in front of our girlfriend, he has saved me from a through beating, as I am clearly unable to defend myself, and now he is being punished for it.

He is the calmest of all of us, totally unfazed by the presence of the police. He is the one doing all the comforting, and he pulls away from me so that we are facing each other. I am touched as he lifts up his arm and tenderly wipes away the blood from my face with his shirtsleeve, his hand lingering on my cheek.

'It's okay Al,' he soothes, 'I know you'd have done the same for me.'

I like to think I would have done, but nowhere near as successfully. He gives me a strange smile and touches my bleeding eyebrow with his fingertips. His brown eyes are studying me, I had no idea he could be so gentle.

'Hey, I hope that's just a flesh wound,' he says, 'We wouldn't want to spoil that pretty face.'

He leans closer and softly kisses me squarely on the mouth, before turning away towards the police car. I am not sure what has shocked me more, the assault or his kiss, but I know which I prefer.

Sophie and I walk home in silence. I can tell she is as shaken as me, staggered at how Jasper's temper has flared and then dissipated just as quickly. We have scarcely ever heard him raise his voice before, let alone almost strangle someone to death. And then to kiss me, on the mouth, out of the blue. I am confused beyond measure.

I slump in a kitchen chair whilst Sophie retrieves the first aid kit from the boot of Jasper's car. She cleans my face carefully with some damp cotton wool and then patiently applies Steristrips to the wound above my eyebrow.

'For a small cut, it certainly bled a lot,' she remarks, 'I think it's going to heal fine - you probably won't even have a scar, but you're definitely going to have a black eye by tomorrow morning.'

I nod in agreement. I've hardly said a word since it happened. She puts her arms around my shoulders, hugging me tight. There is nothing I need more at this moment.

'Come on Alex, let's get to bed. Jasper will be home by morning - maybe even sooner. He'll be fine, honestly.'

She leads me into my room and joins me under the covers, where I lie with my eyes closed. All I can think of is Jasper.

'If I hadn't set up Samira, none if this would have happened, Sophie. It's my fault that Jaz has been arrested.'

Sophie props herself up on one elbow. 'That's ridiculous Alex! If Jasper hadn't gone out with Samira in the first place, then none of this would have happened anyway, so you can't blame yourself - you were just trying to help. Jasper won't blame you. The real person at fault here is that psycho Samira, not you or Jasper, so you can stop that line of thinking right now.'

She speaks sternly and holds my hand tightly.

'I just froze, Soph, when he hit me. Because of what he called me. No one has ever called me that before. Maybe I should grow my hair again - it was absolutely horrible having that sort of abuse thrown at me.'

'No Alex!' exclaims Sophie. 'You are not doing that either! You have told me so many times how proud you are to be deaf. You are amazing the way you refuse to let it stand in your way - and all the people who love you are proud of you too. No way should a nobody, drug dealing twat like that make you change how you are. I won't allow it!'

I smile at her support for me and close my eyes with a sigh. Being beaten up is exhausting. We lie like that for several more minutes.

'Jasper kissed you, Alex. A proper kiss.'

I open my eyes and stare up at the ceiling. 'I know Sophie, I was there.'

It is a feeble attempt at a joke, and it falls flat.

'I'm not sure I can think about that right now,' I say, closing my eyes again. She strokes my hair and kisses my forehead tenderly.

'Don't worry. We'll get through this. We're a team remember?'

CHAPTER 48

JASPER

I let myself quietly into the house just before dawn. Sophie joins me in the kitchen, emerging from Alex's room wearing one of his soft shirts. I am waiting for the kettle to boil. She hugs me wordlessly. I smell sweaty, feel dirty and have Alex's dried blood on my sleeve. The feel of her in my arms is overwhelming. The shirt smells of him.

'They've let me off. They were good guys actually. Funnily enough, the bloke wasn't keen on pressing charges - probably because his pockets were stuffed full of baggies of coke. He couldn't get out of the police station quick enough to be honest. He made a statement though, for what it's worth, so the Samira stuff is all on record. He was pathetic really, I felt sorry for him in the end.'

'Oh Jasper, thank goodness, that's such a relief! I've been worried sick all night.'

The police are the least of my worries. 'Yeah, just the med school now to sort out. I have a feeling that's not going to be quite as straightforward.'

I reach for a mug as I explain further. 'I guess I'll be packing my bags at the end of the week and not coming back, Soph. They don't take kindly to their students getting arrested for GBH.'

Dismay is written all over her face. This scenario had evidently not occurred to her at all.

'That's crazy! No way that can happen Jasper! This wasn't your fault, and surely you can explain that? You were being a good Samaritan!'

I hold her close. 'I'm not sure they're going to see it like that, Soph. I could have nearly fucking killed him. I was bloody strangling him! Not very doctorly of me, was it?'

'Where did that anger come from, Jasper? I've never seen you like that before. You frightened me.'

I am ashamed. 'I'm sorry Sophie. After my dad left, I guess I used to get very angry at stuff. A troubled teen, if you like. I was angry with the world.'

This is putting it mildly to say the least, last night was not the first time I'd been in trouble with the police. I pause.

'I thought I'd grown out of it or at least learnt to control my temper. It would appear that I haven't. But that bloke attacking Alex like that, for no reason at all - I just saw red and I needed to protect him.'

I pick up my coffee. 'I'm going for a shower and then to bed - I'm done in. I can't think about all that now. Come and join me?'

She lies with me, her head on my chest. Surely this isn't all coming to an end. I've worked so damn hard to just throw it all away in a flash of temper.

'How's Alex?' I ask eventually. I can't hold off any longer.

'I don't know, really,' she replies, 'He's doing what he does best - sleeping it all off. But seriously, he's fine physically, the cut will heal, and yet he's hardly said a word. To be attacked and abused like that, out of the blue, well, it's a massive shock isn't it? I can't believe for a second he's ever encountered anything like it. It was more than horrible. And you know what Alex is like. He wouldn't hurt a fly. Hopefully he'll be feeling a bit better when he wakes up later.'

'I'm not sure he'll have much to say to me, though,' I say quietly.

She knows what I'm referring to and I am glad the room is still in darkness.

'Fuck, fuck, fuck!' I say loudly, banging my fist down.

Sophie puts her hand on mine, restraining me. 'Forget about it, Jasper, let's sort all this other stuff out first,' she says soothingly.

We are silent for a while before I speak.

'I don't know what I was thinking, Soph. It just all happened so quickly. He looked so...I don't know.... scared, hurt, whatever, with all that blood on his face, that I just.... just.... needed to kiss him. It felt right....it felt like the right thing to do. Fuck. I fucking wanted to kiss him Sophie! I wasn't even pissed - I'd only had two pints! I've never felt like that before with a bloke - where did that fucking come from?'

My voice is rising as I speak, and I am almost crying now.

'Hey, Jasper, it will be fine, honestly, calm down, don't get upset. You're tired, so much has happened. Get some sleep - you will be able to think much clearer afterwards. You love him, that's all, we both do. Everything will be fine, honestly, I promise. We can get through this.'

CHAPTER 49

SOPHIE

Alex retreats into his non-hearing world all weekend. He lies in his own bed, facing the wall with the door closed, either sleeping or feigning sleep, his eye swollen and turning an impressive shade of purple. I can't persuade him to put on his hearing aids and talk to me, although he must have done so at some point, as I hear him on the phone to papa on several occasions, my own name and Jasper's frequently mentioned. Even though I can't understand the conversation, it is clear from his tone that he is extremely upset. I hardly speak to Jasper either. He also disappears to his own room for much of the weekend, with a six-pack of beers and the door firmly closed. He avoids Alex entirely. But, at night-time, it is like the clocks have been turned back a year; he creeps into my bed when I am already asleep and curls up behind me.

Bad news travels fast, no doubt speeded up by Samira. By Sunday evening, Jasper has received a phone call from the office of the Dean of the medical school, asking him to attend a meeting first thing on Monday morning.

'Let me come with you, Jasper,' I plead, 'I can at least help explain what happened.'

His lips brush mine gently. 'It's okay, Sophie, I can go on my own. I think they will probably have made up their minds anyway. I doubt much will change. And anyway, you never know, they may just give me a warning.'

I don't feel like going to my tutorial on Monday morning, so I put on my gym kit and go for a run instead. Jasper texts me and Alex whilst I am sitting on my familiar bench in Lenton park, reluctant to return home. The message is short and succinct:

'Not good. They've asked me to leave. Jx'

I feel physically sick and burst into tears, much to the surprise of a nearby dog walker. God, it is so unfair! How can they do this to him? He will be a fine doctor - the best! I get up from the bench and begin running in the direction of home. I need to speak to Alex, surely there is something someone can do.

But when I open the front door, the house is empty, and Alex is gone. His old leather rucksack is missing from the corner of his room. I find a note propped up on the kitchen table in his beautiful loopy writing.

'Gone to London to see my parents. Sorry, AV-Z x'

My tears turn to tears of rage and frustration. How could he do this now? Jasper needs him, I need him! And he just runs off to mama and papa when the shit hits the fan? I fling myself onto his bed, inhaling his wonderful Alex smell; Chanel, gin, coconut shampoo. I angrily pummel his pillows. How could I have been so wrong about him? He is just another spoilt rich kid after all - Jasper is ten times the person he will ever be. Life is so bloody unfair! I love him so much, but he's let us down, just when we need him most.

Jasper comes home after lunchtime. He's been for a drink; I smell beer on his breath as he hugs and kisses me. I don't blame him at all. His face is pale, the dark circles have returned under his soulful brown eyes.

'I'm sorry Sophie, I've ruined everything,' he says sadly.

I begin shaking my head, about to speak, but he stops me.

'And the worst thing? I'm going to lose you too, and Alex. I've let my mum down and I've let Christian down. It's going to kill her when I tell her. As if she doesn't have enough problems. The thought of me being at med school and making something of myself was about the only good thing she had left.'

He walks over to the window, looking out over the small patch of lawn. 'I had an opportunity to do something really good, you know? I wanted to make something of myself. I didn't want to be a loser like my dad. I had a future, and do you know what? You were in it too, both you and Alex. Now I've got to go back to Kinsale and start all over again, I'll go back to being just another fucking labourer on a building site.'

'It doesn't have to be over with us, Jasper!' I cry, 'I'm not going to leave you. Kinsale's not too far away is it? Or maybe you could stay here in Nottingham and get a job in town or something. Or maybe get a place on another degree course?'

'I haven't got the money for that,' he responds, shaking his head. 'I'm in debt up to my eyeballs as it is, but at least as a doctor I knew I'd make some decent money and be able to pay it off one day.'

We kiss after that, long and hard. I break off, panting, and taking his hand, lead him upstairs. We make love urgently, not Jasper's usual style at all, not even taking off any clothing, clinging onto each other. When we have finished, we are both crying, our faces wet with tears.

'God, I love you Sophie. I feel like you're all I've got left.'

The next day we both begin packing up our belongings and cleaning out the kitchen in preparation for the Christmas holidays. I'm not taking much home, but unsure of his return, Jasper is taking everything. He doesn't have much at all once he's carefully boxed away his textbooks and filled a bin liner with folders of notes. He dumps the bin liner outside the back door, ready to be carted away. When he isn't looking, I retrieve all the folders and hide the bin liner in the bottom of my wardrobe. I can't bear to see all that hard work thrown out.

For want of something to do, I scrub away in the kitchen all afternoon and by the time I've finished, it is sparkling clean. Neither of us hear anything from Alex.

'He's too scared of me to come back,' says Jasper bitterly, 'That's why he's legged it. I don't blame him for running off - he probably thinks I'm going to jump him in the middle of the night or something.'

The kiss shocked me to the core, almost more than the attack, but I can't tell him that - he's eating himself up over it enough. I have no idea what is going on - or what the hell will happen next. We just need to bloody talk to Alex!

'Don't be so silly,' I say briskly, 'I don't think that's the issue at all. He's just being precious and spoilt - I'm bloody furious with him for ditching you like this. He must have looked at your text. Yes, I know he's upset that he got attacked, but this is much worse, and he should be here facing it with us, not running off to mama at the first sign of trouble. And anyway, he's always kissing you and pretending to fondle you and everything. He's the most metrosexual man I know.'

'I know Sophie, but this was different. That's just him fooling around, but this meant something. I could see in his eyes, he was shocked. He was looking at me strangely, I couldn't tell what he was thinking, it was all over so quickly. I shall fucking regret doing that until the day I die.'

I place an arm around his shoulders. 'No, you won't, silly. You love him and you were just showing it, that's all. He'll understand that when you explain it to him. For what it's worth, Jasper, I feel the need to kiss him all the time, even now, when I'm so bloody cross with him!'

We are both set to leave the next morning. The house is strange and soulless without Alex. The evening ahead looms large, so later on we catch a bus into the city centre and have a cheap dinner in the huge, bustling Wetherspoons on Market Square. Neither of us feel particularly hungry, but it is something to do to pass the time.

We walk around town for a while afterwards, admiring the Christmas lights and gazing into shop windows. Brian Clough has been festooned in red and white tinsel. I reckon he still looks like he is changing a light bulb. I have grown and changed so much since the first time I saw him. The Sophie from eighteen months ago, who was unsure about Nottingham, scared of living with strangers, not certain why she chose to study art history is long gone. I love this town for a start, it's lack of pretension, its pubs, shops and even its football teams. I realise I love my studies too and have a direction for a future career. But most of all, I love my two men and our unconventional relationship, confident of my place within our little team of three.

The town is busy, party season is in full swing and we pass several crowds of happy drunken revellers. When it starts to rain, we catch a packed bus home, I'm squeezed onto Jasper's lap. I would happily stay on that bus all night, if it means that tomorrow can be put off for a little longer.

As we walk up Johnson Road, I can see every light blazing in our house. I quicken my pace.

'I'm sure I only left the hall light on. Hey, Jasper, do you think Alex is home?'

As we get closer, we see a sleek black Range Rover parked up on the pavement outside number five, incongruous amongst all the familiar shabby vehicles lining both sides of the street.

'Yes. I think we are about to have a close encounter with the Van-Zeller family,' observes Jasper, gripping my hand tightly. 'He's probably just come back to grab his stuff.'

With his free hand, he fishes in his trouser pocket to locate his front door key. As he inserts it in the lock, it is flung wide by Alex himself, wearing a smart tailored navy suit, the collar of his crisp white shirt undone, revealing a tantalising hint of smooth chest. The bruising around his eye has almost faded completely. I can't remember when I have ever seen a more arresting sight. If I thought he could rock a pair of jeans, then Alex in a suit is pure dynamite. He looks very relieved, but cross at the same time.

'Where the hell have you two been? I've been waiting for ages!'

He reaches out and envelopes me in his arms.

'I'm so sorry, my sweetheart, that I ran out on you like that. I really am. I can explain everything though.'

He turns to Jasper, holding out his arms. 'Your turn, big boy. God, I've been so worried about you.'

They exchange a manly hug, Jasper looking pensive and deliberately holding back. Alex steps aside.

'Come in, come in, there's someone who wants to see you both.'

He ushers us into the kitchen, where two well-dressed men sit at the table drinking coffee. I silently congratulate myself on having cleaned the kitchen so thoroughly earlier in the day.

The older of the two, a rotund man wearing a plain charcoal suit over a shirt and tie stands up and shakes hands with us both.

'This is Herman the German,' says Alex grinning, giving the man a friendly pat. 'He's our driver and my oldest friend. He's been in our family since forever and he knows everything there is to know about everything. I'm not sure the Van-Zellers can function without him.'

Herman smiles at Alex and then at us. He speaks with a very strong accent.

'It's great to meet you both. I'm sure we will meet again. But now you are here, I go wait in the car. I'm not happy leaving it on this street.'

Alex turns to the other man, who also stands up.

'And this is my papa –Wilhelm. Jasper you have already met, of course.'

Alex's father reaches over and shakes hands with Jasper.

'It's really good to see you again, Jasper.'

He turns to me. 'And of course, you must be the beautiful Sophie. I have heard everything about you from Alexi. Well, maybe not everything.'

His English is smooth and confident, and he has a twinkle in his eyes as he shakes my hand. He is a big man and he effortlessly commands the room. His light grey three-piece wool suit is immaculately tailored to his large frame; he sports a discreetly elegant gold watch on his wrist and a large ruby coloured signet ring on his pinkie finger. Alex has certainly not inherited his dashing blonde looks from his father; Wilhelm's hair is black and peppered with grey; a hooked nose dominates his rugged features. The clear deep blue eyes are the same though, and he regards me carefully.

'Now to business, as Herman and I are flying back to Zurich tonight. Alexi's mama will not be happy with me if I arrive home very late.' He motions to us to sit.

'Alexi has told me everything that has happened to you Jasper, and firstly I must thank you for intervening and preventing Alexi from becoming badly hurt. His mama and I are grateful beyond words. If you hadn't been present, it could have been much, much worse. We are not just grateful for that; we are grateful for everything the both of you have done for him. He is very special to us and it is good to know he is being well looked after here in Nottingham. His mama worries always about him.'

I glance sideways at Alex. I have never seen him blush before, but his face is discernibly redder as he gazes adoringly at his father.

'So,' continues Wilhelm, in his deep measured voice, 'It is my turn to do something for you, Jasper. Today, Alexi, my lawyer and I had a very interesting and profitable meeting at the university medical school. The Van-Zeller Foundation makes lots of charitable donations to many, many good causes. It gives me great pleasure to announce that we have proposed a substantial financial donation to the University Hospital Medical School neurology department, so that they can continue their excellent research into Sudden Unexplained Death in Epilepsy. This, I think Jasper, is a subject probably very close to your heart. Alex actually asked me to look into this a while ago, but recent events have expedited it somewhat.'

Alex puts his hand on Jasper's shoulder. 'It's a huge donation, Jaz, it could make a big difference for other children like Christian, in the future.'

Jasper is visibly stunned; he looks at Wilhelm incredulously. Neither he nor I had expected this. I reach out and take his hand in mine, giving it a squeeze. Wilhelm is still speaking.

'We took the opportunity, whilst arranging the finer details of the donation, to ask the Dean to reconsider the case against a certain medical student named Jasper Coutts. I explained that his own personal tragedy had inspired the donation and that it would be a great shame if he couldn't continue his studies at this august establishment.'

He turns to Jasper and pats his shoulder. 'He hasn't made any promises, Jasper, but he will reconsider the case. That is the best we can hope for. I am quietly confident, however. He mentioned anger management training....'

Alex can't hold it in any longer. 'You're staying Jaz, you're staying here with us!'

Jasper is so overcome with emotion that he can scarcely speak. 'But Mr Van-Zeller - Wilhelm - this is unbelievable, thank you. I don't know what to say. I can't believe that someone like you would do something like this for me. My mam, she's going to be...' Tears form in his eyes; he can't speak, and he shakes his head.

'You do not need to say anything, Jasper,' says Wilhelm gently, 'The Van-Zellers believe in taking care of the people who take care of us, and you have done that for my dear Alexi and me. We all need a bit of kindness occasionally. All I ask of you is that you become the best doctor you can be. Alexi tells me you are possibly thinking of becoming a paediatrician. I will be following your career with great interest.'

With that he stands up again and embraces Alex.

'I will see you in a couple of days, Alexi. Be good, have fun.'

He tenderly kisses Alex on the forehead, and I smile at the familiar gesture. He winks at me, pats a dazed Jasper on the back and disappears out into the night.

Alex returns to the kitchen. 'He's also sorted Samira out too. Our lawyer has been in touch with her and her family and suggested that unless she wants her recent antics exposed, then she should take a year out of her studies for treatment. She needs professional help. He will keep an eye on her progress, and if she follows a treatment programme, then the medical school will accept her back. Everyone deserves a second chance; we are all allowed to fuck up sometimes.'

I am thoroughly exhausted. The last seventy-two hours has been an emotional roller coaster and I am ready to get off, curl into a ball and sleep.

'Okay, Alexi,' I say grinning at him, 'What now?'

Alex laughs. 'It's very sexy when you call me that Sophie, I like it a lot. I think we have some talking to do.'

CHAPTER 50

JASPER

The sloe gin flask is passed round, it comes to me last, and I drain it. Alex gets a top up from the seemingly never-ending supply in his bedroom. Sophie has her arm protectively around me. I am recovered slightly, at least I am now capable of speech, although I am still bewildered. I think I am staying; I think he implied that the Dean is letting me stay, but, fuck, I was lost at the epilepsy donation.

'Alex, I just can't take it in that you have done this for me. The epilepsy research, it's truly incredible - I don't know where to begin. My mother won't be able to believe it when I tell her. It will help her so much to know that Christian hasn't died in vain – that something good has come out of his death. It will be a great comfort to her. I'm not sure I can ever repay you or thank you enough.'

I'm struggling to find the words; my voice is cracking, and I attempt to mask my imminent tears by taking a big gulp of gin and fail miserably. 'Why didn't I drink anything this fucking good in that bloody gin bar?'

Alex takes a smaller sip of his own. 'You don't need to thank me, Jaz, that's what friends are for. And it's my papa's doing anyway, not mine.' He hesitates before carrying on. 'Let me tell you something. You have probably realised by now that he is a very rich man and that comes with some big responsibilities. I am his only heir, which is pretty scary. You may find that hard to believe but actually it is very true.

'When I came to Nottingham, neither of you two knew that about me, and you have become, without the shadow of a doubt, the best friends I could ever have wished for. You both love me because I am your ridiculous deaf housemate Alex, and not because I am Alexi

Van-Zeller, heir to a massive fortune. And that, let me tell you, is absolutely priceless; all the money my papa has in the bank cannot buy that.'

Listening to his words, it is frankly no surprise that Sophie is in love with him. She kisses him and of course, he responds, his hands wandering automatically to her waist. He is looking at me anxiously.

'And Jaz, you've let me have a chance with this beautiful girl. You didn't have to do that, and it nearly killed you to do it, but you did it because you are a good guy, the best in fact. And we've turned out all right, haven't we? This threesome thing we have, it's good, right?'

He's anxious, because he wants me to say that everything is all right. He wants me to tell him that him being with Sophie is all right. He's going to like what I say, because I've realised that I can really do this sharing thing with him. I am happy if she never chooses and we stay this way.

'Yes, Al, it's good, really good,' I say and he lets out the breath he has been holding.

And now it is my turn to look anxiously back at him, and not because he has his hands on our gorgeous girl. The subtext of our conversation is shouting to be heard. There is something I definitely need to get off my chest.

'Al, I need to say something. I've got to get it out in the open. It's about that kiss, outside the pub.' The words come out in a rush and I let out a deep breath of my own. 'I'm sorry, I don't know what happened or why. But I just need you to know, it won't happen again, it was a moment of madness. I'm a fucking idiot.'

Alex sits up straighter and takes his hands off Sophie. She tenses, not sure what is coming next. But she need not be worried, and nor should I, we should have both understood by now that nothing ever seems to faze Alex.

'Hey, big boy, relax. What can I say, you couldn't help yourself, I'm unbelievably seductive, even when I've got blood all over my face!'

His tone is light as he stands up and walks around the table to where I am sitting. He hesitates, chewing his lip, and I briefly wonder what he is thinking, what funny, throw-away line he will come up with to lighten the mood and make everything okay again.

Yet instead of speaking, he reaches down and places a warm hand on my shoulder. He eyes me uncertainly for a split second and then suddenly his lips are crashing down onto mine with an urgency and hunger that takes my breath away. The kiss is hard, hot and clumsy and tastes of gin, and he holds it there, his hands now deep in my hair, forcing my mouth up to his. His clear blue eyes are wide open, boring into mine, gauging my response. And a hundred fireworks explode in my head.

Sneak Preview

Book 2 of the Johnson Road Series

Stepping Out

CHAPTER 1

SOPHIE

'The four best looking blokes in Nottingham are half naked in your front room, Soph,' declares Katy, swigging from a bottle of cheap white wine, 'Not a bad way to start our last year at uni by any stretch of the imagination.'

'Couldn't agree more,' I nod and take the bottle from her.

It is the second night of the new term, and the beginning of our final year at Nottingham University before graduating. The impromptu party at 5, Johnson Road is in full swing. Seb and Hugo have dropped by unexpectedly, to catch up with Alex after the long summer break. They are sweet boys, and I have become increasingly fond of them over the last year or so. During Alex's heavy drinking, promiscuous party days, I had done them a disservice, lumped them together as Alex's posh drinking buddies and nothing more, but slowly they have separated out into two extremely attractive, interesting individuals.

Hugo's company has always been easy to enjoy – he is witty, confident, always up for fun. And extremely easy on the eye - Katy refers to him as Hot Hugo for a very good reason. Seb is no slouch in the looks department either but is much quieter, more reserved. I am gradually getting to know him too, and Alex definitely has a soft spot for him. On their arrival, I had immediately and surreptitiously texted Katy and Amy to alert them to this spur of the moment visit, and unsurprisingly, they also just happened to turn up not long afterwards, with hair washed, faces made up and dressed to impress.

Towards the end of the previous term, and much against her better judgement, Katy found herself in Hugo's bed at the end of a night out on more than one occasion. She is mortified that she has unwittingly developed a crush on him and has sworn me to secrecy. Of course, I have ignored that directive and confided in Alex, who already knew far too many of the intimate details, courtesy of Hugo.

Privately we are both highly amused by this burgeoning relationship. Hugo is a floppy haired, handsome old-Etonian from the Home Counties, whose interests revolve principally around rowing, drinking and generally floating through his privileged life with as little effort as possible. Katy on the other hand, is a smart, sharp talking, down to earth Mancunian and card-carrying member of the Labour Party, who has until now shown great disdain for the likes of Hugo. She manages to tolerate Alex, but only because he is my boyfriend and has the body and face of a Greek God. Jasper of course, she has always adored.

Whilst I'm excited about Katy and Hugo's secretive liaison, I have to concede, that at this point in the relationship, it is entirely possible that the attraction between the two of them has not gone beyond a purely physical level, as it is apparent they are yet to exchange a sober conversation. And so far, tonight is not shaping up to be an exception, as Alex is being his usual generous host when it comes to sharing out the booze. Heady champagne cocktails have been swiftly followed by wine and beer, and none of us students are now in a fit state to seduce anyone with our fine intellect and clever discourse.

Alex has returned from the long summer break looking as bloody gorgeous as ever, and we spent almost all of yesterday in his bed in The Swamp, making up for lost time. Contemplating him hungrily now, I almost wish that everyone else hadn't turned up, so we can retire to bed again. I don't think there will ever come a time in my life when I don't crave his lean golden body on top of mine or his kiss on my lips.

Jasper has been back at university for a few days already and is working hard as usual, but he has broken off his studying for the party and it is clearly a welcome diversion. Frankly, with the racket that we have been making, it would have been too difficult for him to continue studying and ignore it. He has always stayed slightly apart from mine and Alex's friends, but appears more than happy to join in with us all tonight. Hugo finds Alex's close friendship with Jasper a bit of a mystery, and the fact that he is willing to share his girlfriend with him is utterly beyond his comprehension.

I haven't had a chance to be alone with him since my return – hopefully later this evening I will be able to rectify that. Cuddling up on Jasper's broad chest, safe in the harbour of his warm embrace, is possibly my favourite place to be in the whole world.

Alex and I are already fretting about him. It is his final year at medical school and the work is seriously piling up. As well as travelling to placements every week in hospitals all across the region, where he shadows doctors and becomes schooled in the rudiments of good patient care, he then spends his evenings studying and having to prep for what I consider to be a crazy number of exams. The breadth of his learning is mind boggling, and the textbooks are enormous. So, we were both thrilled to see him return from Kinsale tanned, refreshed and ready to tackle the hard work ahead. Once again, from what I can detect through the soft cotton fabric of his T-shirt, the long hours working on the building site have only served to improve his toned physique even more.

Everyone at the party is in various stages of undress, as some hours earlier we had started and then abandoned a drunken game of strip poker. It had been Hugo's suggestion, and he is manfully trying to conceal his satisfaction that Katy now looks extremely beguiling in a black lacy bra and a washed denim miniskirt. Frankly, he is struggling not to openly drool. Alex commenced the game at a significant disadvantage to the rest of us, as he began the evening clad only in a pair of loose jeans, thus is now sprawled provocatively in an armchair wearing just his white Calvin Klein boxer shorts, his well-defined tanned torso and long elegant limbs being fully appreciated by all the girls present. And he is loving every minute of the adoration. Someone has turned up the volume of the music pumping through the house and I smile to myself as I watch him surreptitiously turn it down a notch from his phone. His ability to hear conversation through his implants is at its worst in this sort of environment, but he is far too polite to ever let on and spoil the party for everyone else.

Suffice to say, I have no worries concerning Alex and his studies at all. He is planning on scraping through his English degree by doing as little work as possible and at the same time by having as much fun as he can. After all, his life when he leaves uni is completely mapped out for him already, and has been since the day he was born – firstly to carry on the good work of the Van-Zeller Foundation, and then, when he is ready, to take over the reins one day at the private Swiss bank owned by his family. No degree qualification in the world will change that secure inevitability. He frequently reassures Jasper and I that there is a place for both of us in his future plans and I fervently hope that remains the case. I can't imagine a life without him or Jasper now and I pray desperately that they both feel the same.

'Let's play spin the bottle 'truth or dare',' suggests Katy, tipping her head back and draining the dregs of the bottle of white wine.

Stepping Out will be available in 2020

For information on the Johnson Road series and for a link to a free story, visit the author's website at:

www.fearnehill.com.